LONG ISLAND NOIR

LONG ISLAND NOIR

EDITED BY KAYLIE JONES

This collection is comprised of works of fiction. All names, characters, places, and incidents are the product of the authors' imaginations. Any resemblance to real events or persons, living or dead, is entirely coincidental.

Published by Akashic Books
©2012 Akashic Books

Series concept by Tim McLoughlin and Johnny Temple
Long Island map by Aaron Petrovich
"Boob Noir" ©2012 Jules Feiffer; "Summer Love" ©2012 JZ Holden

ISBN-13: 978-1-61775-062-5
Library of Congress Control Number: 2011943446

Akashic Books
PO Box 1456
New York, NY 10009
info@akashicbooks.com
www.akashicbooks.com

ALSO IN THE AKASHIC NOIR SERIES:

FORTHCOMING:

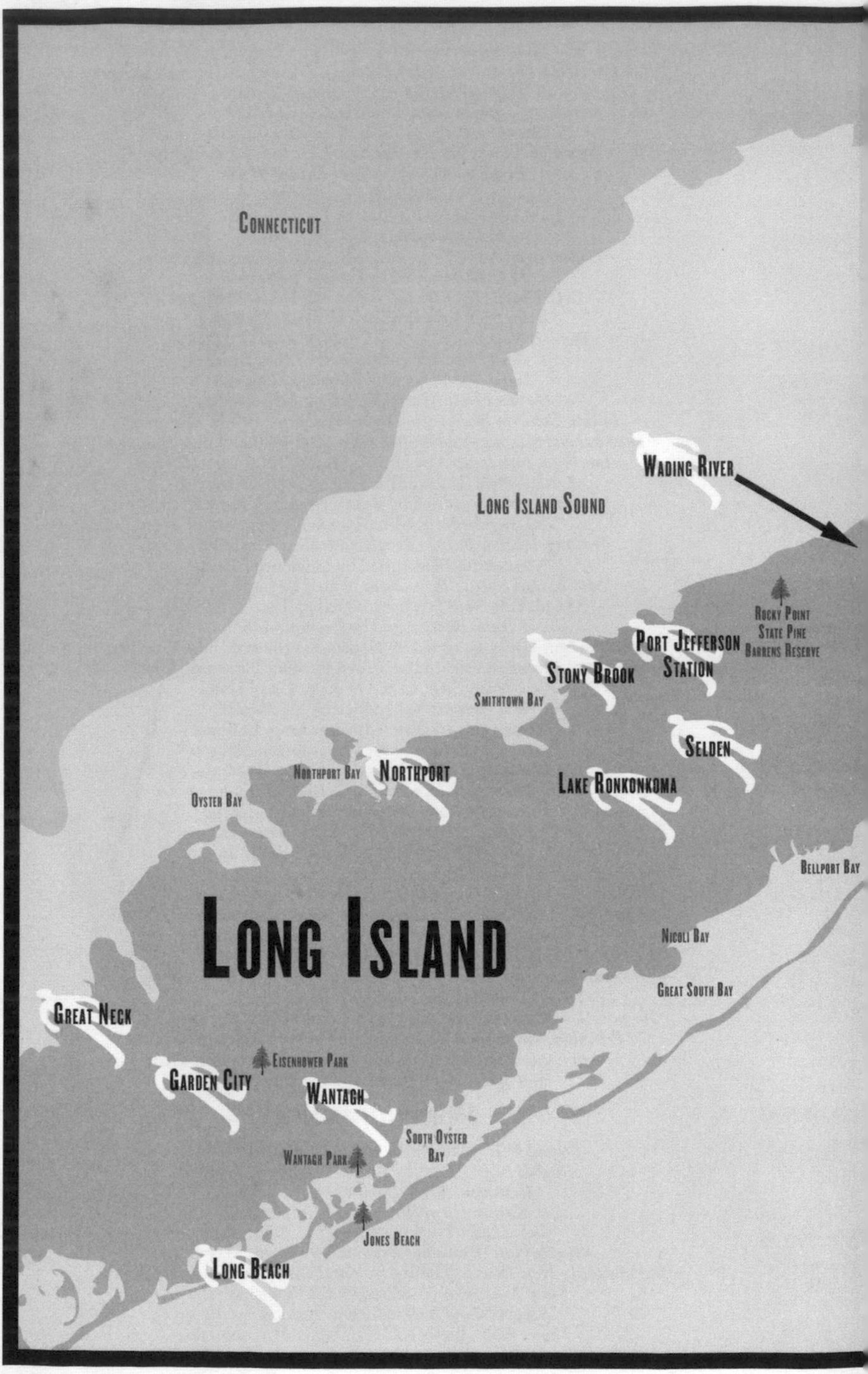

Connecticut
Wading River
Long Island Sound
Rocky Point
State Pine
Barrens Reserve
Port Jefferson
Station
Stony Brook
Smithtown Bay
Selden
Northport Bay
Northport
Lake Ronkonkoma
Oyster Bay
Bellport Bay
Long Island
Nicoli Bay
Great South Bay
Great Neck
Eisenhower Park
Garden City
Wantagh
South Oyster
Bay
Wantagh Park
Jones Beach
Long Beach

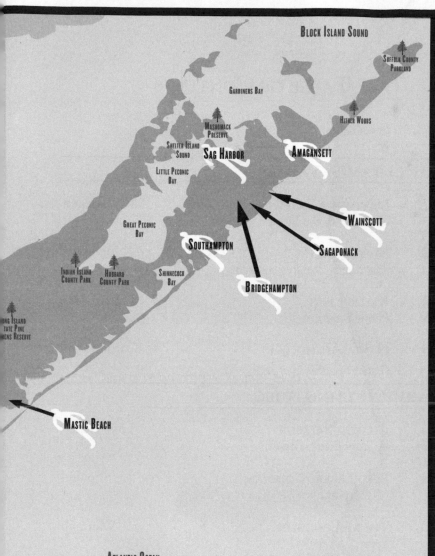

BLOCK ISLAND SOUND

SUFFOLK COUNTY
PARKLAND

GARDINERS BAY

HITHER WOODS

MASHOMACK
PRESERVE

SHELTER ISLAND
SOUND

SAG HARBOR

AMAGANSETT

LITTLE PECONIC
BAY

WAINSCOTT

GREAT PECONIC
BAY

SOUTHAMPTON

SAGAPONACK

INDIAN ISLAND
COUNTY PARK

HUBBARD
COUNTY PARK

SHINNECOCK
BAY

BRIDGEHAMPTON

LONG ISLAND
STATE PINE
BARRENS RESERVE

MASTIC BEACH

ATLANTIC OCEAN

N

TABLE OF CONTENTS

PART III: LOVE AND OTHER HORRORS

PART IV: AMERICAN DREAMERS

INTRODUCTION
A New Kind of Greedy Tension

Summers in the Hamptons were always wild and crazy, even in the late '70s when my family moved out east to Sagaponack. On the weekends in July and August the crowds would surge in from up the island and the city, and the bars, restaurants, and beaches were abuzz with an easygoing excitement rife with possibility. But as the Hamptons became more popular with a richer crowd—Hollywood stars, financial magnates, even politicians—a new kind of greedy tension filled the air, and even the locals were infected. Once, when I was out visiting my mother, I overheard a guy I'd known in high school, a builder, telling people at a bar that last year he'd put in a brand-new brick deck for this CEO prick's wife, but this year the guy's new girlfriend wanted to make a statement, so she told the builder to tear out the bricks and put in a cedar deck instead. "I told her $150,000," he laughed. "She didn't blink an eye." Then he tried to sell us the bricks.

Pretty soon the fields in Sagaponack were gone, replaced by mansions, each one bigger than the last, as if it were some kind of pumpkin-growing contest. And still, no one seemed content; not on the beach, where mobile phones were constantly ringing; not in line at the supermarket or outside the nightclubs; and certainly not stopped dead in stultifying midday traffic. Well, it's still traffic, whether you're in a Mercedes-Benz or a Honda Civic. Now, the truly rich fly out in private planes, adding to the general racket.

It's almost as if the whole world has caught Gatsbyitis. And what an amazing, prescient book that was. *The Great Gatsby* could be seen as the first noir novel of Long Island—a poor boy who doesn't have two cents to rub together falls for a rich girl who would never marry him. So he makes himself a massive fortune the only way he can—illegally. And buys himself a mansion on Long Island. Despite his fortune he is never truly accepted, never truly safe, comfortable, or content. And of course, she leaves him because he'll never be part of her set.

F. Scott Fitzgerald's mansions of Great Neck and Little Neck are still there, lording imposingly over their lesser neighbors. The American dream of suburban bliss has never died, only grown more desperate, more materialistic, and less romantic as it has shoved its way further east, until now there is literally nowhere left to go. The Hamptons I knew and loved are gone forever.

The most die-hard fans of *noir* fiction may find a few of these stories a little *gris*. Not everyone here is literally down and out, though spiritually, they'll give you a run for your money. A wealthy grandmother abandons her young grandson on a public beach in a moment of rage, putting his life in danger. A Northport hood is willing to murder his own brother for ratting out the local mob. An upper-class Pakistani woman almost dies in childbirth, a victim of severe marital abuse, yet she refuses to speak out. The president of a wealthy synagogue robs his donors blind in a ponzi scheme, including his staunchest supporter, a Holocaust survivor. They are all characters driven by some twisted notion of the American Dream, which they feel they must achieve at any cost. This is real-life noir. These people are our neighbors.

* * *

I heard this story at a dinner party once. Kurt Vonnegut, who lived on our street in Sagaponack and was a family friend I wish I'd known better, was invited to a summer cocktail party at the Hamptons home of some billionaire CEO. At the party, someone asked Kurt, "How does it feel to know this guy makes more money in a day than you will ever make in your life-time?" After a moment, Kurt responded calmly that he didn't mind at all, because he had something the CEO would never have.

"What's that?" the person challenged.

"Enough."

These are stories about people who will never feel they have enough, whether they have everything they ever dreamed of, or nothing at all.

Kaylie Jones
February 2012

PART I

Family Values

GATEWAY TO THE STARS
BY MATTHEW McGEVNA

Mastic Beach

Great with fear, Nick was deliberate about getting out of his car just as the policeman had told him. The order came after Nick was ordered to cut the engine because the noise from his broken muffler was "waking up the neighbors." It was seven p.m. Late January. Nick was just about to cross over the Jessup Lane Bridge, which led to Dune Road in Westhampton Beach, a strip of wealthy homes built on a barrier island. Nick knew that the gravelly sound of his muffler roaring past Main Street would draw the attention of the village cops. He had no delusions. Even if he'd somehow gotten over the bridge, he'd still have the bay constable to deal with. It wasn't that he picked his poison—his poison had picked him. He'd seen the reflector strips on the doors of the cop car just as he rounded the tall hedgerow and he knew he was caught—no time to debate whether he should try to make for the bridge, before the lights spun suddenly behind him. They illuminated the interior of his car. He could practically read the e-mail he'd printed out—between his sixteen-year-old brother Jeffrey and the lowlife who'd invited him to his beach house. In the dead of winter, it wouldn't be hard to narrow down the few houses with the lights still on inside, and fortunately "The Famous Mr. Ed" provided the address and a description of his house (which he warned Jeffrey he'd never find—buried as it was behind all the ivy and scrub pine). A white, circular observation tower rising from the roof *where I do all my meth and meditation*, he'd written. Thank you, Facebook. Nick was lucky Jeffrey was somewhat readable—lucky that he'd paid attention one day to Jeffrey's favorite song, Janis Joplin's "Summertime." Nick was only half-listening.

"One of these mornings, Nick, you're gonna rise up singing," he'd said.

"By rise up, you mean OD and choke on my puke?" Nick remembered joking.

But Jeffrey shot off, "You don't get it," before he could detect Nick's humor. Trying to have one of those brotherly moments.

Earlier tonight, somehow Nick had remembered this, and with his mother sobbing in the other room, he went on Facebook and tried to hack into Jeffrey's account, using any variation of Joplin's song he could think of, before finally getting in with *RISEUP*. He'd gone straight to Jeffrey's inbox and found two messages. One from their father. It had been awhile, but Nick recognized the shape of his own mouth in his father's profile pic and shook his head in disbelief. Dad wasn't on Jeffrey's "friends" list, but there was a message waiting nonetheless, and the photo was an old one, from back when their father still lived with them. Back when he was a fairly quiet spectator, moving when Nick's mother told him to move, remaining still when it seemed best to do so. It was taken before his father finally muttered to Nick in the middle of the night that he'd measured out his life in coffee spoons, and then got into his truck and pulled out of the driveway.

The note was brief but infuriating to Nick. *How are you, where have you been, what're you doing?* For a moment Nick felt the urge to delete it. Instead, he rolled his eyes and moved on to the second message. *Mr. Ed. Age: 16. Hometown: Oz.*

Quote: "Haytas only make me stronga." The message to Jeffrey was written in the voice of God.

> *Good and faithful servant Jeffrey. Thou willest visit the house of true Dionysian worship: the 1333rd house of Dune Road, and thou shalt participate in much celebration and mirth, and thou must see that it is good, when one ascends Jacob's ladder to the observation tower, where I myself do all my meth and meditation . . .*

Douche bag. Nick printed the message and Googled the address. A photo of the house popped up in the search. From one of the local newspapers. It was a photo of two old men and an old woman. The caption read: *Donna and Leonard Katzenberg donated $5,000 to Edward Schiffer's charity at his home reception at 1333 Dune Road this weekend.* Nick printed the article and read it while he drove out of Mastic Beach.

Edward Shiffer, the Famous Mr. Ed, hadn't seen sixteen since 1970. An investment broker who owned a string of hotels. Nick had no idea what he was going to do when he got there, but before he even found his keys and told his mother he was bringing Jeffrey home, he'd grabbed his old Ken Griffey Jr. Rawlings bat—thirty-two ounces, and cherry-stained, with dings in the barrel from hitting rocks when he was younger. As he read the article he began to form in his mind exactly what he wanted to do, but probably wouldn't. At the very least, the bat just might scare Ed Shiffer enough into getting facedown and not moving until he and Jeffrey were gone.

It was never going to work, Nick thought, and getting pulled over just before he crossed the bridge didn't come without a little bit of relief. Perhaps he'd get the cop to do something legal. A little less violent. Something that might get Jeffrey some help and nab a pervert at the same time.

But the conversation got off to a bad start. The moment Nick said good evening, the cop said, "Stick your good evenings, give me your license and registration," which Nick had at the ready. The cop took them. Said nothing until a smile of disbelief washed across his face and he shook his head. "How did I know you were from Mistake Beach?" he said. Nick said nothing. "I'm from there originally," the cop added.

Nick said, "Oh yeah?" and the cop looked at him suddenly.

"Originally," he repeated. "Pineway."

"I'm on Mayfield," Nick said, though he knew the cop had his license and could read. The cop gave him another look, as if to close the gap of familiarity.

"Are you bragging or complaining about that? Hope you're complaining."

"What?"

"All right, step out of the car," the cop said, backing away from his door. He tucked Nick's information into his front pocket. Nick tried to ask him what he was stopped for, but the cop barked his order again and it startled him. Then he told him to cut the engine—that he was waking the neighbors—and, for the third time, to step out of the car.

"I know it's not the quietest muffler," Nick said when he got out, but the cop cut him off by nudging him back against the car.

"It's not just the muffler. You also got a broken taillight, and you got a sticker on your back window obstructing your view, and your insurance is a week expired."

"I didn't notice all that."

"Of course you didn't—just like every other kid from Mastic I stop out here. What are you doing here?"

"My brother—"

"You robbing houses?"

"No, my brother—"

"What about your brother?"

"My brother has been missing for the past two days, and I think he's up in a house on Dune Road."

"Why would he be there?"

"He's got a drug problem."

"Are you bragging or complaining about that?"

Nick paused. "I guess I'm complaining," he said.

"Well, complain to your psychiatrist, not to me. Okay, what's the rest of your bullshit story?"

"It's not bullshit, there's a guy on Dune Road who met him over the Internet and invited him to a drug party. Look, I'll show you the e-mail." Without asking permission, he turned and ducked through the open window of the driver's side door. He felt a sudden force yank him back, and he was instantly on the ground with a knee in his ribs.

"You looking to get shot!" the cop screamed. "You never reach into your car like that—what are you reaching for?" The cop jerked him up off the ground and slammed him on the trunk. Nick yelled that he was sorry, but the cop told him to stick his sorries; to keep his palms and his right cheek down on the trunk. Then he went around to the passenger's side of Nick's car and yanked the door open. He grabbed the papers, including the e-mail. Stuffing them into his back pocket, he ripped open the glove box and pulled everything out. He moved to the seat cushions, the door pockets, and ran his hands under the seat.

"Where's the weapon?" he yelled. Nick said he didn't have one, keeping his face on the trunk. "Bullshit, everybody in your town's got some weapon. Never stopped one that didn't."

From then on Nick would only answer direct questions. His knees could hardly hold his weight. His chest ached. He wanted to vomit.

He was reminded of why he'd never tried to help his brother. The last time was in the sixth grade. Jeffrey was eight. It was the day after the Fourth of July, and Jeffrey had gone off with friends to collect fireworks that hadn't exploded—either because they were duds, had bad fuses, or were dropped by someone in all the excitement. His friends kept beating him to the prize—grabbing the spare firecrackers, bottle rockets, and jumping jacks before Jeffrey could reach them.

He came home crying, holding out three broken firecrackers in his palm while he rubbed his eyes and told Nick his friends weren't being fair. One of them even tackled him to the ground, punched his ribs, and snatched the jump rope Jeffrey had found fair and square.

Nick rode his bike down to the kid's house and called him out, shaking his fists at the front window. But the kid stepped out with his three older brothers: thirteen, fourteen, and sixteen.

Nick limped back home. His bike had been thrown over the fence into a sump. And the only thing Jeffrey could think to do was get mad that Nick hadn't recaptured his jumping jacks for him, and storm into the house, slamming the door. He didn't even stick around to hear Nick's side of things.

The front door of the car slammed, and the cop had opened the back door to continue his search. It took seconds for him to see the bat lying across the backseat and exclaim, "Ah, I thought so!" He showed Nick the bat with a satisfied smile.

"I play baseball from time to time," Nick said, which was a lie.

"And what were you planning to do with this tonight?"

"Nothing," Nick said, which was the truth.

"We've had three smash-and-grabs this month on Dune Road. Think I got the guy who did 'em?"

"What's a smash-and-grab?" Nick asked.

The cop came around the car, grabbed Nick's shoulder, and flipped him over so he was faceup. Then he waved the bat at him.

"You're in enough trouble as it is, you wanna be a fuckin' wise-ass, I'll jam this bat right down your throat. You've been smashing windows and stealing shit from cars."

"I have not!" Nick said.

"Then why do you have this?"

"I told you, I was heading over to that guy's house. He's got my brother."

"So you *were* gonna do something with it—a minute ago you play baseball, now you're gonna use it on someone?"

"I don't know why I took the bat," Nick said.

"Just shut the fuck up before you make it worse on yourself. You got any drugs on you?"

"What? No!"

"I'm going into your pockets, if I stick myself on a needle you're a dead piece of white, Mastic trash, you hear me? I'll ask you once more."

"I don't do drugs," Nick said "I'm a sophomore in college."

But the cop said that meant nothing, and after the lie about the bat he didn't believe a word he said. He had probable cause to search him. He recited his legal cover all while clutching at the outside of Nick's pockets. Nick could see the cop's breath pulsing into the cold night past his shoulder, as the cop rifled through his pockets. He came out with a few dollars and put them on the trunk. The wind blew them onto the street. Nick reached to catch them, which earned him another face-plant onto the trunk.

"Are you seriously on something?" the cop asked. Nick thought it was rhetorical, until the man stepped back and told him to undress. Nick must have looked as if he'd never heard English before. The cop repeated it, and told him he needed to complete his search.

"It's January," Nick said.

"You wanna cooperate and get undressed here, or in jail? It makes no difference to me—I still get a paycheck."

Nick pulled his jacket off, slowly, while shaking his head. The cop told him to throw the jacket on the ground toward him. He did. The cop picked it up. Same with the shirt. Then the pants. He collected them all. His dirty sneakers, his socks. He told Nick he could pull his underwear down below his balls, turn slowly around, and then pull them back up. It was then that Nick first felt the cold—when a solid wind coming in from the bay slid through his underarms.

"Good—sit on the trunk of your car."

Nick asked for his clothes back, but the cop was already making a retreat to his squad car, with Nick's clothes held in a heap in front of him, like evidence. The cop asked Nick if he had a record, and Nick shook his head.

"Bullshit. You wanna tell me now, get your clothes back, or you gonna make me look it up?"

"Look it up!" Nick yelled. "I don't have a record."

"We'll see," the cop said, and slid into his car with Nick's clothes.

Seated on the ice-cold trunk, Nick stared across the bay at the scattered lights that rose above the shoreline—like white holes punched into black paper. He could only hear the bay, leaping up with a spray to kiss the wind, while reeds sang softly between them, lined like Christmas carolers along the foot of the bridge.

What about afterward? he thought, when he tried to imagine his brother. He hugged his arms, now leathered from the cold. If Jeffrey is rescued, will he ever be saved? Will he appreciate it? Alter, or change?

He pulled his knees up—to fold the parts of his body not normally exposed into the parts that were. Get the back of his thighs elevated off the trunk. He thought to move to the hood, where it was likely still warm from the engine—but he stared into the cop's windshield and thought better of it. Instead, he forced his mind away from the cold again, and thought of the ride out—the tree-lined boulevards, the loop through Main Street, and the theater marquee he'd driven past. The old-fashioned bulbs mounted beneath, pouring yellow pools onto the sidewalk. As if they'd blink and John F. Kennedy would suddenly be alive. Be superb again. Be hoisted on shoulders. Back before everyone had given up on the cure for death.

As he'd passed the marquee he was reminded of his first movie. Being taken by his father to see *Snow White*. He was ten, and Jeffrey was six. Nick had begged to see the movie all week. They were between paychecks, so his parents decided to leave Jeffrey home with his mother. On his way out, Nick turned in the doorway and saw Jeffrey's blank face peeking out from behind Mom's legs. Nick started to cry and asked if Jeffrey could come, but they said it was the only way.

Shivering now—his mouth stiffening at the jawline—Nick could only remember those few things. Jeffrey's unmoved face staring quizzically back at him while he wept. His father finally "putting an end to this dinner theater" by shutting the door. And the dry taste of popcorn he barely ate.

Even in the cold, through clenched eyes, he pictured Jeffrey's face staring back at him. Blank as lions from the kill. Could there be an afterward, after that?

In greater nightmares, Nick often fixed his mind on one solitary image. A cop coming up to his mother's door. Wipers would nod across the windshield of his squad car. The only movement Nick would notice on the dull gray screen behind the officer. *Are you Mrs. Mahler?* he'd ask. Whatever the outcome. Dead or arrested. Nick had never allowed himself to imagine what would happen after.

But those nightmares had stopped awhile ago. Nick wasn't sure when. He figured the mind could only hold so much before it either stops dead or says: *Do what you must. I can't feel you anymore.* But since he was only twenty, midway though his sophomore year at college, his mind didn't stop, and so he did the latter. Jeffrey drifted in, and through him, around him. Left when Nick arrived, arrived when Nick left. Somehow the milk in the fridge needed replacing. The cereal was left out. A door slammed. Someone turned on the shower and a voice mumbled from it. That voice, which never asked a question. Shouted. Sang. Needed something—a ride to the store for cigarettes, even. Nothing. Mumbles. The occasional hums from its room late at night, when the stuff hits the veins and the limp body leans back against the baseboard. *Mmmm. Mwahhh.* The numb sound of the voice breathing, as if through a straw.

Somehow a door would be locked, and Nick's mother would bang to be let in. She'd know, but not really know, what he was doing in there. She'd suspected often, but only caught him once. Jeffrey had found his old skates and his hockey stick one day, and rolled through the house laughing, out onto the porch, sloshed across the grass like wading through water, and moved into the street. Nearly hit by a car, he spun around.

Slap-shot a rock as it passed. Ducked away from another car that honked. Then he skated off. Crashed into the mailbox and bounced the back of his head off the street. When his mother ran out to him, some blood had trickled from his ear.

She was too nervous, sitting in the waiting room, to wonder about how they would pay the bill for his stupidity. That was Nick's father's job—staring up at the TV as if he were paying attention to the woman on *Maury* obsessed with knitting dog clothes. Her family crying and begging her to stop. He shook his head and stood up, muttering, "How the fuck does this happen?"

It happens, so said the doctor, because acid makes it happen. They found it in his system. It was complicating his concussion. Nick's mother wanted to see him. His father was pacing the floor, repeating stories of wrapping the bleeding heads of drunken sailors back from shore leave before they got shipped off to Vietnam. He hated the sight of bandages. He'd go in, he said, and make sure to only look at Jeffrey's feet. But the doctors wouldn't let either of them visit just yet. There were "hurdles," they said.

After that, Nick's mother put Jeffrey in all sorts of therapy sessions, which made the ghost in Nick's house seem like a ghost finding final peace. Drifting away. Only the stories of him began to fill the rooms. How long he'd been using. How poorly he fit in at school. And another piece of puzzling information that had somehow been tucked away from his parents all these years: he had a vastly above-average IQ. A "superior genius" rating, said one doctor—and he asked if they hadn't noticed this. They hadn't. Nick's father had actually suspected the opposite. The doctor asked if they'd ever witnessed Jeffrey pick up a violin, or sit at the piano and start making sense of it, but they admitted that they never had instruments lying around the house. They weren't really music people, Nick's mother said, though that wasn't really what she meant.

"If you had instruments, you might have caught this. It's generally where extraordinary intelligence plays itself out," the doctor said. He shook their hands after the meeting.

Nick could offer nothing to the investigation his parents launched after that—to get to the bottom of who knew about Jeffrey's genius. The only thing Nick was able to contribute was an instance when they were in elementary school waiting at the bus stop, and fat Danny Yukely was challenging other kids to fight, and Jeffrey told Nick that Danny was the only person he would never fight because he had no "triangles." He was only circles. When they boarded the bus, Nick asked him what he meant. Jeffrey—second grade and laughing all the time—went into an explanation of a system of his own making, that people are made of shapes, mostly triangles, and you can beat people who have a lot of triangles because triangles are clumsy. He could see when people had triangles and when people didn't, and fat Danny Yukely didn't. He was all circles. And circles could not be knocked over. No one's ever seen an upside-down circle, have they?

When Nick's mother finished listening to this story she told Nick it sounded idiotic. Nick agreed. "Except," Nick said, squinting, "I still remember that because it's sort of true."

The car door slammed again. And the cop—all circles, Nick suspected—was carrying his heap of clothes in front of him. He stepped a little closer and threw them at Nick, who instantly snatched as much as he could from the air and started to dress. His jaw shook terribly.

"All right," the cop said. "Doesn't look like you have a record." Nick nodded. The cop noticed and added, "So I was right again." Nick was too cold to question his logic.

"My brother," was all he could mutter, and the cop pulled the e-mail out from a pile of things he'd grabbed during the car search.

"Your brother's doing drugs?" He shook his head in disgust. "Younger or older?"

"Younger," Nick said.

"So this is your fault. Okay, here's what's up. As far as I'm concerned he's over on Dune Road, he's the bay constables' headache. If he's still alive. I'll radio his name to the constables. If he turns up, we'll let you know. But you should know, I'm keeping this e-mail and he will be under arrest."

"What about Ed Schiffer?" Nick asked.

"Don't worry about him—I'm telling you about your brother—he's out here, he's using substances, if we find him, he's ours. But you'll be notified."

"He needs help," Nick said, though he knew it wouldn't matter. "He's a prodigy—he's supposed to do better things."

The cop asked him what a prodigy was.

"A genius," Nick said.

The cop made a fart noise. "Some genius."

"Will he get help if we find him?"

"Not up to me." The cop was writing something. "And what do you mean we?"

"Can't I go look for him? On Dune Road?"

"Are you drunk?" the cop asked. "Say the alphabet." Nick said it. "Here's what's gonna happen. These are yours." He handed Nick four tickets and his information. "You're gonna get into your car and you're gonna swing the front end around so it's facing north, okay?" Nick nodded. "Then you're gonna take this road all the way up to the roundabout, and you're gonna take the left exit. Got it?" Nick nodded again. "That road leads straight into Mastic and Mastic Beach. Go there. Stay there. We'll call you if we hear something."

Nick, realizing he'd been listening to false directions, shook his head and looked at the tickets.

"You in college?" the cop asked. Nick nodded. "Get good grades?"

"Dean's list," he said quietly.

"Are you bragging or complaining?" the cop said with a slight smile.

Nick laughed a little. He started to walk away. The cop called out to him. Nick stopped. The cop walked closer.

"One of these days when you get a house out here, you'll realize why we're so by-the-book. This is the gateway to the stars; there's a lot of money out here, and they don't want just anybody drivin' around. Sorry I had to be a hard-ass, but you understand, right?" He waited for an answer, but none came. "I mean, look at me, I come from the same town as you—I didn't get it either, but these people, they're real intense about riffraff coming into the village. People bringing fights and stealing shit—people like your brother, all due respect, you know?" The cop was again answered with silence. "No hard feelings," he said, and turned to walk away. "I hope we find your little bro."

Minutes later, Nick was reaching the roundabout where he needed to yield, and noticed that the cop had followed him out. He locked stares with him in the rearview mirror, and the cop nodded to him just as the circle cleared. They parted ways.

His body warmed as he blasted the heat and watched the slick surface of Twin Ponds glide by his passenger window—frozen under a foot of ice. Winter birds waddled with their young through paths cleared by skaters. Every star was visible. It made everything inside Nick seem immense. Earth, a place to be swallowed. Mastic Beach, a labyrinth. Guilt, anger, love—unavoidable. Life . . . long. Stars . . . mighty things to hide between. Waddling birds and their roost . . . sage in their simplicity.

It stuck in his chest to think so, but just then he wanted Jeffrey to run. Run and hide, and disappear. Even if it meant he would never see him again. Jeffrey wasn't part of the same world, Nick knew this now. He'd break spirits that tried to ground him. Was bigger than all of them—Nick was mistaken to try and find him. For what, and who would he find? And do what? And how would he convince something that had sailed away so long ago to come back over the bridge? To his own destruction? The cop even told him so.

He shook his head at how, just hours ago, he was praying to find him—a short while ago he breathed with relief that a cop might be able to help him. Now he couldn't imagine a worse fate, and wasn't that how the world he lived in really was? Always having to wait for a bad thing to happen so it makes way for something potentially good?

He pulled into his driveway and idled there. The heat was still on. Light bled white and silver onto the frost-speckled lawn when his mother pulled the front door open. He watched her peer through the reflection of their glass door, shield her eyes, and press her face against the glass.

She focused on Nick. The exhaust pulsed—spat clouds of mist around his car. Nick watched her and then looked over at the empty passenger's seat where he knew his mother was hoping to see her other son. He looked at the seat and half smiled at Jeffrey. Not there, but never before so close.

THY SHINY CAR IN THE NIGHT

BY NICK MAMATAS

Northport

My father told me around the time I seriously started reading books as a teenager that he used to know Jack Kerouac. "When I was a young man, he was living right here in Northport," he said. When we were next on Main Street, he pointed to Gunther's Tap Room as we passed it and said, "Petey, Kerouac used to play pool in there all the time, and sometimes he'd hold court on whatever subject bubbled up in his writerly brain." There were even a few photos of Kerouac in the window, and a sign reading *KEROUAC DRANK HERE*, which I'd never noticed before. I was a kid; I had eyes only for Lic's Ice Cream, the Sweet Shop, and the little newsstand that carried comic books alongside *Newsday* and car magazines. But then I started noticing the other Northport, the one day-trippers don't see.

That's about when I figured out what my father did for a living. "Waste management, middle management," he'd tell me, "boss of all the garbage men on the North Shore." I'd repeat that line in school, knowing it wasn't quite the whole story. I knew we were semiconnected, since Uncle Peter, for whom I am named, couldn't stop talking about it. He was a cliché, central casting for *The Sopranos*, with a thick-tongued accent my father didn't have, a penchant for tracksuits, a ridiculous silvery Cadillac, and rings too gaudy for even the Pope to wear.

I'd be working on my Commodore 64 or have my nose in a book when he'd come over for dinner and say, "That's right. You do good in school, you hear me, and get a good job. A *career*." Career was a three-syllable word to Uncle Peter. "Work to get laid," he'd say. "Not to get made. It's no life." Even I knew what getting made was.

Uncle Peter said he knew Kerouac too. "That guy? Ha! Jim said he knew him?" Granted, my father was a little man, balding with a bundt cake of hair around the back of his head, and he dressed like an accountant. Not the kind of guy you'd think would be hanging out with the king of the Beats.

"Yeah," Uncle Peter continued, all wistful. "Me and this friend of mine, we'd seen Kerouac on TV, then two days later in his garden, wearing coveralls like some kid, then that night wandering down the street like a real stumblebum. The guy was *stunad*, so I thought we'd give him a shakedown."

"Why, Uncle Peter?"

"Eh, we were just dumb kids. We thought writers had money! Anyway, he was a pretty big dude. A lot of muscle, and he could take a punch. I was waling on him, my friend was holding—"

"Who? Dad?"

"Pfft, no way. Nah, you don't know this guy. He was my friend who died before you were born. Anyway, Kerouac was just standing there. It was like punching a car through a pillow. There were definitely muscles under all that fat, and he was just going on about Buddhism and how he was a pacifist. Anyway, your *nonna* had sent Jim to go find me, and he pulls me off and tells me that writers don't have any money, and plus Jack is the only one left to take care of his old mother, so don't hurt him, and especially don't break his thumbs as he won't even be able to do any writing if we did. Kerouac looked like a friggin' bum—unshaved, ratty old navy coat, smelled like a vineyard, so I felt bad and I ended up putting fifty bucks in *his* pocket." Uncle Pete ran his big palms over his face. "Man, that was a time." Then, conspiratorially, "Don't tell Elaine about any of this."

Elaine was Uncle Peter's fiancée. The wedding took place a week after that conversation, in Queens where they lived. We had to park four long Queens blocks away from the church because every spot on the street was taken up by a sedan—some belonged to guests, others to pairs of men who sat in their cars the whole time, eating sandwiches, writing down notes in little pads, and occasionally taking photos of the church, the street, or one of the other cars.

My mother fixed my tie, put a tired smile on her face, and said, "Stand up straight. Pretend that you're famous and that the men across the street are paparazzi." Left unspoken was . . . *and not federal agents.*

It was a great wedding. Tons of food, and dancing, and all sorts of guys coming up to my father at our table and shaking his hand, telling me what a good guy my dad was, how fair and honest and sweet, and that I'd be lucky to grow up to be like him. "Keep that nose clean! In the books!" My father bragged to them about my grades and that I had free access to the adult section at the public library. "Adult, eh?" a few of them said, snickering.

That was a Saturday, June 16, 1984. Back in Northport Ricky Kasso was torturing and killing Gary Lauwers out in the Aztakea Woods. Kasso was the high school "Acid King," a drug dealer and user who was into heavy metal and, supposedly, Satanism. Kasso stabbed Lauwers over a dozen times, demanding that he say, "I love Satan!" Lauwers was the good boy of the story—he would only say, "I love my mother!" The body wasn't discovered till the Fourth of July, his eyes ruined, maggots in the wounds, animals picking at scraps of flesh. Kasso, who had been bragging to his friends about "human sacrifice," killed himself in jail three days later. Then Northport really went crazy.

Uncle Peter cut his honeymoon to the Old Country short. He was now always at our house, going off on sudden errands my father needed done. And Dad was on the phone constantly, talking to guys in the city. "Satanists in the fucking woods!" he bellowed, angry for the first time ever as far as I knew. "We got to get them out of there."

The local priest came over for dinner; I had to wear my wedding suit again. We'd only ever gone to church on Christmas Eve, but Father Ligotti was attentive to my father's questions about Satan and "today's kids" to the point of seeming frightened. Then it clicked—my father wasn't just some pencil pusher in an office in charge of waste management, he was definitely part of the Mothers and Fathers Italian Association, and probably pretty high up. The town longhairs—that's what they called themselves; us normal kids called them dirtbags—didn't spend much time outside that summer, but when I'd see one on Main Street or over by the harbor or in the rich neighborhood pushing a mower across the lawn of someone else's house, they'd be sporting black eyes, a missing tooth, or a broken hand. They never walked alone. There were strange things happening in the woods, all right, and soon enough every kid in town knew to stay the fuck away from Aztakea.

I was too young to know the older kids except by face and reputation. They'd picked on a lot of us freshmen, but I never had any problems, thanks as I now know to Dad. I heard all the Kasso stories, most of which were just hysterical rumors. But one was true—Kasso was probably on drugs when he committed the murder. There was a boulder by the scene where he, or someone anyway, had tried to scrawl *SATAN LIVES*. But he spelled it wrong; it read *SATIN LIVES*.

We had an assembly when school started that year to talk about drugs and watching out for one another. There was a big sheet hung in the hallway by the principal's office and we were told we could write whatever we liked on it, as long as it was positive. No pentagrams, no band names, nothing like that. I wrote, *Whither goest thou, America, in thy shiny car in the night?* from *On the Road*. My English teacher that year, Mrs. Hartman, congratulated me on my "apropos epigram." I ate lunch in the library every day, so it was easy for me to look up *apropos* once I figured out how to spell the word.

My mother went through my records and tapes, demanding answers. "What's this?" she asked. "More heavy metal?" It was Van Halen's *1984*.

"Mom, that music's on the radio all the time! It's not Satanic. There's even an angel on the cover," I said, probably whining, definitely embarrassed.

She snorted. "An angel! That's just the Devil's way to lure you in." The Stephen King paperbacks went into the trash, so did *The Savage Sword of Conan* back issues. She had her hands on *Desolation Angels* too, but my father slid into the room and grabbed her wrist, my hero. "Mary. Maria. That one's fine. That one's okay. It's a college-level book."

I read a lot of college-level books. They were still allowed; fantasy novels, Dungeons & Dragons, Freddy Krueger, Rambo, that was all contraband. I started reading *real* books, literature, more intently than ever, so looking back I guess I don't mind. My parents, ever overprotective, didn't want me to go away for college, or even to the city. "Between the *mulignan* in the projects and the fruitcakes in the Village, you'll end up a vegetable if you go to NYU," Uncle Peter said. My father told him not to talk that way at the table, but he agreed with the sentiment.

So I went to Hofstra and did well, then hit the road. I did a lot of scut work—janitor; a baton-twirling Wackenhut security professional for a town dump in New Jersey (my surname helped); out to Chicago as an SAT tutor; then on to California to work in a bookstore. And I wrote. I always wrote. I got over romanticizing poverty, and the road, but I never got over Kerouac. Like the book says, *I knew there'd be girls, visions, everything; somewhere along the line the pearl would be handed to me.*

I got a few things published too—poems in a haiku journal, stories in *Oakland Hills Review* and one in a C-level men's magazine about D cups that ran the occasional lurid fiction feature. It was called "Satin Lives," that story, and it was about a thinly veiled Ricky Kasso I'd turned into what Uncle Peter called a "real smart-ass" and over late-night coffees during Christmas when I visited for a week or three I let my father know what I thought of his work. My mother was already in bed. Cooking for forty fat cousins and their kids always took a lot out of her, especially after the lumpectomy. Nobody would lift a finger to help her either, not even me, I'm ashamed to admit.

"I don't hurt anyone, Petey. If not for me, there'd be a lot more people hurting, I'll tell you that much," my father said. "It's what we call *property rights*. There's a lot of money to be made hauling trash on Long Island. People here are pigs; they certainly generate enough garbage. The island used to be beautiful, all trees and little towns. Now it's just a hundred-mile-long dump for hamburger wrappers and toxic waste. A lot of people want in on sanitation, and I keep everyone happy, working a certain territory."

"And if someone steps out of line?" I asked. "Or wants to just run an honest business?"

He snorted. My family was full of snorters. My mother was the champion, but Dad was a top contender. "Honest business? Good luck. Look at Wall Street. And anyway, you weren't complaining about ethics when I paid your college tuition; when you were able to gallivant around the country without a penny of debt thanks to me."

"What about the government? What about the law?"

"Listen, if the government cared, they'd just municipalize garbage collection and put us all out of business. We're more efficient than they are, even with the occasional *present* we have to buy, or a labor action here and there. You think garbage men could afford to live out here if Suffolk County paid them? Pfft."

"That doesn't mean what you're doing isn't illegal. The law, the American way—"

He laughed. He had a great laugh, my father. "You sound like Kerouac now. He was a real Republican near the end, all that beatnik business aside. He *hated* hippies, hated liberals. Let me tell you, what does the government do? It organizes property rights just like I do. And yes, it threatens violence when it has to. The difference is that the government doesn't care about the people—they're a violence monopoly, they don't have to. We have to watch out for ourselves; we can't just go crazy and invade the next town over for no reason, not like the Bushes invading Iraq whenever they want to feel tough." George W. Bush was rattling the saber just then for what would be the 2003 invasion, just like his own father had back when I was in college.

"It's not the same, it's just not the same." I was tired, itching for a fight. "The government . . ." What? I thought to myself. The government doesn't bully people? Doesn't tax the hell out of them? Doesn't dump toxic waste out in Aztakea Woods and pollute water tables and give nice suburban mothers breast cancer? The rest of my sentence hung in the air like steam from my mouth. Dad knew where we could take the conversation if I wanted, and so did I. It was nowhere good. I went outside to smoke a cigarette and stare up at the Long Island sky. *The stars were pinpricks in the woolen blanket of the night here, but not in the metropolises of America, where you never dare look up.* I wrote that down, and put it in an (unpublished) poem.

I don't know exactly what happened; it surely wasn't our arguments. But the following summer my dad went to the DA and turned rat. He wasn't offered a deal or pressured. He just showed up with a zip drive full of evidence and an eagerness to explain where "all the bodies are buried"—as it read on the front page of *Newsday*—right after he buried my mother. It was the breast cancer that killed her, like so many ladies from Long Island. *No cancer cluster on LI, my prostate!* Listen to that. Here I am, turning into Uncle Peter, who was coming tonight to kill my father, his own brother. Uncle Peter was always a kidder, always ready with a joke or a smart remark. But he took his oath seriously, more seriously than marriage or blood. Not like my dad, not like me.

I was waiting outside, on the porch. I didn't smoke anymore, but I smoked that night to keep my lungs warm. The sky was brighter than when I was a kid, thanks to the big-box stores and strip malls dotting the highway. My father didn't rate any police protection—though it took a few months, the government got all they wanted out of him, and the local uniforms could be bought off with grocery money. He was inside, drinking his best wine, the stuff he used to kid he was saving for my wedding, and waiting to join his Maria. Uncle Peter's giant boat of a Caddy, still all polished and gleaming, drove up the curve of the driveway. My mother always loved this house.

"Hey kid," he said conversationally. "When'd you get in? Haven't seen you since your poor mother, bless her in heaven, passed." Uncle Peter wasn't as huge as he used to be. He looked partially deflated, like a Macy's Day Parade balloon half an hour after the crowds left.

"I just got here this morning. Took in the sights. Had some fresh snapper; the fish are better out here than in California, you know. Had a Crazy Vanilla ice cream down at the store, went to Gunther's, that sort of thing."

"Gunther's, eh? You a pool hustler now?" He edged forward, keeping his hands in front of him. Maybe he wouldn't kill me here on this porch. Maybe Northport was still a nice small town, where a gunshot wouldn't be written off as a car backfiring, where porch lights might blink on and screen doors swing open at one in the morning.

"Nah, they had a reading tonight. I was one of the readers." I lit another cigarette. "It was even listed in the paper; they ran my picture. *Homecoming for Local Author*."

"A reading?" He was confused. Good. Maybe a little drunk too. I hoped he'd have to be to kill his own brother in cold blood, never mind having to kill me too. "Like, people just sit there and read?"

"No, Uncle Peter; we read aloud. It's like a show. It's for Kerouac's memorial anniversary. They do one every October at Gunther's."

"Was Louie there? Jess?"

I shook my head. "Nah, the regulars clear out when the poets hit the stage. You know how Northport is . . ." I waved my right hand, the cherry of my cigarette bobbing along in the shadows, so he didn't see what I reached for until my old extendable baton telescoped out and smacked him right in the shin. Uncle Peter was still a large man—it's like trying to chop down a tree with a baseball bat. *Something he would say!* But he was old and slow, and I got up and swung the baton down on his head three, four times, and I shouted. I shouted, "I love my mother! I love my mother! I love my mother and father!" No porch lights went on. No screen doors swung open, except for the one behind me.

"Pete . . ." my father said, his mouth heavy with wine. I didn't know which of us he meant.

The Cadillac is eating Pennsylvania for breakfast by the time the sky lightens. My father's next to me, leaning his head out the window like a dog. His son's crazy, the craziest man he's ever known, but he's alive. Alive and free and on the road. Forget property taxes, chemicals on the lawns to keep them green. Forget the police, forget the families of New York, who are all dying or senile or in prison or watching better versions of themselves on the television and saying to themselves, *Yeah, yeah. Al Pacino, that's me.* Forget Long Island, that little turd hanging off the end of America. *California, here we come!* We have a suitcase full of unmarked bills my father had hidden behind the drywall in the garage, my bandaged-up uncle in the trunk banging away on the lid. We have nothing to lose, everything to live for, my father and I. Dad figures his brother will calm down by the time we get to Ohio; then we can let him out and have a little "sit-down" about his future. I hope Uncle Peter decides to come with us. We'll fall asleep and wake up again a million times. In the West, the sun peeks out distantly on the horizon, a great white pearl.

HOME INVASION

BY KAYLIE JONES

Wainscott

That first winter in Wainscott, my dad and I both read Vincent Bugliosi's book about the Manson murders, *Helter Skelter*, which had recently come out. I was so terrified I didn't sleep for three days, even with all the lights on in the house and the doors and windows bolted shut. My dad brought out his revolver, a beautiful Colt pistol with a blueish tint and a little gold medallion of a rearing horse embossed on the brown handle, which he kept in his bedside table, just in case. He believed every man had a right to defend his home and every home was at risk in one way or another. He drove me out into the Northwest Woods of East Hampton and nailed a white paper with a circular black target to a birch tree. It was sandy land, mostly birches and scrub pines, no one around for miles. The first thing he told me was never, ever point a gun at anyone unless you intended to fire it. He showed me the safety and then taught me how to stand with my legs slightly spread and breathe, keeping my knees a little bent, and how to sight down the barrel with both eyes open. "Anybody ever breaks into your house, shoot 'em. And never let anyone tie you up, no matter what they promise." He believed home invaders were cowards at heart, and standing up to them was the only chance you had, whether they ended up killing you or not.

He took me out into the woods once a week and let me

fire the pistol until I could hit the center of the target at fifteen yards, four out of six times. He also taught me how to load the gun. He promised to eventually teach me to make my own bullets, but we never got around to that.

One evening in late February my dad was sitting at the bar in Bobby Van's with my stepmother Yukiko—this was long before the dark old tavern decided to turn fancy and move across the street. My dad was moping because he'd recently been told by his heart doctor that he couldn't drink anymore. Mick Todd, a local guy who filled in sometimes behind the bar, suggested my dad try a little smoke. A little smoke never hurt anybody, Mick said; in fact, in some states pot was starting to be prescribed to cancer patients.

Mick had taken a special liking to my dad, because his dad, like mine, had been in WWII. My dad had fought on Guadalcanal with the 25th Infantry "Tropic Lightning" Division, while Mick's had been in the Battle of the Bulge with Patton's Third Army. But Mick's dad had become "a mean drunk" and Mick would have nothing to do with him. The Todds, it was said, used to own half of Shelter Island. Mick never seemed to be hurting for money. He drove a little light-blue BMW with a surfboard rack on top. He had those perfectly symmetrical, slightly austere WASP features—thin, aquiline nose, strong jaw, fine mouth, blue irises that always swam in a sea of red, and blond hair like straw growing every which way out of his head. His skin was burned to a crisp, even in February, and he wore extremely old and faded preppie button-down shirts with pot-seed burns speckling the cotton. He looked like a WASP kidnapped by Apaches.

My dad told me later that he decided to take Mick up on his offer, and they left Yukiko at the bar (she wanted nothing to do with this nonsense) and went out back into the parking lot without their coats. Mick lit up a joint in the freezing cold and had to show my dad how to suck in the smoke and hold his breath. At first, my dad told me, he didn't feel anything and went back to his barstool a little disappointed. A while later he realized everyone around him was drunk, having incomprehensible discussions, shouting, repeating themselves and spilling drinks, and all he could do was sip his fresh-squeezed lemonade and contemplate his unbearably profound thoughts. He liked the clarity of his thoughts, though their intensity made him feel alienated from everyone else who was drinking, and it unnerved him. He told me he wanted to shout, *Don't you understand what's going on here? The world is turning beneath our feet and no one cares!*

He got up and went into the men's room to pee and locked himself in a stall, grateful for the sudden silence. He started to pee and thought he was taking an awful long time but convinced himself that it was only the pot that seemed to be slowing time down. He decided he wanted to order a dessert at the bar. He was thinking about what kind of dessert to order and that really this pee was taking an awful long time, but no, it couldn't be, it was just the pot, when a man outside the stall muttered, "What the hell is this guy trying to do, get his name in the *Guinness Book of World Records*?"

My dad knew I smoked a little pot with my high school friends so he started asking me about the different kinds and what was the best way to smoke it. Was a pipe better than a joint? Had I ever heard of a bong? "What do I know?" I told him. "I just smoke whatever anyone hands me." I was only sixteen and totally self-involved. Did so-and-so really like me and would I be asked to the junior prom and would someone offer me a ride to the basketball game Friday night? But I found it extremely amusing that my dad was becoming a pothead. When he took an interest in a subject, he studied it to the very core, be it the Civil War, about which he'd written three best-selling history books, or the U.S. attack on Iwo Jima, or how to put up shingles on the side of the house.

He started collecting film canisters of marijuana, asking everyone he knew who smoked to sell or give him a little. A few days after he died, in his attic office I found a Romeo y Julieta cigar box filled with carefully labeled film canisters with stickers written in bold, capital letters. *PANAMA RED. THAI STICK. HAWAIIAN PURPLE. SINSEMILLA. CO-LOMBIAN GOLD.* He even had a little pot pipe someone must have given him that smelled of resin and smoke. I appropriated all of it, smoked it by myself, down to the last fleck. I watched the clouds sail by outside the window and contemplated the future, while downstairs Yukiko lay on their bed in a doctor-prescribed twilight state.

Mick liked my dad a great deal, so that spring, when my dad asked him to help grow some weed in our backyard, Mick took the job seriously—well, as seriously as Mick ever took anything. First, he selected the very best seeds he could find, from some Hawaiian Purple he'd scored off a Samoan while on a surfing trip. We lived at the edge of Mr. Wisnowski's potato field, on the only hillock in Wainscott, the shingled saltbox house protected by an ancient hops hornbeam, maple and horse chestnut trees that in the summertime were like giant shimmering green parasols. There were lilac bushes and a tall privet hedge on two sides, so the spot was well protected and concealed, and the topsoil perfect for growing. On the day of planting, Yukiko, in silent protest, chose to remain in the house. Yukiko had been my dad's Japanese history specialist on his Iwo Jima book; she took his work very seriously, even now that she was his wife. She thought this pot-growing idea of his was a folly; pot was illegal, after all, and my father was a well-known writer. What if he got arrested?

Mick poked little holes in the turned soil with his index finger, about a foot apart, in even rows. "Water them once in a while," he told my dad and me as we stood watching, fascinated. "If you think of it. But lightly. A light spray." He wriggled his fingers in the air over the patch of ground. "And dig a hole, you know, and bury your compost at the edges." What was compost? I had no clue; I wasn't a country girl, having just moved out to Wainscott from the city the previous fall. When my dad's heart had really started acting up, Yukiko decided the quiet country air would be good for him, and they gave up New York City and the literary scene and enrolled me in East Hampton High School, where I was already ahead of everyone except the Advanced Placement and High Honor Roll seniors. This was okay; I didn't have to work too hard and could spend more time with my dad.

By mid-May the pot plants were four feet high and the stalks beginning to thicken. It turned out all three of us were watering them, and also burying compost, including Mick's contribution of the refuse from Bobby Van's restaurant. These were some richly fed pot plants.

One weekend in June a fierce nor'easter was predicted on the news. Intense winds and rain. Mick was delighted for the surfing possibilities but worried about the pot plants, and the day before the storm he brought over a tarp and some iron posts and clamps and stood out there, hammering away until the plants were safe. The next day, in wind and teeming rain, his car rolled up the driveway with the headlights on. He had surfboards tied to the roof. He was coming to check on the plants. A few minutes later he knocked on the kitchen door, his blue T-shirt soaked through and clinging to his torso. He was in an ebullient mood, the tarp had held.

"Hey," he said to me and my dad with a big white-toothed grin, clearly the product of expensive braces, "you guys want to drive out to Montauk with me and watch me and my buddies surf?"

"Surf, in this?" I asked, aghast.

"Well," he explained, "the storm's movin' out to sea. By the time we get there, should be pretty clear."

My dad said he wasn't feeling up to it, and he wasn't so sure it was a good idea for me to go alone, being that I was only sixteen, but I begged him. He was big on new experiences and this promised to be a once-in-a-lifetime event. He made Mick promise to drive slowly and to bring me back by nightfall.

The first thing I learned on the way out to Montauk was that Mick Todd was twenty-seven, much older than he looked or acted. The second thing I learned was how to snort coke off his leather wallet, the straight lines cut by an American Express credit card and the crisp dollar bill rolled evenly while he was driving one-handed in the teeming rain. The third thing I learned was that he'd recently gotten his license back after a year's suspension. He'd driven his previous car, a 1967 Mustang, a little too fast around a curve on Sag Harbor Turnpike and ended up in "this old couple's" living room, crashing right through the wall. They were sitting there watching TV; it was a miracle they didn't die of a heart attack. The worst part of it, besides getting arrested for drunk driving and losing his license, was that his Mustang was totaled. A real pity, a car like that, it just couldn't be replaced.

There was very little I could say to any of this except, *Wow*. He told me the cops hadn't pulled him over in this new car yet so we should be okay, but I'd better snort up quick, just in case. He'd kind of burned his bridges with the cops, despite the fact that they'd known his family for generations.

I also learned, watching Mick surf off Ditch Plains Beach in Montauk, that he was completely fearless. Boy, could he surf. He glided effortlessly over the crests and into the barrels, and several times I thought he was going to die, drowned or crushed on the ocean floor as the blue-green mountains rolled down over his head. But each time he emerged with a shake of his wet hair and a whoop of adrenaline-fueled happiness.

He took off his wet suit and swim trunks standing beside his car and slipped on a pair of battered shorts and a T-shirt without drying off. He got in, cut some more lines on his wallet, and that was the first time he kissed me.

He was too old for me, I realized that. There was no reason at all he should be interested in me. I was a virgin; I knew absolutely nothing. But I did know my dad would blow a gasket if he found out. We kept it pretty chaste, making out a couple of times in his car in the Caldor parking lot or down at Wainscott Beach, when we were supposed to be out running errands. Mick felt alien to me, not like the boys my age I'd kissed and let feel me up. His body pulsed with energy that I wasn't sure he could, or knew how to, contain. I'd come home from these excursions with my head in a fog and my clothes twisted up. My dad was no fool; I wondered how much he'd figured out.

My dad's health deteriorated and this became his constant preoccupation, along with wondering if he would be able to get back to his new book. Pretty soon he couldn't catch his breath to climb the stairs to his office. Yukiko drove him to Huntington, which had the best hospital and the best heart specialist on the Island. The doctor decided to check him in, mostly for tests, and Yukiko stayed with him.

I hung up the phone and turned on all the lights downstairs although it wasn't dark out yet. I was sitting in the kitchen watching *The Bionic Woman* on TV when Mick walked in through the back door, without knocking. He must have seen that by dad's VW Rabbit was gone; he must have known they weren't home.

"Plants are looking excellent!" he said with his usual enthusiasm.

"My dad's in Huntington Hospital. They're running tests."

"Oh. Whoa." He put out his hands as if attempting to stop the charge of a big dog.

He stood behind me and placed his warm hands on my shoulders, kneading the muscles there, which were tighter than I'd realized. "Wow, you're tense! Come on, let me give you a massage."

Mick opened a bottle of my dad's French wine, which he could no longer drink, and in one hand carried the bottle and two long-stemmed elegant crystal glasses into my bedroom downstairs, his other hand around my waist, guiding me. It felt sacrilegious, letting him lie on my bed in my room while my dad and Yukiko were at the hospital. It felt wrong but Mick didn't seem to think so and pretty soon he'd expertly slipped off my shirt and bra. He pulled his own shirt off right over his head. His body was thin, his muscles strong and taut. He pressed my hand against the bulge in his jeans, which felt entirely too big and unfriendly. I wasn't ready and I was scared. I pulled my hand away. Already I'd let this go too far. I'd let it get out of hand.

"You have to go," I said uncertainly. "If someone sees your car in the driveway they'll tell my dad."

"Suck me off," he whispered hoarsely.

I said no.

"I don't care about your dad," he muttered. He unbuttoned my cutoffs and started to tug them down my legs. I didn't know what to do. This was my fault. I'd let him into my room, into my bed. I'd let this go too far. People would blame me no matter what.

"Oh, baby," he said against my neck, his mouth wet and sticky, "you're so hot."

I started to struggle, trying to push him off. He was not a tall guy, but his muscles felt like steel. "Oh, yeah, that's it."

What was he talking about? The rest happened so fast it was like one of his juggling tricks. The same way he rolled joints while driving, or cut lines on his wallet, or could carry a bottle of wine and two glasses in one hand. One second we're just lying there rolling around and I'm struggling a little, and the next he's got a lubricated condom on and he's pressing his fat penis into me, ripping me in two.

I couldn't wait till it was over. I couldn't wait for him to leave.

No one would think rape. My dad would surely have shot him, but my poor dad had problems of his own. I couldn't impose this upon him now, in his weakened state. What if it killed him? It would kill him.

I finally convinced Mick he had to leave (it wasn't too hard once he'd finished); I bolted the front and back doors behind him, and all the windows in the house. I called my dad in his hospital room. My voice was shaking and his sounded distant, vague, but perhaps they'd drugged him. I told him I loved him, my voice breaking. He told me to take good care, to lock the doors and leave on some lights. He told me to sleep in their room if I wanted to. "No one is going to try to break in," he said calmly, "this isn't L.A. But just in case, if it makes you feel better, you know where the gun is."

My dad came back from the hospital looking thin and worn. But his spirits were good; he wasn't giving up hope. By mid-August, the pot plants were seven feet tall, branching out in all directions thanks to Mick's careful pruning. Their stalks were now as thick as celery. My dad brought out his old Lica and took pictures of me in front of the plants, for posterity's sake, willing to take, but not to be in, the photographs. Mick stopped by around sunset every day to check on the plants, and his demeanor with me was easy and unconcerned. I made sure to never be alone with him. I could feel my dad watching, considering this new development.

My dad was growing concerned that Mr. Wisnowski the potato farmer might become inspired to call the police. It was time for his pot-growing experiment to come to an end.

"Nah," Mick insisted. "He wouldn't know what they are anyway." Then he said the plants needed several more weeks, a month at least, to reach their maximum potency. They had to flower, but not seed. My dad sat there at the kitchen table, shaking his head slowly, trying to decide. He finally agreed to wait a few more weeks.

Over Labor Day weekend I turned seventeen, and we had a little party. My dad had a friend from the city who owned a summer house down the street on Georgica Pond, an art dealer who was an aficionado of marijuana. Richard had a little joint holder made out of silver that he passed around the crowded table after dinner. Yukiko put her hand up and backed away as it went past her.

I got up from my place and went over to my dad at the head of the table and bent down and asked him if I could have a hit. He thought about it and I could tell he was struggling with his decision. It would be hypocritical to say no, on my birthday no less. But what would Richard think? He'd known my mother before she died. Eventually my dad passed the joint in its silver holder to me under the table. I crouched down low and took three hits, the deepest, fastest hits I could, and passed it back to him, still under the table.

Good thing that's all I smoked, because this was some serious weed this guy Richard had. It was some kind of hydroponically grown special pot that he purchased from some old hippie upstate. I was practically hallucinating. My dad and I sat in the kitchen long after Richard had left and Yukiko had gone off to bed, shaking her head. We slowly dug our way with soup spoons through an entire gallon of vanilla ice cream. We could taste the different flavors, the soothing vanilla beans surging forth out of the sweet, icy cream. If we could just freeze time, right here, I thought, everything would be right with the world.

Two days later I noticed Mr. Wisnowksi's John Deere tractor idling by our pot plants. I crept over and watched from behind a tree as the old farmer gazed up at the towering plants, hands on his hips. I ran to my dad. That afternoon, he had Mick uproot the plants. This was done under protest, for Mick felt they were being cut down before their time. He took them away in six black garbage bags, stuffed round like balloons. I was overcome with relief. The plants were gone; Mick would no longer have a reason to stop by every day.

The next morning an East Hampton patrol car cruised up the dirt tractor road adjoining our property, and made a show of driving slowly by the area where the plants had been. We'd had a narrow escape.

One morning I kissed my dad goodbye and drove his VW Rabbit to school. He wasn't feeling well so he let me take the car instead of the school bus. At 2:36 p.m. over the PA system I heard my name, and was ordered to present myself at the principal's office. My first thought was that they'd found out about Mick's pot plants and wanted to interrogate me. When I got to the office I was told to drive to the Southampton Hospital emergency room as fast as I could. By the time I got there it was all over, and Yukiko wouldn't let me see him. She thought it would be better for me to remember him as he'd been that morning, sitting at the kitchen table with his hands around his cup of steaming black coffee, in his checked flannel bathrobe and matching slippers.

Yukiko, who was kind and quiet by nature, took to their bed, started wailing, and didn't stop. I called our family doctor and he came over and gave her a shot, and then he handed me a prescription to fill the next day. It was for Valium, twenty milligrams. I thought I'd take some myself. We still hadn't called anyone, still hadn't accepted what had happened.

Worried for Yukiko, I took the gun out of my dad's bedside cabinet and hid it between the mattress and the box spring of my own bed downstairs.

Late that night, I heard glass shattering in the kitchen. I'd left lights on in every room. I heard the back door swing open and bang into the wall and then someone crashing into the hanging pots and pans above the butcher-block island. I reached for the Colt, which felt reassuring in my hand. I crept toward the kitchen and stood in the far doorway, feeling like the last barrier between sanity and utter madness.

It was Mick, his blue eyes swimming in a sea of red. He was completely lit, practically falling down as he crashed his way across the kitchen toward me.

"You can't come in here like this, Mick. My dad's gone now."

"I . . . heard about your dad on the police scanner . . ." He banged his hip on the corner of the stove. "Shit. Fuck. I . . . Uh, here . . . let me give you a hug . . ." he uttered, coming forward.

I lifted the pistol, sighted down the barrel as my dad had taught me, and shot him twice in the chest. He gazed at me without the slightest surprise, as if he'd been expecting this all of his life.

ANJALI'S AMERICA

BY QANTA AHMED, MD

Garden City

My eyes were gritty. My feet ached in shoes made tight from hours of standing. Palpitations clattered helter-skelter within me, skidding slipshod on waves of caffeine. I was wired with the barren exhaustion with which only a physician is intimate.

It was two a.m. My patient had made it out of the OR. I was hurrying to her in the intensive care unit. A young Pakistani woman, Mrs. Anjali Osmaan, was already the mother of several. This last delivery had nearly killed her. The labor had advanced slowly, and partway through the evening the baby turned, obstructing his own passage. After a brief struggle, the tired uterus ruptured, splitting across an old scar. There was a lot of blood. The EMTs said her mother-in-law had looked on in silent disapproval as the ambulance screamed away. Mrs. Osmaan had arrived in extremis, raced to the hospital by the ashen-faced men. Nobody wants a mother to die.

I prepared to war with young death. As nurses moved her from the gurney, I began gowning, gloving, tying my face mask, focusing my thoughts in the silence of age-old battle rituals. Frank had operated on her. I smiled at my friend. Tearing off his paper hat, he rushed up to fill me in.

"Christ, what a disaster—a complete uterine rupture! I don't know if she'll survive the hysterectomy but we had no choice. Baby's dead. She was peri-arrest half the time, we didn't think we'd make it out of the OR. Good luck with this, Yasmine. The anastamoses are secure but her coagulation is shot. And her kidneys are dicey. We ran some labs, pending now, should be back any moment. You know the drill. Gotta run, kiddo, an ectopic in the ER." Thrusting the chart into my hands, he clattered off in his clogs to answer his pager.

With my team of nurses and residents, therapists and orderlies, I began the work of resuscitation. An earnest medical student watched from the corner of the room like a frightened kitten. Seamlessly, the team enacted my terse orders. Ours was a familiar ballet—most of the time it was a dress rehearsal that ended in death; but this was a live performance. We were wrapped in the struggle to win back life.

Within the labyrinth of lines and tubing, Mrs. Osmaan was spectral. Drained of blood, her features were sallow. Arched brows crowned sleeping eyes, lush lashes gleamed moist with Vaseline, as though she'd been crying at her own dismal fate. Her hair was long and unstyled, dull, her premature aging typical of multiparous mothers. This was not a woman with appointments in shrill Long Island salons, who jostled with fur-coated wives. Her nails were unmanicured, but filigree henna patterns ascended both arms, rooted in a deep amber plunge of color at the fingertips. She must have attended a wedding recently. Her pale skin placed her among the elite of Punjab. She was Pakistani, like me. I imagined she had arrived in Long Island after an arranged marriage. I shivered unexpectedly, for hers was a fate I once defied.

I began the examination. She was icy cold, the shock having driven all the blood to her core. Her thready pulse coursed to a furious 160 on jet streams of adrenaline. A firm mouth revealed a determined woman. Chapped lips clasped reflexively around tubing, which shuddered with each mechanical breath. Only the tide of moisture in the tube confirmed the feeble tendrils of life persisting beyond the assault. A clear tube emerged from her nose, ferrying bilious liquid out of the stomach. A tiny stud gleamed in the left nostril of her Mughal nose. In the postoperative nightmare that was now her world, the young Pakistani mother retained her dignity with this glittering decoration, the brave little sparkles escaping the surgical tape overlying it.

The belly wound was dressed, already oozing with thinned blood too weak to clot. Staples gnashed at her anemic flesh, struggling to knit her back to life. Fluids escaped through the futile seams, soaking the dressing. A pristine catheter bag waited for the precious elixir of urine—the first clue of returning life.

Turning her hands over I could see purple flecks speckling her flesh: a very bad sign. Frank was right—after losing her entire blood volume several times over, what circulated was refrigerated blood; her system was badly diluted, distressed, and maybe would never be restored. My patient was punctured, perforated, and powerless to plug the holes. Like sailing a scuppered boat, we were bailing out water as fast as we were taking it in. It was all hands on deck to keep this woman afloat.

Soon we called for more blood products; started antibiotics; added drugs which would drive her heart faster and further; inserted lines to infuse and lines to measure. We dialed up her oxygen and pored over X-rays. We stabbed arteries and cannulated veins. We checked her pupils and emptied her rectum. We pushed and prodded, listened and pondered. Locked in our hive of fervent activity we concealed our worries and fears from each other and ourselves, assuaging our anxieties with yet more intervention. We cross-consulted other physicians, rousing them from fragmented sleep. We wrote orders, dispensed drugs, and finally put her violated body in a clean gown and crisp sheets. Between our many efforts, we suspended the wounded mother in a fragile web of life, wondering if we had built it strong enough to bear her weight.

I settled myself on a swivel chair at the foot of her bed and began the long process of recording the cramped fury that is our work. A silent nurse placed coffee at my elbow. I rubbed the back of my neck to rid it of knots, and pulled my bloodstained gown closer, fending off the special chill of the early hours. Bright lights became dim. The ICU returned to its baseline hum. At last, I allowed myself to uncoil a fraction. Soothed by the unit's background buzz, I permitted myself a momentary satisfaction, for ours is worthwhile work. From time to time, as I scribbled my thoughts and checked my calculations, I studied this woman, this Muslim woman, this Pakistani woman, whose fate could have been mine.

Anjali Osmaan and I were of the same heritage. Both of us had traveled from East Punjab to Nassau County, she on marriage and its trousseau, I for my training in medicine. I looked at her date of birth—we were only months apart in age, yet in such short years our paths had parted and diverged as if separated by an abyss. Where her family had succeeded in making her marriage a priority, my family had spectacularly failed. Where for her, education had been a means of biding time for the right suitor and increasing her marital market value, for me it had been the breakneck getaway car screeching away in clouds of Punjabi dust. We were from similar backgrounds, of that I was certain, yet while I had escaped in noisy defiance, she had acquiesced in silence.

A buzz at the door announced a visitor. Mrs. Osmaan's husband was outside. Someone murmured, "He's an MD." So, finally he had turned up. I prepared to explain her condition, but before I could greet him, he burst into the room with the misplaced authority typical of a doctor finding himself suddenly a relative to the sick. Striding up to me, he demanded to know what was going on. I was struck by the odd mixture of anger and dispassion in his tone. He extended a fleshy hand in cursory greeting, his tight grip twisting my fingers. I winced in pain. He didn't apologize. His was an arrogance nurtured on cream supped at the knees of a doting Christian ayah. I knew the type well—a family who could afford schooling at Aitchison but without the pedigree to find themselves accepted. This was a man who would never be admitted to play with the boys at the Lahore Polo Club; his wealth was not welcome, his circles excluded. He harbored bitterness, but also a sense of entitlement to his mother's money, and a desperate need to conceal his humdrum Punjabi origins. Glancing over my name emblazoned on my coat, he immediately recognized in it his own background, and, repelled, turned away. Nothing was more loathsome to him than to behold a woman from his discarded world who had made it here too—Pakistani women were to be married or bedded, and always without voice.

Our revulsion was mutual. French cologne masked Budweiser and Marlboros, the preferred armor of the Pakistani male failing to find his place in the massive currents of America. A well-cut suit strained at the seams, his thick neck bulging over the collar. A Bluetooth earpiece flashed rhythmically, underlining his self-importance. Silver hair cut a sharp contrast to his deep-brown pockmarked skin, a legacy of the acne that had surely shamed him in adolescence. It was clear he was wrestling with his gentleman's disguise. He never took his hands out of his pockets. Something deep inside me turned.

"So she is in hemorrhagic shock? Any DIC yet? How many

units of FFP did she get? Have you given her any Vitamin K? Not making urine right now? And you have her on adrenaline and dopamine? What's her acid base?" From his questions I gathered he was a fellow specialist.

Falling prey to his authority, I responded with facts. He jangled car keys in his pocket. He was dying for a smoke.

"Anyway, as long as she can still have kids after all this is over." He finally stopped talking, meeting my astonished stare. He paused, gazing coldly at me, the silence heavy with unspoken threat.

"Oh, I am sorry you weren't informed," I began, knowing full well my staff had been trying to reach him for hours. "Your wife ruptured her uterus completely. She had an emergency hysterectomy to save her life. She won't be able to have any more children." I wondered how I would tell him about the dead baby. Worse, I realized I was wondering if he would even care.

Without saying another word, he turned on his heel and left, stony-faced. The woman had failed him completely, now his barren wife would be a shame and a burden. He brushed off compassionate nurses attempting to stop him, wives and mothers themselves. I turned to my abandoned patient. How desolate must have been her years here. I saw it clearly: an arranged bride; a maladjusted Pakistani expat. Grasping at stability in the confusion of America, he handled it the only way he knew how—by dominating his dispossessed bride, far from her girlhood home.

Hours later, as I drove home in the late morning, I thought about Anjali Osmaan. Mineola was bustling with delivery vans and ambulances. The banks were open, bagels were being toasted, traffic was beginning to snarl. I drove past the

Garden City Hotel, its lawns soothed by cascading sprinklers. I followed the tree-lined curving road, always so refreshing after an airless night trapped in fluorescent lights and beeping machines. Passing the most beautiful house on Cathedral Avenue, I slowed the car to take in its symmetry. The colonial columns rose sharp and white from the crisp lawn. The shades were pulled as always, but pretty pink flowers fluttered in the morning breeze. For a thousandth time I wondered about the family within, but as usual the home yielded no clues.

Finally, I reached the hospital housing just at the end of Cathedral Avenue, where the neighborhood changed in a sweeping curve, from Wall Street wealth to working class. I pulled into the garden apartments, one of which was mine. Inside the garage, I switched the engine off and listened for a moment to the *tick-tick* expansion of the uncoiling motor, beginning to feel my own unfurling. Would my unconscious patient survive to tell me her tale?

Soon I was pulling the cold duvet over my head, obliterating daylight. I savored the precious moments before sleep, perched at the cusp of the deep, dreamless state that follows a night on call. As I slipped off the edge, floating into reverie, I thought of the woman I had left behind in the mechanical orchestra of the intensive care unit, where perhaps she was tumbling through a dreamless sleep of her own. As I drifted down into deeper and darker blue canyons, her turbulent battle to stay with the living continued. Would she swim back up of her own will or would the currents finally pull her down into permanent void?

"Bed five is coding. Code 99! Code 99!"

"No pulse! Rhythm: V-tach. Shock her!"

"Epi!"

"Atropine!"

"Pads!"

"Bag her! Are we charged?"

Charging.

"Stand clear. Stand clear, everyone!"

Paralyzing silence.

"Sinus rhythm. She's back."

"Thank you, everyone. Get a gas. Calcium gluconate, please. Get me that EKG. Hang some Mag. Would you? Finish that bolus. Call for blood. And the rapid infuser. Stat. Call the family. It's not looking good. She could box out anytime."

I knew her story as if I'd lived it myself. She would be me, had I not made an impulsive dash for my life. With my mind's eye I looked back over my shoulder and followed the curve of the road disappearing into the dark; I allowed myself a rare pause from my perpetual flight.

It all starts with such hope. Summer is well into its ripeness, though Anjali is yet to blossom. She has just been married-by-proxy, an arrangement approved by her family, who always knows best for their sole daughter, their hopes stoked on the fires of her great beauty. He is from Amreekah! they tell her, choosing wedding fabrics and photographers. "Amreekah!" they shout, repeating it out of sheer disbelief. In the midst of their joy, Anjali is an afterthought. Our daughter will go to Amreekah! A place called Long Island, they tell her, triggering images from *The Great Gatsby*, one of her mother's favorite books. She had read it in British India during her Jesuit schooling.

Busy with the end of college, Anjali doesn't have time or energy to think about protesting. She is joining her new husband in Amreekah. She should be grateful, so few girls get a chance like this. She will be a married woman, the only way to carry her special burden, the woman's cargo of familial honor. Marriage is the only way forward.

And yet I found a way out. I won a place in residency to study medicine in New York. But I was no brighter than she—just stronger, hungrier, more defiant.

Anjali's marriage begins as it will continue: she is alone. The plane lands in torrential summer rains, so like monsoon season in Sindh. With precious dollar bills and an address written on crumpled paper torn from a schoolbook, she takes a taxi to her husband's home. After hours of bumper-to-bumper traffic the cab stops before a large house in a place called Garden City. The neighborhood is glossy and rich. Anjali feels suddenly poor, suddenly small. She hesitates, cowered by her own future.

Entering the house with a newly cut key, she closes the door behind her. The silence is total and in it the weight of her distance from the familiar becomes painfully apparent. Sheets of driving rain are now muted behind heavy glass. There are no cars outside. Even the other houses don't have lights on. In her first night in her husband's vast home she searches for food. With a struggle, she opens the American fridge. She has never seen one so big. It unseals with an expensive, icy hiss. She shivers. A few crumbs and some curled cheese greet her in return. The thin clinking of her marriage bangles seems to be the only sound for miles around.

She wanders into the bedroom, the future scene of her abuse. Anjali falls into a fitful, jetlagged sleep, yet still she remains excited at her own boldness. She draws her bridal hopes close to her throat, trying to be warm in the icy air-conditioning. If only she knew how to turn the coldness off. Drifting to sleep, she warms herself with the childish envy of her college friends at home in Lahore. I am so lucky, she thinks, leaving them all behind. And here I am already on the threshold of everything new! Such exciting beginnings: marriage, migration, motherhood. She doesn't know it yet, but her trust for the stranger she has married is already blind.

She has known him for less than half an hour and already they are in bed. She keeps her eyes closed, sealed shut by a bride's mixture of shame and reluctant pleasure. He fondles her roughly from behind, running his hands up and down her torso and venturing toward the perilous region between her legs, the place where all the horrors begin. She can't stop shivering. Adjusting something on his belt, her husband eases a long, thin territorial leg over her hip. Too naïve a bride, she fails to notice his expertise. The sinewy leg is surprisingly heavy, pinning her still, impaling her will. Penetration will become their only communication and her husband's only claim. As he fills with blood and desire, she fills with dread and sudden regret. This must be how all brides feel, she decides.

The act over, she rearranges her shredded fantasies in the face staring back at her in the bathroom mirror. The bedroom light is on. He is stripped off, freshly showered, fragrant, sitting at the edge of the bed. In the bright lights of the room, he looks sated and alien as he picks up the phone to make a call. Anjali goes to join him on the tousled bed, stroking his shin, imagining this to be affection. Her family isn't a tactile one, so all she knows is what she has learned from movies. He is talking to a woman. His voice is strangely tender, a voice she will soon learn he reserves for his mistress. He is indifferent to Anjali's caress.

At last, he hangs up. Anjali is still a mess of shyness and awkwardness; of shame and embarrassment; of desire and satisfaction, and under it all she is sour with the rancor of new jealousy. Expressionless, he stands, wearing the towel around his waist, heads to the restroom, and urinates a long, satisfying stream. He is done with Anjali and doesn't say a word to her as he dresses and departs. This will be the way it is for a long, long time. Eventually, he will degrade her, beat her, berate her; later the margins between marital relations and marital rape will blur. But all things in their appointed time.

Their children are conceived, delivered, and raised; first one, then another, then another, in such rapid succession that her young body doesn't have time to recover. Finally comes this last baby who is bursting Anjali's seams to get out. *Please God, spare my baby, let the child not be a girl*, she prays.

Her husband still has to relent to the one force stronger than he—his mother. She moves in to help with the rearing of his progeny, efficiently making them hers. Though Anjali's brood grows in numbers, the children only add to her isolation. Her mother-in-law runs the home, a queen in her durbar, supervising from the sofa as though holding court from a Maharani's Divan. In her joyless empire, even her grandchildren cannot evoke her love. That is jealously guarded for her only son, the object of her passion. Anjali both hates and depends on her, and her mother-in-law thrives in her knowledge of this painful truth.

Anjali never learns to drive and is not confident of her spoken English, even though she is fluent in her reading. Instead, she practices speaking with the illiterate migrant maid whose English is even worse than hers. They enjoy a pure connection devoid of complex words; somehow this dismantles the worst of her mounting desolation.

In time, her husband grows wealthier, his practice bigger, his hours longer and more erratic. His addictions deepen;

his language coarsens. He no longer bothers concealing his increasing binges of beer, which become bourbon, then Librium, which later becomes high-dose Valium. Some mornings, he snorts cocaine, saying, "It helps me focus," in a thickened voice. Anjali's despair magnifies, variegates, and slowly burnishes over her spirit. Soon her soul is shellacked shut under shiny layers of silence.

Mechanical beeping, murmurs in a language unknown to her, and again she is sinking, falling into the blackness. *Please let me die*, she prays. The finality, the freedom of death, has become impossibly desirable. Something inside her rattles until there is a strange pause, a long silence before an epic detonation. Then: shrapnel, aftershock, automated gunfire shuddering her frame. Cold gel; hot current; burning hair; searing skin. Something profound aches. And then, nothing. A sinking, curtailed at the edge of the abyss. A precarious pause. The brisk sound of a blossoming parachute.

Why am I not dead? she wonders, wishing for the release, hoping perhaps today will be the day that Allah will finally retrieve her.

It was June. Time for me to hand over the unit to a new team. Interns arrived for their orientations, full of nervous enthusiasm. It was the same every year. I guessed my weariness was giving away my age. I looked at the coltish pack, restlessly trying to conceal their fears and the gaps in their knowledge, and the newly promoted residents terrified at being responsible for such novices. Only the seasoned nurses remained unmoved. It was already almost ten years since I was in their shoes. Medicine had an astonishing way of making time vanish.

Making rounds with the young team, I came to the final

patient, Mrs. Osmaan, and outside her door I summarized her course to the residents. They urgently scribbled down everything I said. Like new detectives at a first bloody crime scene, they barely met my gaze, bowed over notepads and clipboards, as if they thought so long they just kept writing, everything would be all right. Endorsement complete, I entered the patient's room, leaving the youngsters behind.

Anjali was staring out the window. Now strong enough to sit up, her frail arms rested quietly on the arms of the chair. Anjali was so regal the recliner could have been the throne of a vanished kingdom. The silence was broken only by the slow hiss of the pneumatic stockings that kept the blood in her legs from clotting. The henna had long since faded, her pale forearms were now hirsute from long courses of steroids. The baby she had never seen, a stillborn son, lay buried by others, months earlier. After we'd told her the news, she praised Allah, Alhamdulillah, that her prayers had been heard and her baby had not been a girl. She never spoke to us again.

In the months I had attended her, she'd had very few visitors. No notes, no phone calls. The husband never returned after that first night. We hadn't been able to contact her family overseas. Social services had ensured the children were living with their grandmother, with their father's permission, while their mother recovered. Predictably, the grandmother also never visited. Nothing isolates like abuse.

In the past weeks the medical team had been evaluating her home care needs. I wondered how she would manage. Soon, she would leave the ICU and transfer to a regular ward. I wouldn't be her doctor anymore—there would be others to take my place. I'd miss her.

Touching her arm, I followed her gaze out the window but could not tell where she was looking.

We would never meet again.

The waves crashed in the lazy July afternoon. Lido Beach was beautiful this time of year; Sunday afternoons lush and vibrant. I stretched out on my chaise lounge, returning to the newspaper. Once in a while, I read a section out loud to my cousin, visiting from Lebanon. Long Beach reminded her of Beirut, she had explained that morning as we walked past the high-rises looking out to sea. As I got to the Metro page, I sat suddenly upright. I couldn't believe my eyes. Hana put down her book.

"What is it, Yasmine?"

A fine-featured woman stared up at me from a black-and-white photo. I scanned it in disbelief. Her brows, her nose—unmistakable: it was Anjali. For the first time I saw in her face the defiance and pride of her Punjabi forebears. Her tiny nose stud caught the flash just as the photographer snapped the image. She was being bustled into a waiting police car. In the background, a majestic house with a manicured lawn was being sealed in crime scene tape, the same elegant house I had passed on my drives home from the hospital. An ambulance was reversed into the circular drive, a covered body carried into the back. As usual the shades on the house were down, giving nothing away. I could tell: this was no emergency. He was already dead.

"This woman was my patient, Hana. Five years ago. I never forgot it. She almost died of a ruptured uterus. We suspected she was abused in her marriage. I never knew what happened to her."

Hana put her magazine down and together we read the story. We raced over the paragraphs, interrupting each other. A custody battle. Divorce lawyers. Suspicious neighbors. The doctor husband, drunk and belligerent in public. Rumors of a cocaine habit, a suspended medical license. A practice in ruins. A crumpled Lexus slumped into a tree. A New Jersey woman, hysterical at the death of her Pakistani lover. Anjali had given a statement to the police and plead to manslaughter.

He had been demanding a divorce, seeking an annulment so he could marry his lover, a lapsed Catholic who longed for a church wedding. Anjali could never agree to that. Her children could never be illegitimate in the eyes of the law. She just couldn't accept it. The embattled couple had been fighting on the landing, she retreating toward the stairs, he pursuing. He held the legal papers in his hand. It was not difficult for me to imagine his words:

"I never wanted you, Anjali. I never loved you. I was your salvation, you ungrateful bitch. I married you to honor your father. Without me, you would be rotting in Gulberg instead of living here in Amreekah. You are nothing without me, but I have had enough. There is still time for me to finally have happiness. I am leaving you, Anjali. That's final. You have to sign the papers. You have no choice. *Talaq! Talaq! Talaq!*"

She sees his mouth moving but hears no words. Suddenly all the rage he has silenced inside her rises to a foamy crest and, gathering fury, arrives in her arms. She grabs his lapels. The suits are still expensive, despite his insolvency. With all her might she leans into him, her acrylic nails snapping off under the pressure. Her wedding bangles, shackles to her sorry fate, clatter toward her thin elbows and somehow she lifts him off his feet. The rage pours from an unknown locus. The silenced lamb has become a lion.

Neighbors hear the screaming: "No! I will never divorce you. I would rather die! Ya Allah, I would rather die!" She pushes him and his papers away. His thick arms, trapped in the too-tight jacket, fly backward, grasping at the air. Gabardine and silk tumble through the air. His mouth opens, tobacco-stained teeth surprised at the sudden shaft of daylight. His gold-ringed fingers clutch at the balustrades, snapping first one, then many. Tumbling under his own weight, he snaps first his arms, then his lean legs, on the marble stairs. With a sickening thump, the mound of fabric and flesh comes to a halt, landing on a broken neck. His acne-scarred cheek lies smooth against the travertine. A single molar dislodges from his jaw and tumbles out, skittering across the floor. A brief sputter, a silent drool. And then blood, still warm, spills from his ear and puddles on the marble floor. Looking on the scene from above, Anjali feels the sudden, shocking throttle of euphoria. An alien roar surges within her, deadening all other senses. In the astonishing stillness, the divorce papers flutter in a current of icy air-conditioning, the unpleasant chill the one trembling remnant of their shared life.

Anjali looks at her bleeding nails, then again at the body. Trembling yet calm, she picks her way down the broken stairs. Sidestepping the body, she walks across the marble floor where as a young proxy bride she once slipped in cheap, girlish sandals. She finally turns off the air-conditioning and begins at last to thaw. She reaches for the phone and calmly dials 911 and finds her voice. In a clipped accent, she tells the police, "There has been an accident. My husband is dead. Please come."

And so, they do.

I looked at the photo, meeting Anjali's eyes, marveling that my frail patient had survived on the wiry web we'd once built for her. A death in the delivery room, the destruction of a worn-out womb, the sustained theft of her motherhood, and at the root of it all, the beauty which had sealed her fate. Through it all she had been alone. Everyone had failed her. Yet still she lived, destined to be her own solitary savior.

I put down the paper and stared at the Atlantic. Distant laughter bounced on the foaming surf. Somewhere across these currents I had left my own fate behind, choosing something better. I thought of Anjali's tenacious recovery. There had indeed been a purpose to our work, and I understood now why she had survived.

Anjali had finally arrived in her America. The America that was also mine.

PART II

Hitting It Big

A STARR BURNS BRIGHT

BY CHARLES SALZBERG

Long Beach

G oldblatt, you gonna tell me what the hell you wanted to see me about?" I said, as I watched him shovel another forkful of pasta into his mouth, or at least in the general vicinity of his mouth.

"Yeah. Sure. After we finish the meal."

"I don't know if I can wait that long. Watching you eat is making me sick."

"You got a problem with the way I eat?" he said, as a few drops of red sauce shot through the air and landed on a glass I'd moved in front of my plate for protection.

"Exhibit number one." I pointed to the glass.

"Huh?"

"Never mind," I said, looking at my watch. "Look, I've got things to do, places to go, people to see."

"Yeah. Right. Swann, as long as I've known you that ain't been the truth."

"Time passes. Things change."

He sucked the last tubes of penne into his face, dragged a piece of Italian bread across his plate, stuffed it into his mouth, wiped his entire face with the napkin that had been tucked into his collar, and leaned back. "Good meal, huh?"

"Excellent," I said, not even bothering to hide my sarcasm. I doubted he'd get it anyway. My plate of soggy spaghetti nestled in a pool of oil sat practically untouched in front of me, but I guess he didn't notice that. Quantity was always better than quality when it came to Goldblatt. "Now maybe we can discuss the business you said you had for me."

"I haven't had dessert yet."

"Screw dessert. If I don't hear the reason you got me here, I'm leaving."

"Okay, okay. I need you to do a solid for me."

"I don't do solids. I have rent to pay, food to buy, drinks to pay for. I learned a long time ago that favors never turn out to be favors. They turn out to be work. For work, I get paid. And I doubt that's going to happen with you. How much have you brought in since you got disbarred?"

"That's personal."

"I rest my case."

"Hey, I'm no deadbeat. You wanna get paid, I'll see to it you get paid." He pulled a wad of money out of his pocket and waved it in my face.

"What'd you do, mug an old lady for her life's savings?"

"Very funny. You may not believe this, Swann, but I provide valuable services to people and for those services I get paid."

"What kind of services?"

"They vary. I may not be able to practice law anymore, but I know how the law works. I'm a consultant. I'm a facilitator. I get things done."

"I'm sure you do. How do I fit in?"

"I want you to pick up a package for me."

"Do I look like the FedEx guy? I'm a skip tracer. I find people. I don't make deliveries."

"FedEx don't pick up packages where I need them to."

"Where's that?"

"Long Beach."

"As in California?"

"As in Long Island."

"I'm pretty sure FedEx services Long Beach."

"Not when and where I want them to. You familiar with the town?"

"Yeah. My father grew up there. He'd take us back there to visit my grandmother and grandfather. It used to be a dump, now it's a poor man's Hamptons, overrun with weekenders and religious Jews."

He slapped the table. "I knew you were the man for me."

"Not so fast, Goldblatt. Truth is, it turns my stomach to go out there. I'm not a man who likes change. No more family to visit . . ."

"Do I detect the beating of a heart, Swann?"

"Not unless you've got a stethoscope hidden under the napkin covering that belly of yours. I need to know what I'm getting into and for how much."

"What's the difference? You take the train out there, because I know you don't have a car . . ."

". . . and you're not about to spring for a rental."

"You pick up the package, you take the train back and give it to me. Simple as that."

"Do you think I'm stupid?"

"Why would I think that?"

"Because you didn't think I'd ask why you can't do it? A man like you, Goldblatt, four years of college, three years of law school, knows how to figure out a train schedule."

"There are reasons."

"Give 'em to me," I said, knowing that whatever he said would be a lie or at the very least a souped-up version of the truth. Goldblatt was an operator. And he knew that I knew he was an operator.

"I got a bad knee. You saw me limp in here."

"That's not enough."

"Okay, I've got a little problem with some people who live in Long Beach, so if I show my face out there I might find myself in a little trouble."

"That's almost believable, so you know what, I'm not even going to ask what kind of trouble, because I don't give a shit. What's in the package?"

"That's confidential."

"Find someone else to be your errand boy," I said, as I pushed myself away from the table and stood up.

"Wait. What about dessert?"

I had to smile. There was no way to deal with Goldblatt other than to treat him as a joke. But he was a friend. The kind of friend you can't trust but you know it so you still make like he's a friend. So I sat back down.

"You think you can stuff dessert into that fat gut of yours after what you just ate?"

"I left some room," he said, patting his stomach which seemed to have expanded at least a couple of inches from when we walked into the joint.

"Jesus, Goldblatt, you never cease to amaze me."

"Stick around, Swann, there's more where that came from."

He couldn't make up his mind between the apple pie and the chocolate cake, so he ordered both. Me, I had nothing. Trying to watch my weight while Goldblatt increased his.

The deal was simple, or so he said. The next night, I'd go out to Long Beach and meet someone on the boardwalk at precisely nine p.m., in front of one of the little huts that during the summer months issues beach passes. The person, he didn't know if it would be a he or she, would hand me a package. In return, I'd hand over an envelope, which he'd give me when I agreed. Then I'd hop back on the train and deliver the package to him the next morning in his office.

"I can trust you not to open the package or the envelope, right?" he said, as he dug into the last bite of apple pie, then pushed that plate away and started in on the enormous slab of chocolate layer cake.

"I don't like the sound of this, Goldblatt," I answered, doing my best to look away from the epicurean spectacle going on in front of me.

"What's not to like?"

"You want me to go to the deserted boardwalk, in the middle of the night, in the middle of winter, with no one else around, carrying God knows what, meeting God knows who, for God knows what reason."

"Well, if you put it that way . . ."

"What the fuck other way is there to put it? And the kicker is, you're not even paying me for this. Do I look like a moron to you?"

"You owe me, Swann."

"How do you figure?"

"How many times have you asked me to dig up information for you?"

"Three."

"What're you, keeping count? I thought it was more."

"Three."

"So I'm asking you for one favor and then I'll call it even."

I laughed. Because he was entertaining. And because he was persistent. Would it kill me to do a favor for him? No. Was I going to do one for him? In the end, I probably would. Not because it was Goldblatt, but because I hate owing anyone anything. And the truth is, I'd probably need him again. But I wasn't going to make it easy for him.

"Five hundred, plus expenses," I said, waiting to see him choke on his chocolate cake.

"You gotta be kidding."

"Take it or leave it."

"You're killing me, Swann. But I'll tell you this: I pay you five hundred, which I'm not saying I will, and then you and me are finished."

"What's that supposed to mean?"

"It means you go to someone else when you need information. Because I'm finished letting you take advantage of me and my good nature."

He was right and I knew it. I owed him at least this much. He had helped me out in the past and he never asked for anything but a meal, although with Goldblatt that wasn't a cheap tab. But I wasn't about to let him off easy. "Tell you what, you tell me what this is all about and what's in that package and I'll cut it in half."

He put down his fork, which was unusual for him, since there was still half a slice of cake left on his plate. He almost smiled. "I don't know if I can trust you."

I laughed. "And I can trust you? Maybe both of us ought to give it a try."

He was silent a moment, looked down at his cake, then whacked off another hunk with his fork and stuffed it into his mouth. "The name Starr Faithfull mean anything to you?"

"It's got a familiar ring."

"In June 1931, a beachcomber found the body of this beautiful twenty-five-year-old chick named Starr Faithfull."

"And this has what to do with you?"

"I've got a little something going."

"What?"

He leaned forward. "This is top secret, Swann."

"Cut the crap, Goldblatt. You know and I know it's got everything to do with—" I rubbed my fingers together "—and in that case, we're on the same page. You want me to get into something, I need to know what it is. And I need to get paid for it."

"Okay. Faithfull was a slut and she was involved with a bunch of important people, some of whom might have wanted her dead. Even her own sister said, *I'm not sorry she's dead. She's happier. Everybody's happier.* The DA admitted that lots of people in high places would rest easier with her out of the way. They did an autopsy and found that she was full of Veronal, the Ecstasy of its day. The coroner ruled it was death by drowning, but the DA said it was *brought about by someone interested in closing her lips.* Not long before she died she wrote a friend saying she was playing *a dangerous game*, and that there was *no telling where I'll land.* She was leading this double life, see. She went to the finest finishing schools, but she was also a wild child, like that Paris Hilton chick. She was heavy into drugs and sleeping around. One of her boyfriends was this guy Andrew Peters, a former mayor, ex-congressman, and Woodrow Wilson's assistant secretary of the treasury. His wife was Starr's mother's first cousin."

"Get to the point, Goldblatt."

"Keep your shirt on, Swann. Starr left a couple of diaries along with a bunch of letters, some of them filled with suicidal thoughts. But her father claimed they were forgeries. One of the diaries told all about her fourteen years of sexual, shall we say, adventures, with close to twenty guys, including British aristocrats and well-heeled Manhattan playboys. A lot of them gave her money. Apparently, one of them was Peters. The *Daily News* started an investigation and claimed Starr's stepfather was nearly broke and that a few days before Starr disappeared he'd traveled to Boston to get payoffs from Peters. The question is, for what?"

"I still don't know what all this has to do with you."

"There's another diary. One that no one ever knew about."

"So that's what's in the package."

"Yeah."

"And how did all this come to you?"

"I've got a lot of connections, Swann. That's why you come to me for help."

"Why is this diary important now, eighty years after the fact? Who the hell cares about Starr Faithfull?"

"There's interest, okay? That's all I'm gonna say and that's all you gotta know. You in or out?"

"I want a piece of your action, Goldblatt."

"You gotta be kidding."

"You wouldn't be doing this if it didn't mean you weren't getting something out of it. You make money, I make money. That's what friends do for friends."

"So now you're my friend. One percent."

I laughed.

"Five percent."

I laughed harder.

"Ten percent. But that's it."

"Give me the envelope."

Just my luck, the next day the weather turned bad. Very bad. Okay, it was winter, first week in January, but what happened to the January thaw? It was raw. It was cold. It was windy. It was also depressing, now that all the holiday lights across the city had been taken down. It was back to grim reality, eleven months of it, and I didn't like it one damn bit. Life was bad enough without having the lights turned out all the time. To make matters worse, by the time I got to Penn Station there was the smell of snow in the air.

I didn't trust Goldblatt. It's not that he's a bad guy, it's that he plays the angles. And the thing is, he's not even that good at it. That's why he's not a lawyer anymore. He dipped his hand into his clients' pockets once too often and he got caught. But I had the sense that he might be on to something here. I didn't tell him the whole truth when I said the name Starr Faithfull rang a bell. I knew exactly who she was. My grandfather, who used to be a Long Beach cop, told me about the case when I was a kid. He was one of those who thought it wasn't a suicide, that she was murdered, but he was told to keep his mouth shut. It wasn't easy for a guy who liked to talk, but in the end he did. A lost Starr Faithfull diary might prove that my grandfather was right. I don't know why that was important to me. It wasn't like the guy was a saint, because he wasn't. The Long Beach cops weren't above having their hand out and I'm sure one of those hands was his. But the Faithfull case always haunted him, probably because it was a lot bigger than fixing parking tickets and shutting your eyes when it came to after-hours joints.

To Goldblatt, the lost diary obviously meant some kind of payday. He wasn't above a little blackmail, but who was left to blackmail? Would the families of anyone named in Starr's diary care? Only if someone mentioned was very famous and revered. But it was possible that Goldblatt had other fish to fry. I knew he had publishing and film connections. Maybe he was concocting a book or movie deal. Whatever it was, I was in for 10 percent—plus the $250 and expenses. So any way you sliced it, I would come out with something. That's the way I liked it.

It was a fifty-plus-minute ride on the LIRR out to Long

Beach, which was the last stop on the line. I made a seven-ten train, which would give me plenty of time to grab a bite, then walk the three or four blocks to the boardwalk. The heavy commute was over, so I pretty much had the train to myself, which suited me fine. I took out the heavy-duty manila envelope and looked at it. It felt like there was money inside. And plenty of it. I thought about opening it up to see how much, but then I realized it didn't matter. I wondered how Goldblatt got his hands on so much cash, even the wad he waved in my face. However he did, I suspected there was something funny about it. But that wasn't any of my business.

I knew Long Beach, or at least a good part of it, like the back of my hand. My father didn't talk much, but my grandfather loved to regale me with stories of the town, which had led a remarkably checkered past.

Around the turn of the last century, a real estate developer named William Reynolds, who was behind Coney Island's Dreamland, the world's largest amusement park, bought up a bunch of oceanfront property so he could build a boardwalk, homes, and hotels. As a publicity stunt, Reynolds had a herd of elephants march from Dreamland to Long Beach, supposedly to help build the boardwalk. Reynolds touted the area as "the Riviera of the East," and required every building he constructed to be in the Mediterranean style, with white stucco walls and red tile roofs. The thing was, these homes could only be occupied by white Anglo-Saxon Protestants.

When Reynolds's company went bankrupt, these restrictions were lifted and the town began to attract wealthy businessmen and entertainers, many of whom my grandmother claimed to have seen at a theater Reynolds built called Castles by the Sea, with the largest dance floor in the world, which was intended for the famous hoofers Vernon and Irene Castle.

Later, in the '40s, she claimed she saw the likes of Zero Mostel, Mae West, and Jose Ferrer perform, while Jack Dempsey, Cab Calloway, Bogart, Valentino, Flo Ziegfeld, Cagney, Clara Bow, and John Barrymore lived in Long Beach. Then the town became home to Billy Crystal, Joan Jett, Derek Jeter, and the infamous "Long Island Lolita," Amy Fisher.

But there was another, much darker side to Long Beach, one my grandfather was far more familiar with. In the early '20s, the legendary prohibition agents Izzy and Moe raided the Nassau hotel and arrested three men for bootlegging. Police corruption ran rampant, to the point that an uncooperative mayor was shot by a police officer. In 1930, five Long Beach cops were charged with offering a bribe to a U.S. Coast Guard office to allow liquor to be off-loaded.

By the 1950s, Long Beach had turned from a resort area to a bedroom community. The rundown boardwalk hotels became homes for welfare recipients and the elderly. A decade later, the town turned into a drug haven, as kids from other towns on Long Island flocked there. By this time my grandfather had retired from the force. He was bitter and he was angry. I never knew exactly why, but I think at least part of it was that he regretted some of the things he'd done, the way he'd lived his life. I got the feeling that the Faithfull case might have turned things around for him, if he hadn't been muzzled.

Over the last couple decades the town had undergone a renaissance. Most of the drug dealers had been run out and in the summer the boardwalk and beach became a magnet to those who couldn't afford to summer in the Hamptons or Fire Island.

By the time the train arrived at the Long Beach station, the weather had changed and not for the good. A storm had blown in and the wind was whipping around large, wet flakes of snow that stung my face and assaulted my eyes. It was just after eight o'clock, and I could have waited in the warm, inviting station, but I was hungry, so I crossed the boulevard and ducked into a Burger King on the corner.

I sat alone at the window, watching the streets and sidewalks fill with snow, wondering what the hell I was doing out here. I thought seriously about packing it in and going back to the city. It wasn't loyalty to Goldblatt that kept me. I'd long since given up the idea of being loyal to anyone or anything. It was curiosity. I wanted to see this thing through, just so I could figure out the twisted little scheme Goldblatt had hatched.

I looked at my watch. Ten to nine. I waited five more minutes. I didn't want to be the first one there. I wanted to see what was waiting for me.

I patted the inside pocket of my peacoat to make sure the envelope was there, buttoned up, turned up the collar, pulled my wool watch cap over my ears, and headed out into the storm, a lone figure in blue set out against the blanket of white that covered the streets. I wished I'd worn something more substantial on my feet, because my socks, exposed to the elements, were already damp.

As I headed down Edwards Avenue toward the boardwalk, for every three steps I took the wind blew me back one. I crossed Olive, then Beech, then Penn, till I finally reached Broadway. Only one block left. It was so quiet, the only thing I could hear was the crunching sound my shoes made in the newly fallen snow. Before I crossed the street, I looked back, and my eyes followed my footsteps imprinted in the snow. By morning, my footprints would be long gone and the snow would turn a shade of black that wasn't known to nature.

From the illumination of a streetlight in front of me, I could make out the ramp leading to the boardwalk. I crossed Broadway and started up the ramp toward the boardwalk. All

I could hear was the sound of the wind and the waves. A chill ran up my back, and I pressed my arms closer to my body and lowered my head, as if I were using it as a battering ram against the wind.

The boardwalk, bustling in the summer with joggers, bikers, and beach-goers, was empty. The hut was about a hundred yards to my left. I squinted through the falling snow in an attempt to see if anyone was waiting there. No one. I glanced at my watch. It was a few minutes past nine. Was this all a wild goose chase?

I headed toward the hut, my hands jammed deep in my pockets. Maybe I should have brought a gun, only I didn't own one. Why should I? That's not the kind of work I do. It wasn't the kind of work I wanted to do. But keeping my hands in my pockets might make someone think I was packing and that might give me an edge, if I needed one.

About fifty feet from the hut, I veered toward the railing on the oceanfront. I looked out to see if anyone was on the beach, then peered over and down, in case there was anyone hiding under the boardwalk. No one.

I got to the wooden hut, which was boarded up for the winter, and rapped on the side.

"Hey, anyone in there?"

Nothing.

I checked my watch. Quarter past nine. I'd give it till nine-twenty, then I was out of here.

The wind died down a little, giving me a bit more visibility. I didn't need it. Not a soul around. To my left, about a hundred yards away, there was a series of high-rises, but in front of me and to my immediate right, there was nothing but a parking area and land waiting to be used for new co-ops or condos. It was eerie. I felt like I was at the end of the world.

I thought about Starr Faithfull, as I looked out toward the ocean. On a ship. Fell or pushed. Floating up on shore. It was a good story. Knowing Goldblatt, whatever he was paying for would probably be worth it to him, which meant to me too.

I looked back at my watch. Time's up.

I patted the envelope in my pocket. Once I was back on the train I'd open it up and take out what I was due. The hell with Goldblatt and his crazy deal, whatever it was. I was heading home.

I got to the bottom of the ramp and was moving toward Broadway, when I heard a noise behind me. Before I could turn around, I felt a sharp pain in my side, in the vicinity of my kidney. Someone had punched me. Hard. I lost my balance and fell to one knee, instinctively raising my right arm to protect myself.

"Stay down," a raspy voice ordered.

"Whatever you say," I replied, raising both arms up in submission. The guy was a giant. Or at least he looked that way from where I was sitting. He was wearing an overcoat, a muffler, and a fedora, like he was something out of the '40s.

Another, much smaller figure moved out from under the ramp and stood beside whoever had struck me.

"That's some punch you've got there."

"I guess I'm supposed to thank you for the compliment," he said, with a growl.

"Look, I'm just a delivery boy. You've got something for me, I've got something for you. Am I right?"

He turned at the figure beside him, who was wearing jeans and a hoodie under a black leather jacket. By the build, I figured it was either a boy or a woman.

"Who are you?" asked the smaller person, who I now knew was a woman.

"Henry Swann. I was hired by Goldblatt to make the exchange."

"Why didn't he do it himself?"

"Because he's a coward," said the woman, a cloud of carbon dioxide obscuring her face.

The big man laughed.

"You've got the envelope?" she asked.

"You've got the package?" I said.

"It looks to me like you're in no position to bargain. Sidney here could just take it from you."

"That would be robbery."

"Yes. It would."

"If you just give me what I came for it will be a simple business exchange. Look, my pants are getting soaked here. Mind if I get up?"

She nodded. I stood. I still couldn't catch my breath and the pain had me lurching to one side.

"Search him, Sidney."

I raised my hands. "You won't find a weapon, if that's what you're thinking."

"Better safe than sorry," she said.

"Open your coat," Sidney ordered.

"It's friggin' cold out here, Sidney."

He raised his hand. "Just fuckin' open the coat or I'll open it for you."

I opened the coat, spreading out the sides. He patted me down.

"See. Nothing. And nothing up my sleeves, either," I added, sliding my hands down the sleeves of my coat.

Sidney spotted the envelope in my coat pocket and pulled it out. "This it?"

"Yes."

He handed it over to the woman.

"Now what about what I'm supposed to bring back in exchange?"

She opened the envelope. It was filled with cash, and lots of it. Just like I thought.

"You're not going to give me anything, are you?"

"Nothing but a message for Goldblatt."

"What's that?"

"Tell him the next time he tries to fuck with people, he should think twice. And that payback's a bitch."

"What's that supposed to mean?"

"You seem to be a smart guy, Mr. Swann, you figure it out."

Suddenly it dawned on me what was going on. Goldblatt was being hustled and I thought I knew why.

"You wouldn't happen to be a pissed-off former client of his, would you?"

"Goldblatt has disgruntled clients? What a surprise," she said, waving the envelope in the air. "Sidney, did you know that Goldblatt has disgruntled clients? Clients he stole money from?"

"News to me," said Sidney.

"You mind telling me how much is in there?"

"He didn't tell you?"

"You'd be surprised what he doesn't tell me. Today, I'm just his dumb-ass errand boy. But I've got to tell you, whoever came up with that Starr Faithfull story really knew how to bait the hook. I've got to hand it to you. And you know something, I couldn't care less what you're doing to him."

"Isn't he a friend of yours?"

"Define friend. We're acquaintances who use each other when the occasion arises. He used me and I was going to use him. But I see that isn't going to work out."

She closed the envelope and stuffed it into the pocket of her jacket. "I think we're finished here, Sidney. I'm just sorry Goldblatt didn't come here himself. We wanted to give him some extra interest on his money."

"I could give this dude one more shot . . . you know, for that scumbag."

"No. I think we got what we came for."

"So, just out of curiosity, how much did you take him for?" I asked.

She smiled. "Let's say it was a lot more than he took from me. How about chalking it up to earning interest on my investment? I'm sorry you got into this, Mr. Swann, but that's life, I guess."

"Yes, it is. Especially mine."

As Sidney and the woman turned away, I said, "One more question." They turned back. "Was there ever another diary?"

"What do you care?" asked the woman.

"Just curious."

"It's none of his damn business," said Sidney, cocking his fist.

"It's all right, Sidney." She pulled his arm back. "No. No diary. And you can tell that to Goldblatt. Maybe it'll make him feel worse than just losing this money."

A moment later, Sidney and the woman had disappeared under the boardwalk and I and my aching ribs headed back to the train station.

I didn't care that Goldblatt had been ripped off. I was sure he deserved it. And I didn't care that I wasn't going to get paid. The truth is, the look on Goldblatt's face when I told him what happened might be a lot better than $250 and the cost of a round-trip ticket to Long Beach. What I did care about was that there was no lost Starr Faithfull diary that might have proved that my grandfather, who was long gone, was right.

I don't know why that should mean anything to me after all these years. But it did.

MASTERMIND

BY REED FARREL COLEMAN

Selden

J eff Ziegfeld was always the exception to the rule: the
dumb Jew, the blue-collar Jew, the tough Jew. No matter the Zen of the ethnic group the wheel of fortune got
you born into, dumb and poor was the universal formula for
tough. And he had to be tough because it's hard to be hard
when your name is Jeffrey Ziegfeld. Didn't exactly make the
kids on the block shit their pants when someone said, "Watch
out or Ziggy'll kick your ass." He was extra tough because his
dad liked to smack him around for the fun of it, all the time
saying, "Remember, dickhead, no matter how strong you get,
I'll always be able to kick your ass. I grew up the last white
kid in Brownsville. And where'd you grow up? Lake Grove, a
town with no lake and no grove. What a fucking joke. Kinda
like you, huh, kid?"

J-Zig, as one of the other inmates at the jail in Riverhead
had taken to calling him, could trace what had gone wrong
with his life back to before he was born. Neither one of his
parents had ever gotten out of high school or over moving out
of Brooklyn. Long Island was a rootless, soulless place where
everyone except the Shinnecock, the East End farmers, and
the fishermen came from Northern Boulevard or the Grand
Concourse or Pitkin Avenue. And even the natives were trading in their roots and souls for money. All the goddamned
Indians wanted to do was run slot machine and bingo parlors.

The working farms had been converted into condos, McMansions, and golf courses that no one like J-Zig could afford to play. Not that J-Zig knew a rescue club from a lob wedge. The fishermen? Well, they'd become the cause célèbre of Billy Joel, Long Island's king of schlock'n'roll. Billy Joel, born and bred in Hicksville. Hicksville, indeed.

J-Zig's head was somewhere else as he sat on the ratty Salvation Army couch in his dank basement apartment in Nesconset. Nesconset, a stone's throw from his mom's house in Lake Grove. It might just as well have been a million miles away for all he saw his mom since she'd remarried. He had plenty of reasons to hate his real father, but he hated O'Keefe, his mom's new husband, even more and that was really saying something. His stepfather, a retired city fireman with a belly like a beach ball and the manners of a hyena, was a drunk and more than a little anti-Semitic. J-Zig didn't let that get to him. O'Keefe—if the moron had a first name, J-Zig didn't know it—hated everybody, himself most of all. Jews were probably only fourth or fifth on his list. Besides, O'Keefe's opinion of him was nothing more than the buzzing of mosquito wings. There was only one man J-Zig ever cared enough about to want to impress.

J-Zig had a terminal case of yearning exacerbated by persistent bouts of resentment. But he was a lazy son of a bitch and about as ambitious as a dining room chair. There'd be no pulling himself up by his bootstraps—whatever the fuck bootstraps were, anyhow—not for this likely lad. One way or the other he was a man destined to be a ward of the taxpaying public. He'd already tried on three of the state's myriad options: jail, welfare, and the old reliable unemployment insurance. Truth was, he found none of them very much to his liking. The food and company at the jail sucked. Welfare was okay as far as it went, but since he and the wife and her bastard son by another man's drunken indiscretion had split, he no longer qualified. He liked unemployment fine, but the bitch of it was you had to work for a while to qualify and J-Zig wasn't keen on that aspect of the equation. So he sold fake Ecstasy outside clubs and stolen car parts to pay the bills.

When he wasn't making do with the drugs or the hot car parts, he worked as muscle, doing collections for a loan shark and fence named Avi Ben-Levi. Ben-Levi was a crazy Israeli who put cash on the street and charged major vig to his desperate and pathetic clients. Avi might have been a madman, but J-Zig admired the shit out of him. He admired him not only because Avi was only a few years older than him and had everything J-Zig wanted—a big house in King's Point, a gull-wing Mercedes, and the hottest pussy this side of the sun—but because of how Avi got it.

"Balls, Jeffrey, balls. That's what counts in this world. I came to this country five years ago with three words of English and these," Avi would say, grabbing his own crotch. "Look at me. I am a plain-looking bastard with a high school education. I even got kicked out of the IDF. Not easy getting kicked out of the Israeli army, but I did it. And here I am. Do you have the balls to make good, Jeffrey? Do you have them?"

That was a question J-Zig sometimes asked himself until it was the only thing in his head. Still, as much as J-Zig yearned for Avi's approval, he hated being muscle. Well, except when it came to gamblers.

He had no respect for gamblers. They'd borrow the money and blow it that day and then, when J-Zig would come to collect, they'd squeal and beg like little girls. He liked to hear them scream when he snapped their bones like breadsticks. It was the business types he felt sorry for. All sorts of people borrowed money from Avi, but as broke as he could be at times, J-Zig knew better than to dip into a loan shark's well. Once they had you, they had you by the balls and then they squeezed and squeezed and squeezed until they milked you dry. Thing was, Ben-Levi didn't do the milking himself. It was always left to the muscle like J-Zig. It had been a few months since he'd worked for Ben-Levi because the Israeli had wounded J-Zig's pride. Isn't it always the way: the people whose love you want hurt you the most? He'd come to the loan shark with an excellent idea about how to streamline Ben-Levi's business.

"What, are you a mastermind all of a sudden? Listen, Jeffrey, never confuse muscle with balls, okay? You are good muscle, but show me your balls. Until you do, just do your job, get paid, and shut up." He'd waved his hand in front of J-Zig's face. "This ring and watch are worth more money than you will ever see in your life, so please, either go to Wharton or keep your genius ideas to yourself."

Mastermind. The word had been stuck in J-Zig's head ever since. He burned to prove the Israeli wrong, to repay Avi for mocking him. He wanted to shove Avi's sarcasm so far up his ass that they'd be able to see it in Tel Aviv. It didn't seem to matter what J-Zig did or how hard he tried to please, because his father du jour would always shit on him. He could never remember a time when his real dad had anything but disdain for him. His dad's pet name for J-Zig was the Little Idiot, as in, *Where the fuck is that little idiot?* or *What did the little idiot get on his report card this term?* That's how J-Zig still saw himself—a little idiot. Then there were all the other men who had passed through J-Zig's front door on the way to his mother's bed. Most of them ignored him. The ones who didn't treated him like a case of the crabs. *Hey, can't you ditch the kid? I can't fuck if I know the kid's listening to you squeal through the wall.* Compared to them, O'Keefe was a fucking prince among men. But it was Avi more than any of them he burned to prove wrong.

But J-Zig couldn't figure out how to do it. He hadn't hit upon the right idea just yet, though he knew the right idea was out there waiting for him to find it. He could feel it sometimes like an itch on the bottom of his foot that he couldn't quite get to. If he could only reach it, J-Zig was sure he could finally escape the weight of the gravity that had held him down his entire miserable life.

Then it happened in a flash: the idea hit him like a Taser. When he retraced his steps that day, he even understood the genesis of it. This in itself was a near miracle. Deductive reasoning and introspection weren't usually dishes on J-Zig's menu. The day had started out like most others. Maybe a little better than recent days because he'd fallen into some stolen airbags at dirt-cheap prices. God love tweakers. Meth heads didn't haggle, they just wanted enough cash to keep themselves buzzing for the next few weeks. Sometimes they got a little violent, but violence was something J-Zig could handle. He was better at it than most anyone stupid enough to take him on. He was empathetic to the tweakers' plight. Shit, who wouldn't get edgy when his world was spinning that much faster than everyone else's? Who wouldn't get wound up tight after not sleeping for days on end?

J-Zig had found a body shop in Selden willing to buy the boosted airbags at a fair price. Getting goods cheap didn't mean dick if you couldn't find someone to take them off your hands. The exchange of the airbags for cash went smoothly and the gelt in his pocket meant his expenses were covered for the next two months with a little something left over. Mick, his connection at the body shop, told J-Zig that they could handle as much merchandise he could bring in. In a tough economy everyone was looking to cut corners. This new connection and the cash were cool, but it wasn't his way to prove himself. What it was, was a big weight off his shoulders and that helped clear his head.

For the first time in a long while, he had a little mad money and room to breathe. He decided to head a few miles west, straight down Middle Country Road, for the Smith Haven Mall. In Saudi Arabia, they have Mecca and Medina. On Long Island they have Roosevelt Field and the Smith Haven Mall. Who needs God when you've got the Gap? Everybody on the island, even lowlife mutts like Jeff Ziegfeld, prayed at the temple of conspicuous consumption. *Say hallelujah. Say amen.*

The second piece of the grand scheme planted its seed in J-Zig's brain as he turned left out of the body shop's driveway and toward the mall. A commercial came on the radio for Island World Gold and Jewelry Exchange—Long Island's biggest and most generous gold and jewelry exchange, so the announcer claimed, with branches in Floral Park, Bethpage, Massapequa, Mastic, Selden, Yaphank, and Riverhead. *Selden!* And there it was right in front of him, directly across Middle Country Road from the body shop—Island World Gold and Jewelry Exchange. Funny how he never noticed it before. A sign in the window read: MORE CASH ON HAND THAN ANY THREE OF OUR COMPETITORS COMBINED. Still, it didn't quite register. The only thing he was thinking about was checking out the high school girls parading around the mall in skin-tight pants cut so low you could see the waistbands of their thongs peeking out the back. J-Zig was pretty successful with high school girls who had a thing for bad boys with good bodies. But when he got close to the mall, thoughts of teenage girls and their silky thongs went right out of his head.

There were two white-and-blue Suffolk County Police cruisers blocking the Middle Country Road entrances to the mall. The cops were out of their units, motioning for approaching cars to turn around and leave. J-Zig noticed the vast parking lots were empty and that there were Suffolk County PD cars all over the place, their cherry tops lit up like Times Square on New Year's Eve. There were fire engines and ambulances too.

"Excuse me, officer, what's going on?" he asked one of the cops, slowing his car to a crawl. J-Zig's tone was utterly respectful. He'd learned the hard way how to talk to cops. If you kissed their asses and licked their boots a little, they might tell you what you wanted to know.

"Prank," the cop said. "Some stupid kid called in a bomb threat. Okay, now let's keep it moving."

That's when it all clicked. *Eu-fucking-reka!*

It was week seven of his master plan and so far everything was going smoothly. If everything continued going that way—and he had no reason to think it wouldn't—he would hit Island World Gold and Jewelry Exchange in Selden that coming Thursday at two p.m. J-Zig got stiff just thinking about what he'd been able to manage completely on his own. He was proudest of exhibiting three qualities he wasn't exactly known for: diligence, patience, and calm. He had written out the entire plan, step by step. He'd made a list of the equipment he needed and the research he had to do before even thinking about pulling the job. He went over the lists again and again and again.

First thing he did was get ahold of the meth head who'd

gotten him the airbags, because J-Zig needed a steady flow of funds to help finance the job. He promised the tweaker better prices for his merchandise if he could keep the supply of car parts coming. Mick at the body shop was good to his word and said he would pay top dollar for anything J-Zig could deliver. Greed and drugs were great motivators, and within twenty-four hours the tweaker was knocking on J-Zig's door and J-Zig was in turn knocking on the body shop's door. Everybody was happy.

Over the following weeks, whenever he went to the body shop for a transaction, he scoped out the external security set-up at Island World. By his third trip, he was totally confident he hadn't missed anything. It was pretty basic stuff: a camera on the front door, one on the back door, one on the parking lot, one on the side street. He spent days in the abandoned Taco Bell parking lot with a pair of binoculars fixed on Island World. It got so he recognized the employees, their cars, the times they went to lunch. Most importantly, he took note that the armored car pickup came at two-fifteen p.m. every day of the week.

Next thing he did was turn some of his car-part profits into used gold jewelry at a flea market in Sayville. He knew that the stuff was gaudy crap, but that wasn't the point. He need-ed something to use as an excuse to scope out Island World from the inside. Unlike with the outside security, J-Zig would only get one shot, two at most, to survey the internal security. There would be cameras inside, some he knew he wouldn't be able to see, but that would sure as shit see him. He couldn't risk making too many scouting trips. One, his being there a lot would raise suspicions that he was in fact scouting out the place for a job. Two, he was a convicted felon. Admittedly, a low-class felon, but a felon nonetheless. If Island World's security company was thorough, they might identify him and suspect he was using them to dispose of hot jewelry. He meant to set off some alarm bells, but not that way and not just yet.

He'd convinced a local commercial real estate broker that he was interested in a stand-alone building not unlike the one that housed Island World Gold and Jewelry Exchange. "For coins and other collectibles," he told the broker, who was then only too happy to give J-Zig the keys for a look-see.

When the rep from the same firm that did Island World's security met him at the vacant building, J-Zig realized he shouldn't have wasted time worrying about them being thorough. The rep was so eager to land the account, he volunteered more information than J-Zig could have hoped for.

"We do security for a client right down the road from here in Selden that does sort of what you have in mind for this place. It's roughly the same size and we can do the same setup."

The schmuck practically tripped over his own penis giving out details. And in an attempt to sell an even more elaborate system, the sales rep listed the pitfalls of the Island World setup and explained how a very clever criminal might defeat the system entirely. Some of it was beyond J-Zig's capabilities, but he didn't need to defeat the whole system, just part of it. He thanked the salesman, took his card, and told him he'd be in touch.

The other part of the plan was trickier and more dangerous because it directly involved the police. At random times and on different prepaid Walmart cell phones, he called in various emergencies at the Smith Haven Mall. One Monday it was a car fire. One Wednesday it was a robbery. One Thursday it was a heart attack. One Friday it was a bomb threat. Bomb threat won in a landslide. The police response was incredible.

Every cruiser in the 4th Precinct and half the fire departments on the North Shore of Suffolk County showed up at the mall. That would take care of the cops to his west. J-Zig was smart enough not to repeat the phone-threat routine in the 6th Precinct, the one responsible for Selden, but he was willing to bet they would respond to a bomb threat at the local high school with the same sort of vigor the 4th Precinct cops responded to a bomb threat at the mall. When J-Zig pulled the job, the cops would be so preoccupied they wouldn't know what hit them.

What made this especially cool was how, for the first time in his whole fucked-up life, all the parts were falling into place. The stars had finally aligned for him. All of it, from the bad economy to the kid's bomb prank, from the tweaker to Mick, from the radio commercial to Island World being right across the street from the body shop, had made it pretty easy. But now Thursday was here and the easy stuff was done. It was time to go to work.

He'd made all the calls as he pulled into the body shop's parking lot. When he stepped into the shop to greet Mick, the firehouse claxons erupted, calling for the volunteer firemen to get their asses to the firehouse. Then, as he walked to the back room of the body shop to use the bathroom and establish his alibi, J-Zig heard the police sirens wailing. By the time he slid out the back door, all hell had broken loose. Emergency vehicles were flying down Middle Country Road in both directions: fire engines and ambulances and police cars, lots and lots of police cars. With all of the activity no one noticed him dash across the street. Certainly no one saw him slip into the latex gloves and Obama mask in the shadows along the back edge of Island World's parking lot. He had no doubt that Island World's two female employees were too busy to notice him. Every day at this time, they assembled their cash take and jewelry for the armored car pickup at two-fifteen. It was only when J-Zig threw the brick, lit road flares, and a smoke grenade—much easier to get than he thought it would be—through the side window of Island World Gold and Jewelry Exchange that the employees would sense something was terribly wrong. By then it would be too late.

It was magic. When the two women came screaming and coughing out the back door, he ran in and scooped up the two bags. Before leaving, he checked out the back door and he couldn't believe his eyes. The two women were still running and hadn't bothered looking back. He was out of there and at the edge of the lot, out of sight of the cameras. He slipped the deposit bags, gloves, and his mask into the gym bag he had hidden there the night before with the brick, road flares, and grenade. If anything, the activity on Middle Country Road had intensified. Now there were news and police helicopters in the air. Getting back across the street was no easy thing, but he made it. He tossed the gym bag in the trunk of his car, walked through the body shop's back door—which he had made sure to keep slightly ajar with a small stone—hurried to the bathroom, and flushed. He looked at his watch. 2:06 p.m. The stars were still aligned, but that wasn't the beauty part of the deal, not by a long shot.

The sweetness was that J-Zig was going to get the chance to shove Avi Ben-Levi's own words up his ass after all. He had arranged for Ben-Levi, a man with all the right connections in the wrong world, to fence the jewelry. That's why J-Zig had taken the gold and diamonds and not just the cash—so he could get the chance to face Ben-Levi and gloat. He had fantasized about how the meeting would go for nearly seven weeks. After shaking hands with Mick to reestablish his alibi, he was going to head straight from the body shop to meet with

Ben-Levi at his office in Great Neck. And as a kind of subtle and final fuck you to his former employer, J-Zig had purchased a ticket on EL AL for a flight to Israel. Israel was where he needed to go. He wished he could see the look on Avi's face when he opened the letter J-Zig would send him explaining how he'd pulled off the job at Island World Gold and Jewelry Exchange. He would sign the letter *Mastermind*.

J-Zig slammed the toilet door loud enough to be heard over the sirens and then stepped back into the shop itself. Mick was there waiting for him.

"We were gonna send a search party in there after you, for fuck's sake. What the fuck were you doing?" Mick asked.

"Stomach's been bothering me." J-Zig winked. "I wouldn't go in there for a while unless you get battle pay."

"I consider myself warned."

"What the fuck's going on out here anyway?" he asked, as innocent as a spring lamb, while a few more police cruisers flew by. "I heard all the commotion when I was in the can."

"Fuck if I know. Come on in the office, there's some friends I want you to meet."

J-Zig looked at his watch again. "Maybe another time, I've got—"

"Look, man, for what I've been paying you, you owe me this small favor."

It was tough to argue Mick's point, so he didn't bother. "Lead the way."

He was in the office, the door shut at his back, before he could quite make sense of what was going on. Even after seeing the shields hanging on chains around the necks of Mick's three friends and the 9mms strapped to their belts, it almost didn't register. Then he heard Mick, who was still behind him, say: "Jeffrey Ziegfeld, you're under arrest." J-Zig felt Mick tug his wrists and slap on the cuffs. "You have the right to remain silent. Anything you say can and will be used against you in a court of law. You have the right to an attorney. If you cannot afford an attorney, one will be provided to you. Do you understand these rights?"

J-Zig didn't answer the question, but asked one of his own: "What are the charges?"

"*What are the charges*, he asks," said the fierce-looking detective standing directly in front of J-Zig. "Are you fucking kidding me or what? Hey, this guy missed his calling. He shoulda done standup."

J-Zig repeated the question: "What are the charges?"

"This guy can't be this dumb, can he?" the detective asked the cops behind him. Then he spoke directly to J-Zig. "Are you really that stupid?"

J-Zig repeated the question again: "What are the charges?"

"Okay, rocket scientist, let me give you a clue. My name is Detective Robert Ferraro and we're from the Suffolk County PD Auto Crime Task Force. You think maybe now you can figure it out, or do I have to draw you a picture with crayons?"

J-Zig heard someone laughing. It took a second or two until he realized it was himself.

"Mick, can you believe this guy? He's facing like a ten spot in prison and he's laughing his head off. Hey, shithead, what's so funny?" asked Ferraro.

"I am," said J-Zig.

"You wanna let us in on the joke?" Ferraro asked.

"The punch line won't be as funny to you if I just tell you, but you'll find out soon enough."

"Whatever. Mick, get this moron outta here."

Later that afternoon, when J-Zig's impounded car had been

towed to the 6th Precinct, Mick and Ferraro searched it for more stolen parts. Nobody at the precinct paid the two auto crime task force detectives much mind. Who gave a fuck about some dumb-ass skell who was selling car parts to a police sting operation? They were too busy looking for the guy who jerked around half the first responders in Suffolk County, ripped off Island World Gold and Jewelry Exchange, and then disappeared into thin air. After a minute or two, Ferraro found the gym bag with the money, the jewelry, the gloves, and the Obama mask.

"Holy fuck, Mick!"

"What is it?"

"The punch line."

When J-Zig was arraigned the next morning at the courthouse in Central Islip, he seemed utterly calm. He turned and smiled at the crush of media squeezed into the courtroom. After the long list of charges were read, the judge asked for J-Zig's plea.

"Tell Avi Ben-Levi to go fuck himself!" is what he answered.

J-Zig knew it really didn't matter what he said. He was going to spend a lot of his now somewhat less miserable life in prison.

SEVEN ELEVEN

BY TIM McLOUGHLIN

Wantagh

I was born on July 11 and have therefore assumed that I had no choice but to be a gambler. Although none of us asks to be born, and certainly not when or where, I believe my fate was further cemented by the fact that I was born in 1976, the year that gaming was legalized in Atlantic City. Within a year of my birth, which occurred in Queens, a bus to Resorts International began stopping daily at our corner gas station. Back then the fare was ten dollars round trip, and upon arrival passengers were presented with a roll of quarters, making it a free ride. The quarters, of course, never left the boardwalk. My father enjoyed the slots, and my mother loved the beach, so I grew up in the literal shadow of casinos. Sometimes these decisions are made for you.

Predetermination, superstition, and fate dictate the gambler's choices, and I am no exception. I'm not a stupid man, and am fully aware of the perception of foolishness attributed to an emotional investment in games, but in the larger picture, don't we all celebrate the random nature of the universe? We fear hurricanes and heart attacks, and revel in unexpected pregnancies and promotions. I'm everyman, but more so. I am simply honest about my reliance on the vagaries of chance.

I might have been the CEO of a huge corporate empire if the winds of luck had blown my way. They did not, and that is why, at present, I am homeless, and contemplating the robbery of an armed and somewhat vicious man. I have been standing in the parking lot of the Wantagh station, across the street from his bar, for some time now, and I weigh the odds of my success every few minutes. They are not good.

Wantagh has, to my way of thinking, always been a place where people go to die. Its population has grown dramatically in my lifetime, and Jones Beach has gone from bucolic to nightmarish, but it is still essentially the elephant's graveyard of the lower middle class. When I was a child my family referred reverentially to the enclaves of Nassau County. These were the towns to which my parents' childhood friends from years past had fled, abandoning New York's outer boroughs and scattering to the suburban winds in the white flight of the 1960s. It wasn't until decades later that my mother and father left their deteriorating neighborhood and joined them, everyone reuniting in geriatric, single-level bliss.

My father died before my mother, and that occasioned my first visit as an adult. My parents had been living in Wantagh for six years at that point, but I'd gone to college in California, and decided to settle on the West Coast. I hadn't been back for a while.

I worked in the world of finance then, but repeated the same unfortunate scenario in every firm at which I was employed. I always exhibited great promise and remarkable early success, but my investment strategies would become increasingly volatile, and finally, when the risks had become enormous, some decision would not pay off, with dire consequences for the firm, and I would be let go. After three such incidents, I was barred from working in the industry.

Now it is my mother's death that has brought me back, though I would have been better served following my instincts and remaining in San Diego, where the climate is reasonably suited to outdoor living. But I knew my mother had a will, and as my sister had been killed in an automobile accident when I was still an infant, I was the sole heir. Or so I'd assumed. There was certainly no estate to speak of, but my parents' meager ranch on White Birch Lane would sell quickly and generate enough income that I might have a comfortable winter. And if I could double or even triple it quickly, who knew where it might lead?

I had not counted on my mother's increased devotion to Catholicism following my father's death. That, and the fact that I'd only contacted her once in the past four years—and then to request money—led her to bequeath the house and her modest savings to Saint Francis de Chantal Church. So here I stand.

I was married once, and had a son. That was probably my grandest effort at integrating myself into mainstream life, but it was ultimately futile. I could not maintain with any regularity the mundane jobs necessary to support a family; and sex, with women or men, was really only a pale distraction from gambling.

My wife remarried, after our divorce, a large, stupid man with a quick temper. He sold quantities of steel pipe to other large, stupid men. One night he got more drunk than usual and began beating my wife with a piece of pipe that he carried in his sales kit. When my son—who was six years old—attempted to protect his mother, her husband struck him in the face with the pipe, killing him. The director of the funeral home apologized to me for not being able to make his body presentable enough for an open-casket viewing.

My wife's husband was sentenced to fifteen years, and it seems that he will have to serve eight. He has been in prison for four years now. When he is released, if I'm still alive, I will kill him.

Since our son's death my wife has sustained herself with marijuana and wine. I attempted to do the same, but have found that neither drugs nor alcohol can cut through guilt and grief with the laser precision of gambling. It is only in those moments of action that I can still lose myself. That I can exist outside myself, in a world where my son is still alive, because my wife did not marry a brutal drunk, because she did not leave me, because I have no gambling problem.

This Sunday is Super Bowl Sunday, and for the first time in more years than I care to remember, I will be a winner. I will be a winner because I have an edge. Not an edge in the traditional sense, like receiving a beneficial point spread. This is more like inside information. It's like knowing that a key player has an undisclosed injury.

Suffice to say, my only interest in sports is a sporting one. That could broadly be said about my interest in almost everything, but with sports it defines a love/hate relationship. I find physical competition, between humans or animals, a pointless exercise unless the element of chance and risk of one's capital is inserted into the equation. There is no particular reason why any sane person should care, for example, who the fastest human being on the planet might be. If it were about traveling from one place to another as quickly as possible, wouldn't you simply take a taxi? Yet I have, on two different occasions, won five thousand, and lost fifteen thousand dollars, because of the results of competitions to determine that very fact on a given day.

My addiction requires that I process an endless flow of information, from medical reports to pop culture gossip, about people whose lives mean nothing to me and with whom I have no more interest in interacting socially than I would the horses on which I wager. I am like a Roman general preparing for a great battle. Every available scrap of knowledge is digested and analyzed, and at the last hour the most momentous, potentially devastating decisions are based on the reading of a bird's entrails. My life, and my decisions, have to this point been premised in almost as foolish a manner; intelligence perennially trumped by compulsion driven by blind faith. Until now. Now I have an edge.

My edge is this: I recently learned that the bar across the street is owned by one of the largest bookmakers in Wantagh, and that wagering this year—when the Giants are in contention—has been extraordinary. I have learned something else. The police will raid this establishment today, and they will arrest the bookmaker and all his employees. They will seize his gambling records and, of course, his cash. Unless I arrive first.

See, the money is gone, lost, though the bookmaker doesn't yet know it. So the question is, what becomes of it? The police will confiscate it and, after endless legal entanglements and court appearances, it will be forfeited by the bookmaker and dumped into the public coffers, where it will make barely a ripple. Or it will be pilfered by corrupt officers involved in the raid.

Or I will enter the bar in the next twenty minutes, and I will take it.

I tend to be quiet around the police. No good can come from conversing with them at any length, and you inevitably give away more than you get. It's the nature of the interrogator, always taking it all in. I've been arrested over a dozen times, and though I've never gone to prison I have spent more than a few nights in a precinct cell or backwater lockup. Mostly I pretend to be drunk. Police officers are used to people trying to deny that they are intoxicated, but rarely question your motives if you openly confess to being impaired. Since my arrests have generally been for gambling, or gambling-related offenses, being drunk in no way added to my potential punishment, and the ruse has often saved me from tedious and pointless questioning.

I have, as a side benefit, numerous times enjoyed the voyeuristic pleasures of being the proverbial fly on the wall. I've always marveled at the intimacies cops casually share with their partners, but this last arrest was the only time I'd ever gleaned information that I could genuinely characterize as valuable.

Like any degenerate gambler worthy of the moniker, I've got a pocketful of gutter-to-penthouse-and-back-again stories for most of the places I've drifted through, but in Wantagh I knew almost no one. That meant no one to vouch for me if I were to try to peddle my information to the target of the raid, or his confederates, or, for that matter, his enemies.

Besides, the police had spoken about this raid with an enthusiasm for the project rarely seen in law enforcement outside of film or television. It was to be huge for this town, huge enough to engender excitement in civil servants, and I found that excitement contagious.

I've never taken anything in my life by force, be it money, property, or sex, but I realized that even if I had the contacts to initiate an exchange with the bookmaker, my remuneration would be, in the scheme of things, paltry. It would change my circumstances, of course, but for how long? All my life I've dreamt of the big hit, every gambler's white whale. Perhaps I never realized the form it would have to take.

I began to obsess about the robbery the way I usually fixate on a big game or race. It builds over time and you find yourself doing things to insure your participation in the event while still telling yourself you probably won't follow through. In the weeks preceding the event you squirrel away funds, or borrow them, or sell your wife's jewelry, or refinance your home, just to be ready. You probably won't do anything, but you have to be ready. And then on the eve of the game there comes a sign, an undeniable omen that moves you forward and places the bet. Sometimes these decisions are made for you.

This idea, this robbery, has taken on that feel. I have been moving about in a bubble, voices around me indistinct and muffled. I have convinced a social worker at SNG on Park Avenue that I'm a recovering heroin addict from New York, and she has enrolled me in a daily methadone maintenance program. I have been selling the methadone to supplement the money I've earned by cleaning the kitchen and bathrooms of a café in the Cherrywood Shopping Center. Sometimes they feed me, though they are not as generous as one might hope.

It took me only three weeks to accumulate the funds to buy the gun. Three weeks of living single-mindedly, obsessively, telling myself the whole time that I almost certainly won't do this. I won't commit this robbery in a town where no one left alive knows me. Where I gave the police a false name, and the charge was too insignificant to warrant fingerprinting. A town from which I can virtually vanish. I probably won't do this.

As in any high-stakes game the clock dictates the risk level, and my situation proves the rule. I had been staying in my parents' house until last week, when the church engaged a real estate agency to sell the property. They did not respond to being passively ignored with the same patience granted me by the clergy, and they changed the locks while I was out. Since winter has been thus far fortuitously mild and I still had access to the garage, I was able to sleep in an enclosed space and continue using my mother's lumbering Crown Victoria, so long as I kept out of sight and maintained the odd hours that, frankly, have always suited me. When I returned last night from my trip to New York to acquire the firearm, my mother's car was missing from the parking lot of the railroad station.

There are about a dozen taverns and clubs that huddle around Wantagh station, borne of an era which dictated that the suburban response to urban stress should be alcohol consumption followed by driving home. Though that attitude is presently frowned upon, the establishments have rooted deeply and continue to thrive in the new culture of designated drivers and taxis.

I had no designated driver, and though my cash might cover cab fare, I did not need a witness to my breaking into the garage, so I walked the two miles to the house.

Being on foot alone at night, even in the overgrown suburbia of Wantagh, the feeling of isolation was overwhelming. This had been Jerusalem, my parents' promised land. They had traveled here as children, and told me stories of Victorian homes surrounded by forests and farms; a dozen streets laid out with tract housing, then a huge cornfield, then another tract. Friends and cousins with backyards, lawns, well water, and above-ground pools. Success.

I looked for this magic on my own childhood visits, but found only the used dreams that had been inherited by cops and plumbers, bus drivers and bank tellers. Those with the luxury to dream big had already rolled east. We went to down-at-the-heels bowling alleys and the drive-in at Westbury and breathed in the last wisps of the good life. My mother and father were blind to that reality, and I realize now that blindness can be a blessing.

The garage felt vast and soulless without the car. Whether it had been towed by the municipality for some infraction, or seized by the now rightful owners, was irrelevant; it only served to up the ante on my increasingly claustrophobic circumstances. This morning, after the first truly cold night spent on a concrete floor, I walked the two miles back. I have been standing here for several hours, and the clock is about to run out.

Three unmarked vans will have left police headquarters a few minutes ago. Soon they will park on the opposite corners from this establishment and discharge the officers who will execute the raid. Soon. I have timed their arrival to cover my escape, but the schedule has absolutely no flexibility.

The weapon stuck in my waistband feels very heavy, and it digs into my empty stomach. I need to decide now. If I misjudge this I will not live to avenge my son.

There is a crushing moment of self-awareness that descends upon me as I consider my next move. These instants of vicious clarity are thankfully rare, but when they hit it is with the brutal force of unfiltered truth, like visions of dying alone that visit in the night.

It comes to me that it matters not a whit whether I am successful. Wantagh is where my family goes to die. If I fail, I will most likely die. But if I triumph, then what? If this day results in my greatest score in a life spent chasing the great score, then what? I will be penniless in six months or less, living in a shelter, unclean, and again contemplating violence. And violence, by all reputable accounts, comes easier the second time around, and easier still thereafter. Whatever good comes into my life I will destroy. And if some all-powerful deity grants me a second chance, with full benefit of the memories of this life, I'll make short work of ruining that too. Because I am a monster. We are all monsters here. We sacrifice careers and relationships, the bonds of family. We sacrifice our sons. Nothing is left but need, ever growing.

The moment is paralyzing in its weight but mercifully brief. An old green Saturn sedan stops at the light in front of me, then turns. Its license plate is GSB117, and there is a Padres baseball cap sitting on the rear window shelf. Now I am golden. GSB. Giants Super Bowl. 117. 711. Get it? I was living in San Diego.

I open my jacket and shake it once to billow it away from the outline of the gun, and walk quickly toward the bar's side door.

Sometimes these decisions are made for you.

PAST PRESIDENT

BY SARAH WEINMAN

Great Neck

On Monday morning, six days after she was voted the *shul*'s first female president, no one showed up at the annual general meeting. Under normal circumstances, Pamela Rosenstein would have raised a stink about the collective disrespect. She would have been infuriated at being undermined by a group, not just by individuals who had opposed her appointment in the first place.

But these weren't normal circumstances. Pamela had also skipped out on the general meeting. Instead, all twelve members of the *shul* board stood by the freshly dug grave of Morris Cohn, the man whom Pamela had replaced. Morris's retirement after thirty-five bitter, bullish years as the Greater Synagogue of Great Neck's top *macher* had not been voluntary. Pamela's sudden and unexpected ascension came after Morris's wife found him in his study with a bullet in his head and three more in his chest. He'd lingered in the hospital for five days, never regaining consciousness but still inspiring his wife to proclaim he would come out of it "in no time." He never did, and finally expired Sunday afternoon, while his wife had stepped out for a brief bathroom break. Now, at the grave, Mrs. Cohn looked like she was about to relieve herself of a greater load, what with the ferocious stink eye she affixed the *shul*'s collective, Pamela included.

The wind whipped Pamela's red-gold locks into her face,

and as she smoothed her hair back, a terse whisper sounded in her left ear: "You'll certainly be sitting pretty now."

Pamela looked to her left, but no one stood next to her. She nonetheless recognized the unmistakable Southern drawl—and the trail of orchid-scented perfume—of Lyssa Kamp, chairwoman of the social committee. She was loyal to Morris and Morris only, and had been the loudest of Pamela's many opponents. It would be just like Lyssa to suspect Pamela had some sinister hand in Morris's death, when Pamela hadn't even met the old codger until two days before his shooting, during *kiddush* after Saturday services. And that meeting had only come at the insistence of the vice president, who had been one of the first to welcome Pamela into the synagogue community and thought she and Morris should meet each other. "You never know if she'll come in handy," he'd said, as Morris and Pamela stared awkwardly at one another.

Little did the vice president know how accurate his words would be.

As Morris's coffin was lowered into the ground, Pamela took stock of her fellow board members. So much gray hair. So many wrinkles. That usually meant experience and wisdom, but for the past week she'd seen little sign of those traits, instead replaced by bountiful heaps of pettiness and malice. The worst of it had come four days ago. As Morris lay in a coma, Lyssa and her fellow social committee members knocked on her door, presented Pamela with a document, and told her, in Lyssa's sweetly oozing drawl, that fifty *shul* members had signed or would sign a petition to remove Pamela as president.

Three hours later, at the behest of the vice president, Lyssa had apologized, but both women knew this was for show. All it would take was one tiny mistake on Pamela's part and the war would begin in earnest.

It wasn't as if Pamela had asked for the job. No one wanted it. Who could follow in Morris's footsteps? Who could grease community wheels and cajole donations from *shul* members to the tune of $3.4 million a year, which still wouldn't account for the extensive renovations the eighty-year-old edifice needed to heal its crumbling infrastructure? Who could convince an Orthodox rabbi to work for them when the board couldn't decide if they should modernize and downgrade their religious observance to Reform, or stubbornly cling to a 1950s-style orthodoxy nobody practiced anymore? And who'd want the hassle of replacing Morris when so much of what made him effective, however brutal his methods, relied on knowledge he never shared with anyone?

But what rankled Pamela most was why she had been chosen as *shul* president in the first place. It wasn't for her religiosity, acquired only five years ago after a later-in-life epiphany that she should move away from secularism and reacquaint herself with a more Jewish way of life. It wasn't because of her leadership abilities, for she'd pissed people off mightily in her last full-time job, getting suspended three times and eventually asked, more nicely than warranted, to consider some other line of work.

No, the reason Stephen Pascal, who as vice president had been helping to lead the *shul* almost as long as Morris Cohn, asked Pamela to step in six days ago was because of her former job with the 81st Precinct of the New York City Police Department. And specifically, her specialty in homicide detection. That meant Pamela's survey of her fellow board members wasn't just a matter of politics, but of murder. And everyone assembled—even Stephen—was a suspect.

She'd said no, multiple times. It had been easy when the request was straightforward, a little less the next time, when Stephen added a pleading tone to his voice. Then, on try number three, he brought out his trump card: Pamela had been so effective at defusing that precarious situation, when a Satmar *hasid* from Williamsburg wandered into the wrong Bed-Stuy street corner at the wrong time. He got out, but not before Pamela fired two bullets into the neck of his attacker. She was a heroine to the Jewish community then; she could be the same here in Great Neck.

In his many appeals Pamela could see why Stephen was an effective sidekick to Morris's more showy, less politic personality. Stephen flattered. He reasoned. He explained. And eventually, he convinced Pamela that her newly visible position would be a good cover for finding out the truth about Morris Cohn. He persuaded her precisely by underplaying his hand, not realizing it was the very guilt Pamela felt about the Bed-Stuy shooting which bolstered her policing career that prompted her to reconsider her Jewish self, and to leave New York City altogether.

Pamela had no one to consult before accepting the offer. Not her husband, who'd walked out on her when she announced she was *ba'al teshuva*, returning to the faith. Not her partner, who as far as she knew was still a cop, though no longer homicide, and no longer with the 8-8. Not her boss, canned two months after Pamela on embezzlement charges, news that surprised her more than anyone. Not even her dog Marky, a Boston Terrier who didn't care about anything except when he'd next eat and when he could go for a walk.

But she knew the real, awful reason why she'd accepted, an answer trumping curiosity, the desire for justice, or random whim. The truth was, she was bored out of her mind. Pamela had moved to Great Neck thinking she'd be a better Jew there than in New York City, with all its temptations to break *Shabbat* and lead a non-Orthodox life. The ultra-Orthodox enclaves were no option for her because she could only stomach wearing a skirt between sundown on Friday and sundown on Saturday and couldn't stand the total lack of regard for women. But Great Neck was so fucking *slow* compared to the five boroughs. Even Staten Island. It was her choice of bed, she had to lie in it, but she might as well make her life more interesting, more meaningful, in the process.

Even if no one would appreciate the gesture.

The wind wouldn't stop whipping Pamela's hair. She'd thought often of chopping all of her locks off, going bald and embracing it. But she knew she wouldn't. She loved her hair too much to let it go to waste, even if it meant she had to spend an inordinate amount of time keeping it out of her face. It was at this very moment that another voice said, "Don't you know how to act appropriate at a funeral?"

Pamela had her hair out of her eyes, now looking directly at Henri Durocher. *Oh great*, she thought as her heart started to plummet. *Just what I need, a lecture from the synagogue's richest donor*. Any other venue and she would have fought back. His Holocaust survivor status didn't faze Pamela, nor did his position as the owner of the country's largest hedge fund, built from scratch after he emigrated to the U.S., by way of Birkenau, on his nineteenth birthday. Pamela had run into her fair share of powerful old men and the appropriate investigative pressure usually felled much of their formidable nature. But here, at a cemetery, the only words she could muster were: "Clearly, appropriateness eluded me for a moment."

"Don't let it happen again. I sided with Stephen only because he is a very convincing man. Don't disabuse him, and me, of that belief." Durocher wagged his gnarly finger at her. *Finger-wagging!* Pamela wanted so much to laugh, but like so many of her impulses, she'd have to save them for later, when she was in the public role of president and private role of investigator. Even at the age of seventy-eight, Durocher was rich enough, cunning enough, and dangerous enough to land high on her potential suspect list, despite being one of Morris's best friends.

But could Henri, or any of these other graying board members, truly be capable of murder? Pamela knew well that anyone could kill, given the right motivation, the best weapon, and well-timed rage, and she would certainly ferret out all of those variables. Yet looking around the grave, Pamela's first instinct was to rule out all of her fellow board members. It was one thing to stab in the back metaphorically, which most of these members did with astonishing ease. It was quite another to elevate character assassination to out-and-out homicide.

Then an odd movement caught the corner of Pamela's eye. She couldn't turn around, because it happened just as Morris's coffin was lowered into the ground and the aging pallbearers picked up nearby shovels and began to throw dirt into the hole. As Morris's wife and two sons started saying *Kaddish*, Pamela craned her neck toward the cemetery exit. And added someone new to the potential suspect list.

The crowd dispersed after *Kaddish* and Pamela quietly slipped away from the group. Being ostracized had its advantages, she thought as she hurried toward the exit, hoping she could catch the mysterious decamper. It helped that the man's limp prevented him from walking very fast, so that by the time Pamela reached the long train of cars, he was still fiddling with his keys.

"Excuse me, do you have a minute?" she asked.

He looked up at Pamela, startled. Then he nodded, signaling she should sit in the passenger seat.

"I think it might be better if we spoke out here," Pamela said.

"It definitely would be better if we spoke in the car." The man looked frail, but his voice boomed with easy authority. She wouldn't have expected anything less of Stuart Cohn, two years the elder of Morris.

Pamela acquiesced, but not before making sure her smartphone was turned on. It didn't hurt to have the GPS broadcasted out in the event that something happened, a lesson that came in handy several years ago when a scrape in the 88th almost turned out to be her last case.

When the doors shut, Stuart said, "I know what you must be thinking."

"Why don't you tell me."

"That I must be a horrible person to walk away from my own brother's funeral."

"Should I think you're horrible?"

Stuart Cohn lowered his head to the steering wheel. "Maybe. I know I do. But Morris was asking for trouble this last year. He went too far. Pushed too many buttons and made too many enemies."

"Were you one of those enemies?" asked Pamela.

Stuart jerked his head up. He was frail, but the intensity of his green eyes was as formidable as it must have been during his prime in the family business. She wasn't afraid of him, at least from a cop-to-potential-suspect standpoint. But from a shul-president-to-rich-congregant standpoint, she felt a small sting of disrespect.

"You can take the woman out of the precinct . . ." began

Stuart, before he realized what he was saying. Then he clamped his mouth shut.

"It's all right," Pamela assured him. "I think the board knows the real reason I was appointed, and none of them like it much. Even Stephen wasn't happy, and he was the one doing the appointing."

They lapsed into silence. Pamela was patient and used to such lulls. They allowed her focus to sharpen, to think of follow-up questions. And in the meantime, the person across from her would squirm a little as he or she chafed from the strain of silence.

Stuart was a pro too, but even he succumbed. "We weren't getting along near the end," he finally admitted, "but there was a good reason."

"What was it?"

"Morris lost all my money."

"All of it?"

"Ninety percent, which for a multimillionaire is as close to *all of it* as one ever gets."

"I didn't know Morris was that rich," Pamela said.

"The man liked to think he was a genius with money. So he got a little lucky with stock options and hedge funds! Until he wasn't so lucky anymore."

The pain on Stuart's face was real and Pamela didn't know what to say for a moment. It was terrible. And yet, it was so Morris to take his brother's trust and abuse it mercilessly.

"There's no way I can ever make it back," said Stuart. In a smaller voice, he added, "I still haven't told my wife."

"So why should I rule you out?"

"Of course you would ask me that," Stuart snarled. "Because you can never, ever take the precinct out of the woman. And if you must know, I was having dinner with my wife when

Morris was getting himself shot. I'm sure the restaurant will have a credit card receipt to confirm, should you feel the need to check."

"I'm sure I will." More charitably, Pamela then said, "I appreciate you telling me what happened."

Stuart brushed aside her comment with his hand. "I know I'm not the only one he did this to. Find the person who got pissed off the most, you have your man. Or your woman." He unlocked the car doors and laughed without humor. "The fairer sex is probably more capable of killing him."

"Why would you say that?"

"Because there are a number of them who were far angrier with Morris than me." Stuart bobbed his head toward the passenger door. "Now if you'll excuse me, I'd like to spend some time with people I actually care about and impart some news no one wants to hear."

The car zoomed away as Pamela trudged back toward the cemetery's entrance. Stuart Cohn was tough, but his hands couldn't lie. They trembled on the steering wheel in such a way to confirm he couldn't possibly have held a gun, let alone fire it repeatedly.

This time, Pamela was the one who was approached as she was fiddling for her car keys. "Stephen said I should speak with you," said Morris's widow.

Aline Cohn's voice had caught Pamela's attention when she gave a brief eulogy at the service. She barely opened her mouth but her words resonated all the way to the back of the hall, where Pamela had taken a seat. Now, with that voice just inches away, Pamela had the urge to block her ears. No wonder she'd stayed married to Morris the whole time, Pamela mused. Aline was one of the few people who could shout him down and even dominate the conversation.

"If this isn't a good time—" Pamela began.

"There's never a good time," Aline snapped. "It might as well be now. I don't have that much to say except that I gather you're looking to find out who killed Morris, and my suggestion is to look amongst the harpies on the board."

Pamela tried to suppress a smile, but Aline found her out. "This isn't funny, young woman."

"Of course not," Pamela managed to eke out. "It's just, well, your voice carries."

"Do you think I care if the entire world hears what I have to say? So be it!" Aline's arm gestures were almost as loud and frantic as her voice. "Morris was a terrible person. I wasn't much better, but someone had to be an example to our children and grandchildren and he certainly wasn't stepping up. I'm actually amazed he managed to charm so many women when he looked the way he did!" Aline shook her head, keeping a crocodile-like smile. "Especially that one." She pointed her left arm at Lyssa Kamp, who was walking toward them.

"What the hell did you see in him?" yelled Aline. This time Pamela did cover her ears.

"I can't believe you would ask me this," said Lyssa, who moved to face her nemesis. "At Morris's funeral! Aline, we can talk about this later—"

"Oh, I don't think so. We'll discuss this right now. Besides, Miss Rosenstein here is looking for who killed Morris. Why don't you strike yourself off the list for her sake, even if it won't be for mine?"

Lyssa drew back, stunned. Her right foot caught on a rock and she suddenly fell on her side with a loud thump. When she hit the ground, she cried, "Morris was the best lover I ever had. He had so much energy saved up because you kept spurning him!"

Aline didn't say anything, her mouth frozen open in an oval. Lyssa didn't move. The moment suspended in time before Pamela intervened, moving between the two women.

"Ladies, do either of you really want to get into a fight?"

"You stay out of this!" spat Lyssa. "I've wanted to tell that bitch for years what's really been going on with Morris and me!"

At the same time, Aline rushed forward, and Pamela held out her hands to ward off the widow.

"I can't stay out of this. Otherwise I wouldn't be doing my job. And besides," Pamela added, keeping her arms out toward each woman as a physical warning, "neither of you is really convincing me of any innocence in Morris's death."

"Is everything all right, Ma?" Morris's oldest son, Barry, had come up behind his mother, and was now holding her back.

"Take your hands off me, Barry," said Aline. "I'm fine. Let's go home." But before she moved, she had some final words for Pamela: "Don't screw this up."

As if Pamela needed another reminder of what was at stake. When the Cohns left, she held out her arm to Lyssa, who brushed furiously at her suit as she rose from the ground. And if Pamela thought Lyssa would be grateful, she was quickly proved wrong. "This suit cost three thousand dollars and it will be in the dry cleaner for weeks now!" There was no offer of thanks and no goodbyes as the older woman stormed away.

And Pamela was left to wonder what other bizarre scenes would play out as she removed the rock that was Morris Cohn's murder and secrets inevitably began to slither out into public view.

* * *

The 81st Precinct hadn't been Pamela's first choice of station, but that was only because she grew up a middle-class Jew, unaccustomed to those whose fortunes fared far worse. She'd been seconded to the 20th Precinct on the Upper West Side as a rookie cop, spending her first five years dealing with the domestic concerns of Manhattan's most suburban neighborhood during flush economic times. Pamela's reeducation began an hour into her first shift as a homicide detective, when she and her partner were called out to a drug deal turned bad. It was on September 16, 2008, the day after Lehman Brothers went bankrupt, and Pamela's mind was on how the news would affect her husband. He'd switched to Goldman Sachs just six months before, but still had equity in his old firm. That was forty million dollars in stock options now gone up in a puff of economic-meltdown smoke.

The multiple murders, with needle shards strewn all over the floor and blood smeared on the walls, gave Pamela the necessary perspective. The economy would boom and bust and paper money could vanish, but there were people stuck in perpetual ruts, whose choices varied between selling drugs or doing them, having eight kids with six men or four kids with one, and a life expectancy of thirty-five if you were lucky. It was Pamela's first case and it remained unsolved to this day.

She would have preferred to reopen that case than investigate the black comedy that was Morris Cohn's killing. And she certainly would have preferred the long, hot shower she had to forgo when the doorbell rang, causing Marky to morph from sweet little dog into a psychotic bundle of screaming terror.

Pamela quickly threw on sweatpants and a T-shirt and answered the door. She wasn't a stickler about appearance, but still shrank at the sight of her visitor's carefully coiffed copper hair, elegantly structured pantsuit, and narrowed hazel eyes. A mere three hours after a funeral and Iris Tropper looked every inch the Wall Street executive she used to be.

"Sorry to bother you," said Iris, sounding anything but. "I wanted to set the record straight."

"I was just about to jump into the shower—"

"This won't take long," Iris interjected. There was a reason she had been appointed treasurer. She knew exactly where the *shul*'s money was supposed to be and where it actually was. Knowing that key difference, as well as being a strong foil for Morris's more creative, if economically unsustainable ideas, kept the Great Neck synagogue alive. Barely.

Pamela opened the door and Iris came through in two strides, refusing a drink or a seat. Instead, she went straight to the point: "The *shul* is in terrible trouble. Morris left a hell of a mess and it's up to you to clean it up."

Now Pamela really wished she'd had time for the shower. "What do you mean?"

"We're down to our last hundred thousand. I checked the ledger a few days ago, after he was shot, but with everything in turmoil I didn't trust my own calculations. Then I checked again yesterday and was certain. The building fund is gone." Iris's face remained impassive, but Pamela caught a glint of fear in her eyes. A fear Pamela herself now felt, warring with a sense of anticipation.

"Gone where?" she asked.

Iris fished out a set of papers from her purse. "Take a look. There's a shell company called AmFam Associates, based out of Grand Cayman, that's listed twelve times in the last four months. Then the trail disappears."

"Why didn't you notice this before, Iris?"

The other woman stood quietly for a moment, then sank

back into the nearest chair, crossed her legs, and arranged her posture so it was even straighter than when she stood. Quite a feat, Pamela marveled, but it was all defensive armor as Iris struggled with what to say next.

"I've asked myself that question a number of times," Iris said, in a small voice completely unlike her regal bearing. "But that's how Morris was. A fireball of bravado and charisma, whether or not you liked him—as too many did, or didn't, like me." Her eyes flickered away from Pamela's at that moment, and her voice died away.

"How mutual was that dislike?"

Iris cast her head down, her face flushing red. "It's so embarrassing to admit this, but there was a time when what was mutual was something other than dislike. Just once. It was awful. Just thinking about it now, when my husband hasn't been well all year . . ."

"So why," said Pamela, sensing there was a crack in the armor ready to be exploited, "are you being so up-front with me? To rule yourself out as a suspect?" A smile played on her lips. "Who's to say you didn't do the math before and let Morris know of your calculations?"

Iris didn't blink. "You have every right to ask, but if that was the case, why am I here?"

"A lot of people like to play the hide-in-plain-sight game. You're smart enough to do that. I'd say the entire board of directors is capable. So unless you have concrete proof you didn't kill Morris—"

"As a matter of fact, I do." Out came another paper-clipped bundle of sheets. "These are hospital records. I always ask them to provide copies for insurance purposes, but in light of Lyssa's ridiculous behavior at the cemetery, I was glad to have them on hand."

Pamela took a look at the records, and her heart ached a little for Iris. There was her signature on the hospital's log book, once to sign in at 6:35 p.m. on Wednesday, once to sign out at 9:50 p.m. Then a validated parking slip at the hospital fifteen minutes later, and, helpful for Pamela but likely embarrassing for Iris, a speeding ticket write-up at 10:45 p.m. just three blocks from her house in the adjoining suburb.

"My husband has perhaps a month, maybe two left," said Iris. "The last thing I would do is jeopardize what time we have left."

"I appreciate you being so thorough."

Iris stood up, the armor now fully back in place. "You won't when you have to contend with this money mess. Fortunately that won't be my problem." And out came one final slip of paper. "That's my resignation, effective immediately. I won't be part of this sideshow anymore."

The long, hot shower Pamela finally had didn't clear up her confusion. That would only come with a frantic phone call from Stephen Pascal, urging her to meet immediately.

"I thought we weren't meeting up until progress was made on tracking down the killer," Pamela said.

"Now it's Morris's and Lyssa's killer."

Marky barked twice when Pamela put down the phone. When her dog seemed to grasp the situation better than she did, she knew how much trouble she'd gotten herself into.

While Iris was spoon-feeding her alibi to Pamela, Lyssa Kamp had gotten herself killed in her car. A blunt object of some kind had smashed the woman's head from the back as she moved into the driveway of her own house. Stephen's nephew, who was married to a low-level patrol cop who supposedly knew how to get the right people to leak information at the right time, said the going theory was a carjacker. Stephen thought otherwise.

"What carjacker hides in a car at a cemetery and then stays down for the entire car ride?" he scoffed. They sat in Morris's old office, which was now Pamela's, except it was still full of her predecessor's furniture, pictures, and files. No one, least of all Pamela, had had time to change anything.

"I suppose it's possible," Pamela conceded, "but it's pretty unlikely."

"And you shouldn't have left the cemetery when you did. There were still a good half a dozen board members remaining. Any one of them could have jumped into the car to take Lyssa out."

Pamela's shoulders sagged. "The fight ended. Aline and her son had already walked back to their car. Lyssa was on her way to her car when I left. And need I remind you, Stephen, I used to be a policewoman, but I'm not anymore, and there were no police on hand at the funeral. There are limits to what I could and can do."

"Now, Pamela, do you want to be *shul* president or not?"

She didn't answer. She didn't have to. Stephen sighed in dramatic fashion. "I suppose that's the wrong question. But someone needs to lead."

"Well, why not you? You certainly want to control this situation, Stephen."

"Because the city wants to shut us down!" he cried. "Because Morris Cohn fucked us in the worst possible way. Iris is leaving because of his fiscal irresponsibility."

"She told you she was resigning?"

"Of course. Iris called me before she went out to your house."

For Pamela, this was the final straw. She laid out all of

Iris's documents on Morris's desk. "You know what, Stephen, I don't need this headache. I don't want this responsibility. I just wanted to be a good Jew and a good volunteer, but this *shul* is full of vipers, most of all you. I'm done. Goodbye."

"Wait a minute! You can't leave!"

But Pamela was deaf to Stephen's cries, storming out of the office and ready to escape to the refuge that was her crappy little car.

Until she realized she had miscalculated. And to correct her miscalculation, she would have to search Morris's office.

It was foolish, but Pamela couldn't go back into the synagogue while Stephen was still around. She could grovel later, if need be, but now was a time to let the man stew in his own power juice. And for what, when he didn't even want to run things officially? No, Pamela realized, Stephen Pascal much preferred power from a small remove, twisting the puppet strings of those, like herself, who were just figureheads for the real leaders.

"Miss Rosenstein?" said a voice from behind.

Pamela snapped out of her increasingly rage-filled thoughts and found her composure. "Yes?" she asked. It was Stephen's secretary, Marsha, who at six-foot-two towered over Pamela and, though twenty years older, moved with the quickness of a cheetah, judging by how short a time it took to catch up.

"There's a phone call for you, and I saw you leaving—"

"I'll take it. Thanks." Here was Pamela's ready-made excuse to return to the *shul*. "And make sure I'm not to be disturbed, especially by your boss."

"Of course," said Marsha, sprinting ahead.

Back in Morris's office—she would never think of it as hers—Pamela shut the door and got to work on the drawers. The top one was unlocked, the rest were not, but latent lock-picking skills she had learned on a weekend training session during her rookie year as a cop came back, albeit with a significant amount of rust. She was certain everyone, especially Stephen, could hear her drawer ministrations, but she did not care. She had to get at whatever was inside the desk.

At first Pamela couldn't contain her disappointment. The top drawer was filled with junk, tons of it, in the form of a ripped *tallis*, a set of *tefillin* with so much dust they had to have been almost as old as Morris, an ashtray full of moldy cigarette butts and half-empty matchsticks. Even if there could be some useful clues to glean, it wouldn't help Pamela now. She didn't have the weeks required for proper evidence and DNA testing at her disposal.

She was about to open the second drawer when the office phone rang again. Shit. Pamela had been so absorbed she'd forgotten about the call Marsha told her was coming. She picked up and tried her best to be polite, to tamp down her irritation.

"Is this Pamela Rosenstein?" said a timid voice on the other line.

"Yes, may I help you?"

"I'm not sure . . . but I hope so. I called the office and they said you're in Morris's office now, that you've taken over as president?"

Pamela held the receiver away from her ear, exhaled slowly, and then went back on the line. "Yes, that's true."

"I'm sorry it's taking so long to get to the point, but it's just . . . well, I was with Morris that day."

"Which day?" Pamela knew damn well which day, but she needed confirmation.

"The day he was . . . the day he died." The woman's voice was like broken glass. "I need to talk to someone and I gather you're the person to talk to so . . ."

Pamela knew an opening when she had one. "Where should we meet?"

"There's a coffee shop, Dinero's, on the corner of Middle Neck and Northern. I'll be there one hour from now."

"How will I know what you look like?"

The woman laughed bitterly. "Believe me, I'm hard to miss."

She rang off and Pamela held her head in her hands. Dinero's was a five-minute drive and she had thirty minutes, tops, to conduct a search that should really take two hours. But it had to be done. She rifled through more endless junk until she reached the last drawer. The clock ticked and the lock could not be picked. Frustrated, Pamela whacked her purse against the drawer. There was a click.

And true to form, the effect was Open Sesame all the way. A cursory look revealed facts, figures, numbers. Pamela grabbed all that could fit in her purse and rushed out of the office, past a glaring Marsha, and back to her little car.

And when Pamela reached Dinero's there was some crime scene tape waiting for her.

Since Pamela had no badge to flash and the authority of synagogue presidency didn't carry quite the same weight as being a homicide detective, she didn't get much out of the cops at the scene. One, however, did allow the tape had been put up just ten minutes ago, after a hooded figure walked into the shop, took out a gun, and fired three bullets into the head of an elderly woman with a significant facial deformity.

"Jesus Christ," Pamela gasped involuntarily.

"Yeah," said the cop, brushing back blond bangs from his eyes, "seriously cold shit." His eyes narrowed on Pamela's. "Why are you so interested, anyway?"

In that moment, Pamela elected to keep the phone call to herself. She'd tell the police on her terms, but not before. "Occupational hazard," she allowed. "I used to work homicide in the city."

"No fooling? Where?"

"The 8-1."

The cop's ensuing grin was out of place. "I used to live not far from there. It's cleaned up some, but back when I was around . . . hoo boy."

"Hoo boy, indeed," said Pamela, smiling without mirth.

"But you still can't go in there."

"I wouldn't dream of it."

The conversation was over, but Pamela stuck around and let her ears be her guide. From careful eavesdropping and casual exchanges with customers who'd been questioned and were leaving the premises, she learned the woman's name: Esther Danzig. The name rang faintly in Pamela's mind, but she couldn't place why right away. And why had the woman wanted to talk with Pamela? More to the point, was the facial deformity—a bright red birthmark covering a third of her face—what Esther meant over the phone with respect to recognition, or did she know she was marked?

Pamela could guess what had likely happened, though. The woman, Esther, was one of Morris's financial victims. Trusted him with her money and lost it all, and when she found out, she confronted him. Pamela doubted she had been ready to confess to murder; but whatever it was she'd intended to confess worried the killer enough that she had to be shut up. Just like Lyssa. Just like Morris.

The documents, the damn documents. Pamela felt oppressed by the milling around, the crime scene tape, the endless chatter. She had to double-check what she thought she saw and the only way was to get in her car, pull over, and spend quality time poring over figures that might give her the answers she needed.

She made her way to the car, checking the backseat first. If someone was going around carjacking people, even if that theory didn't hold water, she didn't want to fall victim to stupidity. Satisfied she was well and truly alone, Pamela drove to another coffee shop down the way, checking her mirrors in true paranoid fashion and pulling into a spot in the very back of the shop.

The coffee at this place was horrible, unlike the frou-frou stuff Dinero's served, but it was requisite fuel while Pamela contended with Morris's documents. As Iris said, there were the Grand Cayman accounts, registered in other people's names: Morris, Esther, Lyssa, Stuart Cohn, Aline Cohn, Henri Durocher. All that money washed away, never to return to American soil.

Pamela now knew what would come next. Lyssa hadn't been carjacked, and neither had her car left the driveway. She hoped to hell that Marky would prove himself to be an excellent guard dog instead of the softy she knew he really was and loved him for.

Pamela drove quickly but not so fast as to trigger a speed gun. She dialed Stephen on his cell phone and informed him she was close to a solution.

"Are you sure?" He sounded incredulous.

"Very sure," said Pamela, "but you're not going to like it."

Pamela parked her car across the street from the driveway, and when she emerged from the vehicle, kept her gun hand free. It was in her purse, but within easy reach. Darkness had come quickly in Great Neck, as it often did in March, right before spring. Normally this would be a disadvantage, but not for Pamela, who wanted to enhance the element of surprise. She crouched down and slithered through the grass up to the front door.

As she expected, the door was open. What worried Pamela most was that Marky didn't make a sound. Her heart began to plummet.

Pamela pushed the door open, hoping like hell the oil she'd put on the door had worked and it wouldn't squeak. No sound. Good. The front hall was still dark, as she'd left it, but it was quiet, too quiet. She moved to her purse, took out her gun—

And Marky barked, loud and clear.

Pamela hit the lights. Her dog stood on top of the prone body of a feeble-looking old man who had bite marks in his back; his right leg was splayed out at an unnatural angle. Marky wasn't moving but boy was he barking with triumph!

The man on the floor had the audacity to say, "Get that fucking dog off of me."

"I don't think so, Henri. Who knows what you might do?"

"My leg is broken! I can't do anything!"

"All the more reason to let other people deal with the matter. You broke into my house. If I search you, will I find the gun that killed Esther and Lyssa? And Morris?"

Henri Durocher had the grace to stop talking. Instead, he howled in pain, and Marky barked louder.

Pamela wanted to scoop up her dog and declare him a hero, but she had three things to do first: contact the police and report a burglary in progress, get an ambulance for the fallen rich man, and call Stephen.

The ambulance had come and gone and the cops were securing the scene and peppering Pamela with questions when Stephen arrived. Pamela's story made his face turn several shades paler, and his eyes misted over.

"What a terrible shame," he said.

"I think Henri found out he wasn't so rich after all and Morris was much richer than he ought to be."

"And really, no one had any money." Stephen Pascal sighed. "But for Henri it would have been the worst blow of all." Pamela could only nod as Stephen continued. "I think we all forgot that *shul* politics isn't a shell game, but Morris in particular let this get away from him." He looked at Pamela beseechingly.

She shook her head. "I'm sorry, Stephen. But I'm not cut out to run the synagogue. Don't fight the inevitable."

"I'll tell you what's inevitable. The average age of a congregant is sixty-nine. The youngsters are leaving, just like they always do, but it's so much worse now. We have renovations we can't afford and expenses mounting up. In Great Neck! The community was supposed to support us."

"There are a lot of things communities are supposed to support," Pamela pointed out. "Libraries. Firehouses. Roads. And all of that's falling away, turning decrepit. Look at Nassau County. They're nearly broke again, twenty years after building themselves back from the brink. Do we ever learn?"

"We may not," said Stephen, "but that doesn't mean we shouldn't try."

After he left, Pamela mulled over the vice president's final statement. She knew she was making the right decision to leave the *shul* presidency before she even began, and yet this experience would leave a mark on her. Money trumped religion, and cooperation too often seemed an impossibility. Otherwise how could so many die because of one man's single-minded, if strangely justifiable rage over losing his money?

But then, what of Morris's brother Stuart? He was in the same position, and he hadn't acted so rashly, so murderously. Or Stephen, for that matter, who wanted to save the synagogue even though it was a futile exercise.

There were no obvious answers, as Pamela had learned so many times before. But as long as this was a world where dogs could save lives, and love—for a person or for a construct—could rule all, Pamela wasn't ready to throw in the towel.

Marky toddled up and stared at Pamela. "You can't lick me!" she said in mock horror.

Pamela read the dog's look again when Marky wouldn't go away. She reached down, scooped him up in a hug, and realized what to do. And as Marky ate his food in bliss and in near-oblivion over what had just happened, Pamela understood. We are who we are, she thought, and sometimes that's more than enough.

PART III

LOVE AND OTHER HORRORS

BOOB NOIR   BY JULES FEIFFER   *Southampton*

SUMMER LOVE

BY JZ HOLDEN

Sagaponack

I was the managing editor of a new magazine. The intro-
ductory issue had been a great success. While I worked
diligently to make it so, the aging publisher's latest girlfriend, La Diva of the cocaine-induced blow job, who serviced
him assiduously from beneath his desk each day during lunch,
licked her lips sweetly and demanded my job.

There was no contest. After receiving the news, and since
we were at the start of a new season, I was left little choice but
to meet with the editor of our rival publication.

Michael Ashforth was a tall WASP in his fifties, balding
ever so slightly, his remaining hair graying silently. He wore a
salt-and-pepper mustache reminiscent of the 1970s that he
kept neatly trimmed. When he sat cross-legged, you could see
that he had a bit of a paunch. He examined my resume like a
doctor reading a chart while I sat across from him in an un-
comfortable, cool-to-the-touch, middle-school wooden chair.
He peered through the wire-framed pharmacy reading glasses
that made him look like an intellectual while his elegant, ta-
pered fingers gently fondled the sheets of paper resting on his
knee. I quietly waited for him to finish, feeling demoded and
pretending not to care. When he was done, we made small
talk, discussed the weather, where and how long I'd lived in
the Hamptons, and then the conversation took a more personal turn. Where had I grown up and was I married? I ex-

plained that New York City had been my home for most of my life. That I was divorced, and childless. As it turned out, we were the same age and we had both grown up in the city. Coincidentally, his uncle's town house was on the same street as my childhood home.

Since we appeared to be heading down that road, I asked about the photograph of the attractive young girl above his desk. With a note of pride in his voice, he announced that she was his daughter and the love of his life. He made no mention of a wife. I checked for a wedding band. None. No other photos, not even a smiling group shot complete with cats and dogs, posed on the front lawn.

I reminded myself that I was there to pitch my stories. I offered each one as if it were a delectable, handmade chocolate morsel on a silver tray. Energetically, I presented every article I had planned for my own magazine for the season. He devoured them, saying yes to each and smiling greedily. He explained that I would be standing in for a writer who was on vacation for the summer. But there was something in his manner, something intangible, something electric, simmering beneath the surface.

The deal made, we stood up to shake hands and say goodbye, when he gently brushed a loose strand of hair from my right eye. His phone calls and e-mails commenced the next day. After all, we had a professional relationship. I was the new writer, and had to be nurtured. Jokingly, I requested to be sent to The Hague to cover the war crimes trials of deposed despots. His response was, only if he could go with me. Assigned to cover a gallery opening, I asked whether he'd care to accompany me there. He politely declined. But by the time I returned from viewing the exhibition, eight phone messages were waiting in my voicemail.

"Hi. I . . . er, was just thinking of you and thought I'd say hello." *Click.*

All my life I had successfully employed a policy to never fool around with the men I worked with, particularly if those men were married, and especially if those men were in positions of power. But this guy was making it difficult. A haze of ambiguity surrounded the risks involved in becoming lovers; the fact that doing so might cause me to lose my job which I desperately needed, versus my turning him down, which also might cause me to lose my job, added a certain relish to the mix. I was rushed off my feet by excitation and flattery; imagining what he stood to lose if we were caught.

My last relationship had ended over a year ago, and I did not care for one-night stands. Instead I chose to spend time on creative projects or activities like dinner and movies with friends. The transition from magazine editor to freelance writer also left me with more time on my hands than I was accustomed to having. To my surprise, I discovered that I was lonely and hungry for attention. His constant calls not only gave my ego a buzz, they reawakened my sensuality, exposing in its wake a voracious hunger for sexual intimacy. The strength of his ardor made me realize just how parched I had become.

There was no question, he was offering himself to me as a very willing drink of water, slightly toxic perhaps, but water nonetheless.

The next morning at nine o'clock the phone rang.

"Hi. I was wondering whether you'd be available for lunch today?"

"Lunch?" I said. "Well, sort of short notice but okay, yes."

"I'll swing by at twelve-thirty then."

I was still toweling off when I heard the screen door slam

and a man's voice downstairs shout, "Hi! I'm early!"

Running into the bedroom, I dripped water across the floor. The clock read noon.

"I'll be down in a minute!" I responded.

The clothes I'd planned to wear were laid out on the bed. Grabbing the loose-fitting linen shirt and pants, I ran a comb through my wet hair and walked down the stairs, almost breathless. He looked up, came over, took my face in his hands, and kissed me.

"I've wanted to do that ever since we met," he said.

I found his behavior disarming. Moving away, I sat on the sofa.

"I'm starving," I said, "where shall we eat?"

"You tell me."

Things were happening faster than I had expected and I needed time.

"How about Yama-Q?" I suggested. "We can walk."

"First tell me about this painting," he said, pointing to the art above the fireplace.

I felt him stalling.

"That's my Great-aunt Sophie with the red hair, holding court at her nightclub in Berlin."

"You had an aunt who had a nightclub in Berlin?"

"In the '20s."

"Is she still alive?"

"No, but she survived the war, whereas most of my family did not."

"Who painted the picture?" he asked.

"One of her many lovers, a Polish artist."

"What happened to him?"

"He became a scenic artist in Hollywood."

"I'm not worthy of you," he said.

"That's not good."

"No, that's not good."

We sat at a little table in the corner. He asked why I left my previous job. I explained about the under-the-desk, cocksucking, drug-using publisher's girlfriend.

"Are you married?"

"Yes," he said, and looked directly into my eyes.

"You don't act married."

"How do you feel about that?"

"About the fact that you are married or about the fact that you don't act married?"

"The first."

"Depends . . ."

He ate his sushi with chopsticks, slowly, meticulously, taking small breaks between pieces, placing his chopsticks on the side of the plate and tilting his head as if to indicate that he was listening.

"We haven't been together in a long time."

"Sexually?" I asked.

"I no longer love her."

"Why do you stay?"

"It's complicated," he answered, and washed down his last piece of pink tuna with some steaming green tea.

I thought, *He's full of shit*, but said nothing. Beneath the pretense I sensed need, warmth, and something else, sadness perhaps, something tragic. After lunch, we walked the half-mile to my house. It was a sunny June day, the buds on the trees had burst, all the leaves were fresh and bright. I invited him inside. We sat on the sofa and talked about the stories I would write and we kissed again, and hugged for a long time. He was gentle and his clothes smelled of laundry detergent. I felt a mixture of tenderness and sorrow.

"Your experience of working with me will be the antithesis of what occurred at your previous job," he said, "I promise."

I didn't quite know what he meant by that remark, but feeling that it required a response, I said, "Okay."

The next morning we began working together. I agreed to produce two to three stories a week. We spoke on the phone every day. We e-mailed jokes to one another along with stray thoughts and poems. I acquiesced to lunch once a week. Before I knew it, it was July. The temperature was up in the nineties, even at night.

Then he started stopping at a phone booth to call when he'd take the dog out for a walk.

"Hey." The greeting was always the same.

"Hey."

"What are you wearing?" he'd ask.

"A pale pink silk nightgown." It wouldn't matter if I were wearing gray flannel men's pajamas, he couldn't see me.

"Describe it," he'd say, breathing heavily. And telling me that he adored me. That he wanted to make love to me.

"Not like this. Not the first time."

One day he refused to stop. "I'd start at your toes and work my way up. I want to make love to you tomorrow. I'll be there at one o'clock . . . I've fallen in love with you."

The sun rose over hundreds of parched and windless lawns in a season of cloudless skies. The fan had been pushing hot air around all night long and the oppressive lack of a breeze was crushing. We were entering the eighth day of a heat wave. My next door neighbors had spent the last two days screaming at one another, taking intermittent breaks to beat their five-year-old son. The child's screams would sear the air, piercing my heart. I considered running across the street to save him, but believed his parents would have me arrested if I interfered. Eventually the slaps ceased, or I turned up the music sufficiently to mute the sounds of his cries, while praying for the breeze that would liberate the dark and heavy lethargy into which we had all descended.

I pulled on a white Indian shirt that came to my knees and drove to Peter's Pond Beach. I was a lone black sedan on a recently paved asphalt road. The windows and roof were open, the hot air a giant hair dryer against my skin. I parked at the end of a long, sandy street hidden between fragrant beach grass, nestled in a cornfield alive with stalks, motionless in their brackish inertia.

Walking barefoot to the edge of the water, the ocean appeared flattened by the weight of the sun. I slipped out of my shirt and dove naked into the strangely peaceful surf, the blindingly sunlit water like a sheet of aluminum foil. The empty beach was my temple, the ocean my god. Only submerged could I forget myself. There was a bit of time before the others would arrive with their dogs. I remained immersed, floating, diving, skimming, until I heard a Rhodesian Ridgeback's familiar yelp and knew my neighbors had arrived, and it was time for me to go home.

After coffee and a shower, I slipped a silk chemise over my head and headed downstairs to the tune of tires grinding in the gravel driveway, followed by jaunty footsteps on the kitchen stairs. As I stood next to the fridge little beads of sweat formed behind my knees, and my heart started to beat faster when the door swung open. Michael was wearing unspeakable sunglasses. They were a cross between *Goodfellas* and *Miami Vice*, early drug deal gone bad, purple and mirrored, blue plastic wraparounds. He put his arms around me and we kissed. Then, without talking, he took my hand and led me up the stairs to my bedroom.

The fan blew the ninety-eight-degree air. He pulled the silk dress over my head. Then he hurriedly removed his clothes, and left them lying on the floor. Our bodies were dripping with sweat. Finally, he removed his sunglasses.

He was lean, but the muscle tone was gone. His pecs did not stand at attention, and the little hair that grew on his chest was gray. His buttocks were soft and small, and his legs long and thin. He was attentive and sensual, somewhat nervous and overly intent on making me orgasm first. He asked whether I'd like to come again, and I said of course, who wouldn't? We kissed while he was inside me and even though it was the first time, or perhaps because it was the first time, I was overwhelmed with feelings of love. When he said he was ready, I said, "Oh yes."

I wanted to feel his body shake and hear him groan.

"Yes," I whispered, "do it."

Afterward, we lay on the wet sheets lightly touching one another.

"There are some things you need to know about me," he said. "The first is that I am a liar."

I laughed.

"I mean it. I'm an alcoholic. I stopped drinking eight years ago, but there isn't a day that goes by that I wouldn't like to. I was drinking and taking drugs and saw God and made a terrible racket in the process. The outburst landed me in jail in what is my favorite place on the planet, Alabama. They arrested me with way too much cocaine on me."

I was silent.

"Do you still want to be with me?" he asked.

"What was it like being in jail in the South?"

"I detoxed in a cell all by myself, no drugs, no help. They took away my clothes so that I wouldn't kill myself and removed the mattress so that my dick would fall between the springs when I tried to lie on my belly. My parents didn't bail me out, and all in all it was the absolute bottom of my life." He took a deep breath and paused dramatically. "Oh yes. And my father committed suicide. Drank himself to death. So you see, there are reasons why I should stay away from alcohol."

I didn't know what to say.

"I want to see you again," he added.

It would have been so much easier to say no if we hadn't had sex.

"Will you see me again after all the things I've told you?" he asked.

I wanted to say no. Go away, please. But I didn't have the heart. "How can I possibly reject you when you are completely exposed and at your most vulnerable?"

He kissed me meaningfully. I couldn't speak. We dressed and walked downstairs where I'd prepared lunch. The table was set with my best linen and family china. We ate salad and cold smoked salmon on blue-and-white plates edged in gold. He took my hand at the table. We were like an old married couple finally alone with the kids grown up and gone. A part of me wanted this moment to last forever, and part of me wanted to run from the house screaming. Inside my head my grandmother's Yiddish words were going around and around: *You don't lie in a sick bed with a healthy head.*

I must not be so healthy myself, I thought. Or else I wouldn't be here, would I?

"So what did you think?" he asked.

"About what?"

"About me?"

"What about you?" I said.

"How was I?"

"You were wonderful."

He wiped his mouth with the linen napkin, and said he had to go.

The sweltering days of July gave way to the warm and breezy days of August. Michael and I had phone sex every night when he went out to walk the dog. I wondered how he managed it standing in a phone booth. In a strange sort of way, we grew closer. I started wondering whether he needed this sort of distance and risk as part of the excitement? He told me that he loved me, that he was in love with me, that I was his oasis. I started bleeding uncontrollably. I was having a period that simply wouldn't stop.

The gynecologist explained that I had uterine dysplasia and prescribed progesterone tablets for the next ninety days. He reported that the biopsy from the cells of my uterus were abnormal. If the progesterone worked, he said, the cells would correct themselves and the bleeding would cease. If not, it was cancer and I would have to have a hysterectomy. I wondered how they came up with the word dysplasia and contemplated the possibility that my uterus was merely articulating its displeasure at my choice of a lover.

The next day, Michael and I had an appointment for a rendezvous. In the morning I received an e-mail requesting that I not wear perfume. He arrived an hour late.

We sat on the front porch. I didn't know which upset me more, his being late or the perfume request.

"You mean," I said, "when your daughter asked you about the smell, you didn't tell her you were in love?"

"How could I do that?"

"I see it as an opportunity," I said, "to bring things into the open."

He looked at me as if I had just stepped over the line.

"I can't leave," he replied in a restrained tone of voice, "it would destroy me financially."

"And you could never take me to that club you belong to either."

"That has nothing to do with anything."

"Are Jewish girls among the exotics who WASPs reserve for fucking?" I wanted to fight. I wanted to scream my head off.

"What has gotten into you?"

"I've been bleeding heavily all week. The doctor says it's something called uterine dysplasia. The cells are abnormal. There is a possibility that they could become cancerous. I'm taking progesterone tablets. If the tablets don't work, I'll need a hysterectomy."

"I don't want you to die," he said.

"That's good to know."

"I still want you."

"I can't have sex for a week—the biopsy."

"We can do other things, can't we?"

I burst into tears. "I need to feel safe, to feel protected. Do you understand?"

"Ssshhhh," he said as he wrapped his arms around me.

We kissed and I smelled freshly eaten garlic on his breath. We ended up in bed.

He asked me to masturbate while he watched. Then he put a pillow beneath his head while I gave him a blow job.

He growled. "No one's ever gotten me so hard."

When sex was over, he stood and pulled on his pants.

"Afterward," he said, "I want to stay with you. It's getting more and more difficult to go home."

He threw on the rest of his clothes. When I tried to hug him, he backed away.

"I'll call you!" he shouted on his way to his car.

And as I watched him sniff his fingers and check his mustache in the rearview mirror, I knew that he was planning to leave me.

The next day, he didn't call the way he had in the past. No e-mails. No nothing. Two days later, he phoned to explain his silence. His wife—who had a drug problem, he said—took pills that she purchased over the Internet. She almost overdosed. This was not the first time this had happened.

"I married my father," he said.

"I'm sorry."

"My father drank himself to death. She's just like him."

"What can I do to help?"

"Nothing. I've trained for this job all my life."

"Are you sleeping with her?"

"Yes," he whispered. "Do you think I'm being selfish?"

"I can't believe you have to ask."

He had not told me what she looked like, but I imagined his wife to be an attractive forty-year-old brunette with shoulder-length hair and a great figure. I was desperately jealous of her. He went home to her every night. She slept next to him. She had his child. They went out to dinner together, and to the movies and to the beach.

They did all the things that he and I could not do. And on some level, I think she knew about me. I think she knew about all of us. I was willing to bet that each time he had an affair, she tried to kill herself. What a merry ride this was turning out to be.

But the show had to go on. I was still cranking out three

stories a week. I was on deadline. The stories were due the day after tomorrow. I sat at my computer pounding out the first of three, when I felt a migraine coming on. I made some espresso, took my medication, and got on with it. Michael phoned from the office. He wanted to have phone sex.

"Do you miss me?" I asked.

"I miss your pussy."

"My pussy is attached."

"But right now I miss your pussy, okay?"

I was starting to feel as if I were a drug and he needed a hit.

"Okay?" he asked sweetly. "Please? Call me when you're ready to come."

I didn't know how I could have allowed this to happen to me. I phoned him as requested. After I came, he ran to the company bathroom to masturbate. When he was done, he phoned me back, whispering, "I love you."

I tried to go back to writing, but I couldn't. The pain over my eyes was too intense. I felt nauseous, I lay down. I closed the blinds. I threw up. A friend called to see how I was doing and I asked her to take me to the emergency room. Once there, they injected me with Demerol and sent me home.

The headache went on for two days and for the first time in my life, I missed a deadline. Three days later Michael came to see me. My hair was dirty. I hadn't washed or eaten in three days.

"I don't like to see you this way," he said. "Let me get you some soup."

I just wanted to put my head on his shoulder.

"I'm so jealous of her," I said. "I'm jealous of her, and of anyone else you may be fucking."

"There's nobody else."

But it was too late. He was a self-proclaimed liar. And each time he opened his mouth that was all I could think about. What was I doing with a liar? Did I actually believe that this man would change *for me*? He lied to his wife. What made me think he was suddenly going to speak the truth to me?

"Soup sounds good," I said.

He kissed me on the cheek and asked whether I wanted chicken soup or cream of tomato. While I was making up my mind, he said, "I'm sorry I've been such a dick lately, but I needed to keep you off balance."

"What?"

"Can't have you feeling too secure."

"Your need to keep me off balance is going to kill me," I said, "so chicken soup will be fine for my last supper."

When Michael got into his car, I wondered whether he'd be back. But he reappeared with chicken soup for me and cream of tomato for him. We ate in silence. Every so often, he'd reach out and caress my face. I had grown to feel something for him that I called love, but I knew it was the farthest thing from it. I realized that I knew nothing about him except what he had told me. Part of me thought he was an awful man, and yet I wanted to fall asleep next to him, and wake up with him the following morning.

I wanted to go to the movies and hold his hand in the dark. I wanted to see what he was like around other people.

"I'm worried about you," he said. "Do you need me to take care of you too?"

I wanted to say yes. Yes, no one has ever taken care of me, and I need you to be the one.

But I couldn't.

"I can take care of myself," I responded. "I don't want a man to be with me because I need him. I want a man to be with me because he loves me. Do you want to be with me?"

"I don't know how to be in a normal relationship." He looked into his soup.

"I need to feel secure," I said.

He stared at me and put down his spoon. He took a deep breath and sighed as if this news was a personal affront. "It's starting to bother me," he said, "that sooner or later it always comes to this. That I am asked to make up for all the shitty things other men have done. As a matter of fact, I'm sick of it."

"This isn't about you."

"It is now," he said.

"I think you are using me as a Band-Aid to keep your marriage together," I blurted out. "If I had a spouse who was using, I'd grab my kid and get us the hell out of there. If you decide you want to do that, you can come here. *Mi casa es tu casa.* In the meantime, I need a break."

"I understand," he said.

I walked him to his car. I knew this was the last time I would ever see him. I put my arms around him and felt his body stiffen. He glanced up and down the street uncomfortably while he tried to undo my arms.

"Take it easy," he said, "this isn't the last time we'll ever see one another."

"Bullshit."

He reached into his pocket and pulled out the wraparound sunglasses. Then he climbed into the front seat of his car. I turned around and headed for the house. I could hear the engine rev, could hear the gears shift, the grinding of the tires on the gravel, and I was determined not to turn around and wave. I would not allow him to see my tears.

* * *

Now, when I think of him, I remember not our lovemaking, but the dramas we staged for one another. And as I relive them, they transform from the once playful taunts I'd believed them to be, into war exercises, our weapons dishonesty and disrespect. I longed to turn into the selfish man-killer I'd imagined myself to be when we met.

The kind of person who could do things like phone the house to talk to his wife, or appear in his driveway.

But I kept thinking about the kid. About what her issues would be when she grew up. I didn't want to be a part of what she went into therapy twenty years later to get over.

I really couldn't understand how Michael could be happy with this arrangement, as a father or as a man. So eventually it seemed that the only helpful thing I might do would be to exit.

Later that winter, my health improved. I did not have a hysterectomy. Simply getting rid of Michael was enough.

One morning, long after the affair was over, I ran into a mutual acquaintance in the parking lot of a local eatery. It had been awhile and Paul seemed eager to talk. He and Michael were working together again and Paul's need to gossip was overwhelming.

"You know," he said, "his wife committed suicide recently. And throughout the entire ordeal, he's such a horn-dog you know, he chased and fucked anyone he could get his hands on. I mean, do you know Marcie? Well, he was all over her the week after his wife was buried . . ."

"What did you say?"

"He was all over Marcie . . ."

"No, before that. About his wife."

"She committed suicide." He looked at me blankly. "You mean you didn't know?"

"No."

"Took pills and put a plastic bag over her head."

I inhaled.

"What a blessing that you were well out of it by then," he said.

"You don't need to tell me any more."

But he continued: "He had moved out. Then their daughter moved out to join him. They were in couple's therapy together, and the last time she just didn't show up."

I needed to get away from him. He was talking and licking his lips, his big brown eyes bulging out of his head with each detail.

Sweat broke out on my upper lip. Goddamn it. The bead started rolling into my mouth. I caught it with my tongue.

I didn't want to know how ugly it had been, and yet I did. Paul couldn't stop talking about all the women. How many? No, don't tell me. I knew that no woman really meant anything to him. We were pitchers of martinis; we numbed him to his existence. As soon as he was done drinking one pitcher, he simply tossed us in the trash and went on to the next. We all wanted him precisely because *no one* really mattered. Stupidly, I believed that I had been *the one who would make the difference*. It was that old cliché; if only he would open his heart, my remarkable love would redeem him, enabling him, so to speak, to transcend the crap of his life. I think Freud would have called mine a savior complex.

Paul's lips kept moving, but I no longer heard anything he said. I was thinking of a story Michael told me at a diner one afternoon, about a girl he had dated in college, a married woman who had left her husband for him. Once she had actually split from her husband, Michael decided he didn't want her. Two years later she and both her children were dead in a car crash. After relaying the story, he said, "I don't know why I'm telling you this." He chuckled. "You'll be thinking all these women go around killing themselves over me." Then he went on to add, "You know how I want to die? Shot by a jealous husband while I'm screwing his wife."

"You're looking a little pale," said Paul.

"I've got to go."

My hand was shaking as I tried unsuccessfully to put the key in the lock of my old Volvo. Finally slipping into the car, I slumped down in the seat and gripped the steering wheel with both hands.

My palms were sweating and my hands kept slipping. I couldn't breathe. I imagined a woman I didn't know, an attractive forty-year-old brunette with shoulder-length hair, lying on her living room rug, her face blue, spittle coming out of her mouth and nose, the plastic bag over her head tied in a bow at her throat. I thought of her daughter, her parents, her grandchildren, and the Christmases they would now endure.

The car was hot and airless and a swarm of enormous flies were playing tag on the windshield. I hit the open button and the windows rolled down.

ENDING IN PAUMANOK

BY RICHIE NARVAEZ

Stony Brook

M ary hated driving so close to the water. She couldn't
even see it—an incoming storm blackened the sky
and the sea beneath it—but she could sense the
Atlantic pulsing out there, just off the passenger side, moving
like some great predator teasing its prey. "Out of the cradle
endlessly stalking," said Mary to herself.

She stepped on the gas. There was no traffic to weave
through that early in the morning. She took Dune Road to
the reservation, then turned onto Old Point Road.

Tommy Hawk's Trading Post was just where Lawrence
said it would be. A weathered cigar-store Indian leaned on its
side in front.

When Mary shut off the car, her hands were shaking.

Inside, a Shinnecock man sat behind a long counter.
Brown skin, slicked-back kinky hair, red-rimmed eyes. The
Shinnecock had intermarried with local African Americans
so much over the generations you could barely see any Native American in them anymore, unless you got very close.
Behind the Shinnecock man were pallets and pallets of
cigarettes.

"Hello there," Mary said, trying to sound regular, trying
not to sound like a professor. He mumbled a "Good morning."
There was no heat in the store, and she was shivering.

"Eddie sent me," Mary said. "You know—Eddie."

The Shinnecock gave her a once-over with those red-rimmed eyes, said nothing.

Mary pointed. "Let me have twenty cartons of those, the menthol, please, um, fella."

Lawrence chain-smoked those menthols. His mouth stank of it. Thinking of it gave Mary an erotic surge. She blushed, despite the cold.

Oblivious, the Shinnecock moved with glacial speed. He put the cartons in cardboard boxes.

Mary paid him quickly in cash. "I bet my guy and I'll make a bundle reselling these in the city." She wished Lawrence were there with her. She knew she would be believed more if she had a man with her.

Still, the Shinnecock said nothing.

"Thank you, then," she said, giving up the ruse. "You have been singularly helpful."

Mary took the boxes to the trunk of her car. When she set them down, she couldn't help sweeping her hand over the wrapped-up plastic bag behind the pile of textbooks. Of course it was still there. She didn't want to think about what it was, what it could do.

As she got in the car, her cell phone rang. A text from Lawrence. With a picture of himself, just smiling, no doubt naked under the frame. She stared at it for a while. She wanted to speed, but the rain had started and made it slow going.

She took County Road straight up to Riverhead. With the rain, it took most of an hour. She hated being late.

She parked behind the Peconic Bay Diner on West Main, hoping she had arrived on time. It was an average diner, detached from the buildings on either side. A Greek flag and an

American flag hung side-by-side limply on its roof. Her former brother-in-law came here every morning without fail, like an elephant returning to its graveyard.

And there he sat, a plate of pork chops in front of him. Still in his Suffolk County Police Department uniform. Mary remembered when he graduated from the academy—"I want the world to see that the Shinnecock people can be more than just hoodlums from Riverhead," he'd said. He was proud then. And much thinner.

"Eddie," she said, going right up to his table.

"Mary?" His brown bulldog face had once been handsome. But now his features were thickened with age. He kept his coarse gray hair short. He had a big smear of sauce on his cheek. "You're sure far from your hunting grounds."

"Yes, how funny to bump into you here," she said. "Pork chops for breakfast?"

"Nothing like gnawing on something to get your day started right. How are you, Mary? You look . . . good, good as always."

"Fine. Fine. How are things with you?"

"Work is work. Best thing in my life now is Larry. Larry's doing good. Very proud of my boy. In his second year at Stony Brook. You see him on the campus?"

She blushed. She decided to look intently at the sugar dispenser. "Never," she said. "I mean, well, he was in one of my classes last year, but, well, his schedule is probably completely different than mine. He probably takes classes in a different building. What is he, a psych major?"

"An English major, I thought. Last time I heard. No money in it, but—oh, sorry, no offense, Mary."

"None taken, believe me."

"Have a chop," he said, pushing the plate closer.

Mary was starving, but she was in a hurry. She picked up the remaining chop at the edge of his plate. She anticipated something salty and meaty, but instead it was cold and greasy.

"How is Brenda?" she said.

"She left me. She had it already. Two years now."

"Sorry, I really didn't—"

He stopped her by putting up a hand, like a traffic cop, sauce-tipped fingers. "What are you doing here, Mary? You didn't come out all this way to see your old brother-in-law for nothing."

"No, Eddie."

Eddie was the best man when she married Ralph, his brother; was there to help after Ralph got killed, was a much better man than his brother had been. She hated what she had to do now.

But there was nowhere else to go.

"Listen. On the Shinnecock reservation, there's a—I guess you'd call it a trading post, on Old Point Road."

"Yeah." He was using his tongue to work at something in his teeth.

"They sell cigarettes, tons of cigarettes, that they get tax-free. Selling them to anybody, who might resell them in the city for a big profit. They've been doing this for years."

"The laws changed, Mary, what with that crazy New York mayor. The rez is getting taxed for that kind of stuff now." He was digging at his teeth with his fingers.

"Yeah, but your little trading post is still selling cartons and cartons at special prices to special friends. I know, I was just there this morning."

"What do you want, Mary?"

"Let me finish. I know that's your beat and has been for

years. I know you're part of it all, and that's how you get your-self a brand-new four-wheeler every year."

He leaned closer. He was looking hard at her.

She went on, trying to stay focused. "You wouldn't want the Shinnecock to get a reputation for filling the pockets of bootleggers and crooked cigarette dealers. Not when they're on the verge of sealing a deal to build one, two, maybe three gi-ant casinos on Long Island. There are billions of dollars at stake."

He wiped his face finally. "The professor did her home-work."

"I'll put it plain. I need ten thousand dollars."

"You and your new husband both got jobs."

"My husband can't know about this."

"Ahh, I see—"

"Don't try to see anything. This is a private situation. I need the money. I had some of my own, but now it's gone. I need more."

"You can't be serious."

"I am. I need that money, Eddie. I am not fucking around."

He stared at her. She had never cursed ever in his pres-ence, and he'd known her almost twenty-five years, since she'd started dating his brother.

"Let's go out for a smoke," he said.

"But—"

Again the traffic-cop hand. "I know you still smoke. I can smell it on you. Remember how we used to sneak out and smoke behind Ralph's back?"

"He hated the smell of it."

"Let's go outside."

They went out behind the diner. Parked in the back was a brand-new SUV that she knew was Eddie's. She took out a pack of cigarettes.

"Menthols now?" he said. "I thought you liked tougher cigarettes."

"I—I just like them. It's cold out there. Smokers seem to be sentenced to outcast status."

"Well, that's Long Island. All the inconvenience of the city and none of its perks. Let me tell you a story, Mary."

"Okay," she said.

"About us Shinnecock. See, back in the day, they used to hunt whales in these dinky little dugout canoes. Like twenty of these canoes, about a hundred guys. They'd go after a single whale. And you know how they would get it? They had harpoons, yeah, but still. How were they gonna get that giant animal back on shore, you see what I mean? But the Shinnecock were smart, very smart. They would stab the whale again and again. So the whale would bleed to death in the ocean. Just bleed. You know whales are warm-blooded? Imagine all that dark red blood staining the water."

Mary could see it, could see where he was going.

"After it got good and dead enough," he continued, "they would just tow it back to shore. Imagine how that made the whale feel. These people come along and just peck at you and peck at you, till you have no choice but to give up and die."

"I see your point, Eddie."

"Listen, Mary, Ralph was a son of a bitch for the way he laid his hands on you. Life made him pay, it always does."

Eddie had known about Ralph's hands-on approach to relationships from the start, but had done nothing. She exhaled. "The Long Island Expressway made him pay."

He laughed a cold laugh. "We're still family. But just remember, whatever this is, I'm helping you out just this time. Just this once. Come by tomorrow."

* * *

"Hello, Professor Cipriano!"

On campus, one of Mary's sweeter but more mediocre students recognized her walking out of the parking lot in her hat and bright black slicker. She said, "Kerri, hello."

Traffic had crawled on the way from Riverhead. Not paying attention to her driving, Mary had taken 495 instead of 25A and had been adrift in a sea of traffic slowed down by the rain.

"I can't believe you're totally late for class!"

"Errands," Mary said. "Happens to the best of us. How is your paper coming along?"

They walked together under umbrellas to the Humanities building and to Mary's Modern American Poetry class.

The lesson was on parsing Lowell's "Skunk Hour" and Plath's "Lady Lazarus," but Mary could barely focus. The rain drummed hypnotically on the windows.

With ten minutes left, Mary had run out of things to say and questions to ask. She stared at her students for a hazy moment, not really seeing them at all. There was a long silence as the rain stabbed again and again at the windows.

Then the back door kicked in, and Lawrence slinked in, late as always, looking bored, looking as if nothing were amiss in his world. He took his regular seat way in the back, in the middle, so he had a direct line of sight to her.

She felt hot. She felt annoyed. She felt invigorated.

"Well," she said, "I want to remind you about the research paper due next week. Strict MLA standards are to be followed—without fail."

When class was over, the students scattered. But Lawrence, ever Lawrence, slinked his taut body through the sea of chairs, straight to her podium. His slicked-back, wavy hair and light brown skin were wet from the rain.

"Hi, professor," he said. His pretty, angular mouth broke into a smile. He had huge brown doe eyes, a chin framed by beard hair slightly reminiscent, Mary thought, of his pubic hair.

"You look hot today," he said, brushing her hand. He was touching her openly. Was there another class due in? Mary worried. Would anyone walk through the door?

"Lawrence, please. Not here."

"I like when you say, *Please*. Can we do it tomorrow night?"

"Remember—I have to run that errand we talked about."

"Oh yeah, cool. Do that first. I really gotta have that money." He came even closer, if that were possible. You could barely see any Native American anymore, unless you got very close. "We don't want anybody knowing about us, right?"

"No, no, we don't. I—I don't know if I'll be able to get the money right away."

He made a hard fist with his hand, but rubbed his knuckles gently against her cheek. *People will see!*

"C'mon, Professor Mary, he'll give it to you."

His infantile pet name for her. It made her defenseless.

"Yes, darling, I know," she said softly. Damn this boy.

"Will you have time to meet me afterward? In your office?" He was radiant, glittering with barely postadolescent energy.

"We'll see."

"I think you should."

The words themselves were a lover's importuning, Mary thought, but they could just as easily be heard as a threat.

"Yes, of course, I will."

Mary had known Lawrence for years, since he was a child. But she'd thought nothing of him then, just a handsome little boy. She was not one of *those* women, she was not. After her first husband's death, she only heard from Eddie once a year, at the holidays. She hadn't heard from Lawrence at all until he wrote to tell her he'd gotten accepted to Stony Brook.

When he took her American Lit class his freshman year, she found it fun to tease him and be teased by him. She liked his confidence, she liked his strength. She liked the exotic look of him. Then he would linger after class, walk her to her office, to her car. One day, her car wasn't starting. He offered her a ride. She knew by the look on his face that it would be wrong to accept.

But she did.

And so she became the stuff of tabloid headlines.

He listened to her long, boring stories, he brought her bag after bag of unhealthy snacks, and, at the same time, when they were alone, he dominated her in the most masculine way any man had ever done.

"*Victory, union, faith, identity, time / The indissoluble compacts, riches, mystery,*" she said aloud to no one.

A knock. She had been sitting at her desk, staring out the window.

Professor Lee stood in her doorway, in his same old friendly corduroys. "Mary, how go the wars?"

"It's a rout," she said. "Raise the white flag."

"You look a little peaked—really."

Everett was a lovely man, really, Mary thought, given to toking a bit during the day, but still kind, caring.

"Not sleeping enough, I guess, Everett. Finals, you know how it is."

He looked around, then stepped into the room, lowered his voice. "Well—well, did you hear about the chair position?"

She looked up. "No."

"Looks like Gunderson's a lock. Sorry, Mary. You know the department—they need to look diverse."

She was quiet for a while. She stared at his white beard to keep focused. "Well, I don't think if I were also black and handicapped it would've helped. Perhaps if I were a midget lesbian!"

They laughed at that.

"Gunderson is excellent," she said. "I'm a lowly Whitman scholar, and she's all post-post-postmodern. And she publishes like a machine. More power to her."

"Sorry, Mary."

"It's okay, Everett, really."

After he left, she got up and closed the door.

She drove home, to her colonial on Lilac Drive. Eric, the man Eddie called her "new husband," would be home soon. She went out to the back, onto the patio. The rain had stopped, but it was still damned cold. She sat in her favorite Adirondack chair, the one on the left, in total darkness. The house was close enough to the shore that, when things were quiet, you could hear the song of Long Island Sound.

She lit another cigarette—damn Lawrence for getting her back into this habit. Eric didn't like when she smoked. But he wouldn't notice. Men stopped noticing things after the first few months of wooing.

She inhaled and imagined the lit tip was a beacon in the dark, a lighthouse for lost ships, lost sailors.

She had to admit Lawrence's plan seemed to be working. Blackmailed by the son, she was forced to blackmail the father. A perfect circle of extortion. Of fearful symmetry. "He gets mad money from the cigarettes," Lawrence had said. "We just got to bleed it from him."

She went upstairs to change. She took off all her clothes and looked at her body. Not bad for mid-forties. No wattles.

Both of the girls still perky. Not too much gray. A MILF, as Lawrence crudely said. How true. She'd start showing soon. That's why things had to happen now. Poor Eric. He had always wanted children and couldn't. And now this. This would kill him.

It would destroy what was left of her career too.

Before she became Mary Cipriano, professor of English literature, she was simply Mary Cipriano, good Catholic girl from Massapequa. She ate almost every night at the All American Hamburger, spent countless hours getting groped and groping back at Croon's Lake, lost her virginity willingly in the Jones Beach parking lot during a Stray Cats concert. Mostly willingly. Bad boys, bad men. Men like Ralph. Men like Lawrence.

When she came downstairs, Eric was on the couch, neatly shelling and eating pistachio nuts.

"Chinese tonight?" he said, offering her a shelled nut. He made tea for her every morning. He had never been a bad boy or a bad man.

"Yes, that would be divine."

"Movies tomorrow?"

"Yes—oh—actually, I have a reception."

"Need a second wheel?"

"No, Eric, thanks. You'd be bored to distraction."

In the morning, she drove to the diner again. This time Eddie was eating a cheeseburger. He brought her out to his brand-new SUV and handed her a paper bag.

Ten thousand dollars in a paper bag, she thought. *How cinematic.*

"Eddie, I can pay you back," she said. "Not soon. But—I have a promotion coming up. I'll be chair."

"Sure, sure," he said.

Her plan was moving forward, and she felt damned awful about it. On the drive to campus, her phone chimed. A text from Lawrence. She stopped.

No picture this time.

U get it, he'd written.

Yes, she typed back.

KEWL!!! C U 2 nite.

She tossed the phone on the seat. As she drove, she began to cry.

That night, she drove back to the campus. She opened the trunk and tore open a box of cigarettes. She tossed a few cartons out, then unwrapped the gun. It was heavier than it looked and felt evil. She put it on top of the cartons. Then she sealed the box again.

Walking from the lot, she found she was scared. The campus, so green and alive that morning, was different at night. The many trees caught your eye during the day, but at night the institutional gray buildings ruled. The students had scurried to their dorms, the library, the student union. Very few of them hung around the Humanities building on a Friday night.

Lawrence liked being *intimate* in her office. She didn't know why. Maybe it was a rebellion against authority. Maybe it was because he knew it made her nervous. Hell, maybe it was the Georgia O'Keefe print. He liked to look at that.

She sat down and waited, facing the door.

She realized she was tired of being so lost, tired of feeling so dominated, so defenseless.

She was a professor, a woman of culture and literature. She would give the young stud his money, and he'd be gone, she knew. He liked the sex, sure, but he wanted the money more. To spend it on drugs or alcohol, or the other women he no doubt slept with; and on hair products—no doubt about that at all. Money his father was tired of giving him, money she could no longer give him, money she had gone and extorted for him.

She didn't want to think about why she got the gun.

The door flew open. It was a girl. Mary recognized her from around campus. Some scrawny black-haired thing. Stupid upturned nose.

"Hi, I'm a friend of Lawrence. He said you had something to give him and I'm supposed to pick it up."

"Where is Lawrence?"

"He said just to give me the money. That he would talk to you later."

Mary felt her blood rise. She touched the edge of the box opening.

"I will give you nothing, young lady. Where is Lawrence? Is he in the hall? Is he outside?"

"Just give me the money and I'll go, okay?"

There was a sharp, rhythmic jingling sound. The girl immediately reached into her pocket and took out her phone. "What?" she said. "I'm right here. She won't give it to me. What do I do?"

"Is that Lawrence? Let me speak to him—"

"She is totally crazy, Lawrence."

Then there was a knock. Right behind the girl was Eddie, Lawrence's father.

He said, "You think I'm going to fork over ten grand like nothing, without knowing what's going on? You think I'm stupid or something?"

"Not at all."

"So this little girl is blackmailing you?"

"Oh my god!" the girl said, clicking off her phone. "I am so out of here."

"Wait a second," Eddie said, pulling the girl by the arm. "Where is Larry?" He took out his gun. "I'm not screwing around, little girl. I'm serious."

He knows, Mary thought, he knows.

He turned to her and said, "Wasn't hard to figure out. The menthols. The fact that Larry suddenly stopped bugging me for money. The look on your face when I said his name. Don't ever play poker, Mary."

The girl kicked and screamed, and then suddenly Lawrence appeared. Breathing heavy, lips parted. He yelled at his father, the father yelled back. The girl ran. The men struggled for the gun.

Mary reached into the box, touched the weapon she had brought. A small revolver. Her hands were shaking.

Lawrence was hitting his father again and again in the face. Eddie was bloody, going limp. Now Lawrence had the Glock. She pointed. Eddie yelled, "Mary, don't!"

The son getting the advantage over the father. A shot. Eddie flew backward. Then Lawrence turned to face her, his gun pointed her way. *Phallic symbol,* she couldn't help thinking. More shots. Almost simultaneous. She did not remember pulling the trigger. But she must have.

She saw Lawrence's pretty face disappear. Maybe that was what she had planned all along. She couldn't say . . . *The best-laid schemes of mice and women . . .*

Then she looked down to see a bullet hole bursting from the box on her desk, cellophane and tobacco spilling out. She looked down and saw where the bullet had gotten her. *Cosmic irony?*

* * *

The drive home was quick, it wasn't very far after all. She actually thanked God for no late-night traffic on 25A.

She parked at an angle in the driveway, almost hitting Eric's sedan. She stumbled out of the car, the blood flowing slowly out of her belly. It was all over the car. Eric would kill her for that; he liked things clean. She did not stop in the living room. She did not stop in the dining room.

"Mary, are you okay? Where are you going, Mary?"

She did not stop until she went through the kitchen and out the back door and to the patio. She sat in her Adirondack chair, the one on the left.

Eddie wanted to talk Shinnecock. She knew Shinnecock. She knew they have a horrible penchant for dying at sea. In 1873, a freighter called the *Circassian* foundered off the coast, not far from the reservation. The crew was rescued. Then Shinnecock men, known for their skills at seafaring, whaling, were hired to salvage the cargo. Bricks, lime, nonsense. While they were on board, another storm hit. The Shinnecock were ordered to stay, perhaps at gunpoint. None survived. All for nonsense.

They stayed too long.

For nonsense, for nothing, she thought.

She listened to the Sound, its song of companionship, its song of passion, its song of outlawed offenders. *Haste on.*

TERROR

BY SHEILA KOHLER

Amagansett

S he walks from the station and comes up the driveway in the heat of the July afternoon, her leather backpack on her back, her heavy handbag and a carryall in her hands. Her daughter Emma's car glints silver in the glare in the pebbled driveway, and she can hear the gleeful cries of children accompanied by the sounds of splashing. They must already be in the pool.

She feels a stab of pain down her left leg and wonders if she will be able to take care of two children for two weeks on her own. She has turned sixty this summer. She stands for a moment in the shade to get her breath and looks up at her house, a gray, barn-shaped edifice with blue hydrangeas growing in round tubs, as they did in her own childhood house in Johannesburg, on either side of the blue door. There are rosebushes and day lilies growing wild along the white fence, and very faintly she can hear the soothing sound of the ocean. The property, which they bought many years ago, when such places were cheap, is on a secluded and tree-shaded back lane.

She looks up and sees her daughter who waves from the window over the staircase. Each time she sees her only child it is with a little shock of surprise. She still sees the beloved baby, the plump, pink-cheeked pet, with the spun-gold hair, whom she called an angel. Now at forty, Emma is no longer plump or pink-cheeked but slender, as though life has worn away at her like some friable substance. Even from this distance her mother sees her pale skin and the dark shadows under her eyes, as Emma waves to her through the window on the staircase in her blue jeans and washed-out shirt.

Stella smiles and waves back as she listens to the yells. It is the boy, Mark, she gathers, who is making all the noise in the swimming pool, for the girl, Rose, now appears in the open doorway, standing with one hand on her hip and the other lifted to wave in the bright afternoon sunlight, swaying like a vivid bloom between the blue hydrangea bushes. How can this tall, full-breasted redhead with her green eyes be her grandchild? She looks nothing like her grandmother, her mother—both small-breasted, pale-haired, and pale-eyed.

"Goodness, how big you have got," Stella cannot stop herself from saying, as she walks into the shadowy hall, though she remembers just how annoying such a clichéd comment sounded as a child.

But Rose, with her long dangling earrings of somewhat doubtful taste, who appears almost eighteen this year, rather than thirteen, doesn't seem to mind. Damp as she is, she embraces her grandmother warmly. Stella stands back to admire her. Rose's sloe eyes are circled with makeup and her full breasts burst from her tight pink bikini top which is decorated with silver spangles. If her daughter has become increasingly slender over the years, her granddaughter has become increasingly buxom and doesn't seem to mind flaunting her charms. Stella in her faded blue jeans, her white shirt, and linen navy jacket feels a little colorless, dowdy, and inconsequential at her side.

She finds Emma in the large, old-fashioned kitchen with its low-beamed ceiling and the glass-fronted cupboards where

Stella's mother's fine china, cut glass, and silver—what is left of it—are displayed.

"So many of the cups have been broken, I'm afraid," Stella says as her daughter helps her make the tea and puts out the pink shell-shaped cups on the wooden table. "I haven't bothered to replace them. What with the taxes on this place which do nothing but rise."

They live on her professor's salary and not much else, these days. Stella's husband, always a thrifty man, is saving to retire in the next few years from his position as a doctor with the state; then they plan on giving up the place in town and moving out here permanently. Also, they try to help their daughter who has recently divorced a husband who works in the theater. Emma lives alone, the sole supporter of her two children. "Two children are easier than three," she told Stella at the time of the divorce. Stella said nothing but thought that none at all might have been easiest.

Now she takes out the silver teapot and puts the scones she has brought from the city on a platter. The two women sit opposite one another and her daughter tells her she has been up since five, driving out from Montclair early this morning to bring the boy and the girl to the house at the sea. She looks exhausted, her head in her hands, dark circles like ash under the pale eyes.

Her daughter is leaving the next day for Texas to present a paper at a conference. She too teaches history—but at a state college in Montclair. She is leaving the children in Stella's care for two weeks, not something she has ever done before.

But this year, Rose, at thirteen, has become a teenager, and the boy is now almost ten, old enough to fend for themselves, surely. "Low maintenance," her daughter has said over the phone. Stella's husband has laughingly put all her fears into words. "Let's hope you don't send Rose back pregnant, with AIDS, and drug addicted!"

Now, her hand shaking slightly, Stella puts down her mother's pale pink, almost transparent cup. She asks her daughter, "Do you think they can go to the beach on their own?"

"I think you could let Rose go alone, for a few hours, perhaps, if she wants to. She's a great swimmer and quite sensible."

"And what happens if she meets boys there?"

"Well, you'll have to check them out, to make sure there is parental supervision of some sort, if she goes out with them. But don't worry, Mummy, she's very savvy and not likely to disappear with some stranger. She shouldn't be any trouble at all, but you can't really ask her to watch Mark on the beach."

"No, I suppose not. But they are both good swimmers, no?" Stella says, and rises to watch through the window as Mark, a plump nine-year-old, runs and jumps into the pool. He is her favorite, a bright child who beats her at chess, blond-headed and blue-eyed like his Irish father.

"You'll have to keep an eye on him. You know what boys are like. He's totally unaware of danger," the daughter says, and her pale eyes fill with tears.

"You were such a careful child, such an angel," Stella says, grasping her daughter's hand. "They'll be fine, don't worry," she adds, and wonders why she didn't warn her own child more of the dangers in life, the importance when choosing a mate to remember that you choose not just a husband, who might be dispensible, but also the father of your children, who is not.

"The good thing is that they sleep so late," the daughter says as she washes the cups.

"Yes, I remember sleeping like that. Now I wake so early. I'll have a couple of hours in the mornings for my work." Stella is working on a book about the role of women's memoirs in eighteenth-century France. She has a whole load of them in her heavy backpack: the memoirs of the Marquise de la Tour du Pin, the Marquise de Boigne, and Madame Roland. The problem for her will be how to get through the rest of the day, she thinks.

"I don't know how you do so many things at once. I can only concentrate on one thing at a time," the daughter says, looking out the window at the children in the pool. Then she asks her mother how her teaching has been going this spring.

"I like the faculty so much. I made friends with a lovely young Ethiopian woman, Eleni, who is teaching with us now. She must be a little older than you. She came for dinner with her boy who is a bit younger than Mark—adorable. We sat up and drank wine and talked until too late, and the child fell asleep in my lap. Apparently the father, a famous poet, is not particularly interested in him, or her for that matter." Stella offers her daughter another scone. She is always trying to get her to eat.

The daughter refuses the offer and says, "What's the professor's name?"

Stella thinks for a moment and then shakes her head. "Dr. Alzheimer whispering in my ear. I can't remember her surname. One of those complicated, unpronounceable African names. She wrote me a warm thank-you letter, saying how much the dinner had meant to her, which I must answer. She too is on her own with her little boy."

Stella looks up at her grandson, who stands dripping wet in the kitchen doorway. His blond hair is cut short and sticks up on his head, which gives him a slightly surprised look.

"Dry your feet, darling, will you, before you come inside—because of the floors." She adds, "Try not to take out ten million towels, could you, darling?" A friend has told her to install the one-towel rule in order to get through these two summer weeks alone with her grandchildren.

At dinner that night, they sit around the wide eighteenth-century dining table on Chippendale chairs and eat the beef and potatoes Stella has roasted. The conversation centers on one of Rose's classmates, who has, it is rumored, fallen pregnant.

"At thirteen!" Stella gasps.

"I think she's fourteen. These things happen," Emma says, glancing at her mother, who had, after all, married her father for just such a reason, though they were both nineteen at the time.

The first few days without her daughter are unexpectedly easy. Mark strolls into her room well after ten o'clock, when she has been working for three hours in her large bedroom, which opens onto the garden. She likes to sit at her desk, glancing up from time to time at the pots around the pool with the bright petunias, nasturtiums, and verbena. She keeps the door open and listens to the sounds of the birds calling and the water running in the pool.

Mark always looks smart, his hair carefully wetted and brushed back and his clothes, for this visit, obviously chosen with a care which touches her. After breakfast, she goes swimming with him in the pool, doing laps, trying to teach him how to put his face in the water, how to improve his stroke.

The boy leads the way into the village, riding her husband's bicycle, which is much too big for him, pedaling vigorously along the edge of the busy road. Stella follows shakily behind. Though she has several degrees, she has never learned to ride a bicycle properly: she has difficulty managing a turn. Fortunately, the road to the beach and the one into the village, though heavily traveled, are mostly straight, and Mark carries the towels and even the big umbrella across the handlebars for her.

After lunch, Rose appears, looking fresh and rosy, like her name, to eat the croissants which Stella has bought for breakfast at the farmer's market. When Rose has put on her makeup and fixed her hair in some complicated way, piling it up high or wearing it hanging down loose and glossy with little silver butterflies caught in the web, she bicycles down to the beach for a few hours.

Stella makes simple suppers—spaghetti, pork chops—or orders in pizza. She watches the news on her own, with a glass of white wine, and lets the children watch television and put themselves to bed. She climbs into bed early and sleeps heavily.

As the weather is fine, they eat outside under a white umbrella by the pool. Rose eats little and then rises quickly from the table before Stella has hardly begun, taking her plate with her politely, thanking her for the meal, which she has only picked at daintily. She says very little to her or to anyone else and spends most of her time in her bedroom, applying makeup, which she has brought in large quantities.

If she needs anything, she sends Mark to ask Stella for it. He seems willing to do anything for his big sister. From time to time Stella knocks on the girl's door and peers in, catching a glimpse of her on the unmade bed, plucking stray hairs from her legs with the tweezers, the television lit and some youth singing something without melody or comprehensible words.

Sometimes Stella finds her eating bags of chips and drinking Gatorade, which she has apparently bought at the farmer's market across the street.

If anything, Stella feels a little lonely. Her husband had promised to join her on the weekend but is held up in town at his work.

"They are being terribly good. No problems," she tells her daughter, when she calls each day to speak to the children.

Mark sometimes lingers on with his grandmother at the table, particularly after breakfast, which they eat on their own, Rose still lying in bed. He takes the sports section from her newspaper and sits beside her, solemnly reading every word and commenting on the trading of various players and how much money they have been offered to change teams. He wants to be a basketball player when he grows up. "They make millions," he says hopefully and grins at her.

"Such a short career," she responds.

"They can coach and do other things afterward," he explains, and plays with the gold bracelets on her arm.

"I miss my mom," he confides on the third day and puts his head on his hand. He says he has a stomachache.

"I miss her too," Stella says, ignoring the bit about the stomach. She looks at the boy, who does seem pale, the large blue eyes scintillant with tears. She ruffles his short hair and adds, "Tomorrow, let's get up early and go for a run and a swim on the beach—just you and me."

She remembers her mother-in-law saying to her once, when she complained about how much work even one child was, "Each moment with a child is the last."

She wakes early the next day and goes into Mark's room. Rose is still fast asleep in the big upstairs bedroom on the canopy bed. When she puts her hand on the boy's forehead, he springs up immediately.

The trees arch above them, as they run side by side down the lane, and the clear, early-morning light flickers through leaves on the boy's bright face. He is one of those people, she thinks, cursed like her with a guilty conscience and destined always to try too hard to please. She laughs at him, then dashes playfully ahead, turns, and runs backward.

"Next year you will be the one to beat me, I bet," she says. Panting, the boy smiles.

All her anxiety lifts. She feels so young and strong. How could she be sixty? It seems impossible. She doesn't see other sixty-year-old women running. She feels younger than ever, this cool bright morning. The pain in her leg has gone. She remembers so clearly being thirteen like Rose with pimples and crushes on boys. Amagansett. The loveliest place on earth in the summer, and I love these children; I am a lucky woman, she thinks.

Running along the edge of the sea, Mark pants and calls out to slow down. Despite his dreams of being a basketball player, he is not used to running any distance. She slows down, lets him catch up. He complains that his pants are too long and drag. She rolls them up, so that he can run in the water beside her. But he falls back again. The pants are still rubbing; he is getting a rash between his legs. He wants to walk.

She walks beside him, thinking that she would never have complained like that as a child. She remembers her years at boarding school, where she had been sent at his age, and how she had to take cold showers in the coldest of weather, the shock of the icy water like a knife on her tender skin. What would he say to that?

She says, "We were taught as children not to complain. I'll

just go on ahead, and you can catch up," hoping he will, if she sets the example, but he stalks along the edge of the beach, lagging further and further behind, gradually disappearing in the glare.

Eventually, thinking of her daughter's words, she runs back to him and asks if he wants to swim with her. He has not put on his swimsuit, as she had told him to do. It would have rubbed, he explains. She says, "Never mind. Just go in your boxers."

He looks horrified. "What if someone sees me?" he says, though there is only one man strolling on the beach at this early hour.

"Don't be so ridiculous. No one is going to pay attention to a nine-year-old boy."

He looks up at her angrily. "I don't want to swim," he says, folding his arms, standing on the edge of the sea looking at the empty blue sky.

She peers at the smooth cool water longingly and shakes her head. "Then I'm going to run back home. You know the way, don't you?"

He nods and gives her a sulky look.

"And don't look at me like that; it's rude," she says angrily, and takes off as fast as she can. As she runs across the beach she crosses the lone man who wishes her a good morning politely with a foreign accent and smiles at her graciously, showing white teeth.

"A lovely way to start the day," he says.

She nods and notices a tattoo of a snake on his muscled, bare arm.

In her big, cool bedroom she strips off her shorts and her bathing suit and showers. Under the water, she thinks with relief that she will have a little while to work before he returns. She is fascinated by the lives of these brave women who lived through such difficult times with courage and dignity and wrote about it.

She imagines her grandson, strolling slowly and sulkily along the road, kicking at pebbles. She doesn't like children who sulk. She considers she never sulked as a child. Of course, she got angry, but it never lasted.

For a second she imagines how much easier her daughter's life would be if she had only one child. Emma teaches four classes all through the year to large numbers of students who demonstrate little intellectual curiosity. She has to grade hundreds of papers, meet with recalcitrant, rude students, who have little respect for her, and attend endless meetings; the arduous, grueling, badly paid work of the adjunct professor.

She remembers her daughter calling to tell her she was pregnant again, just after she had enrolled in graduate school. "How will you cope with two children and your studies? Are you sure you want to do this?" Stella had asked. Well, she has done it, with great courage and determination, but at what cost to herself, and her children?

She sits down at her desk and notices the letter from her colleague, the young Ethiopian woman who wrote to her so warmly. She opens up the letter and reads the words again.

You cannot imagine how difficult and lonely it feels sometimes, trying to raise this boy on my own. I miss my own family so much. There is no one here who understands or wants to help. People stare at me with a kind of disgust when I take him in the subway or on trains, and he cries. I'm filled with terror most of the time. How am I going to give this child the care and attention he needs and make

enough money for us to live? A little brown boy in this
very white world. How on earth am I going to give him a
good life?

She remembers sitting in the armchair with the little boy
warm on her lap, with Eleni, in her bright orange skirt, opposite her. She remembers saying that it must be so interesting to
be married to a poet. Eleni's large, expressive eyes smoldered
at her unfortunate words. "Interesting for him! Not so interesting for me! He's gone most of the time doing readings while
I have to stay home and take care of the child!" she said with
so much raw rage in her voice, and so much hate in her eyes,
that Stella felt herself clutching onto the child. She can still
see the anger in the young woman's face.

She notices a telephone number at the top of the page,
and reaches for the phone on her desk, hesitates, and then
works on her book instead. She has a small idea, which she
doesn't want to forget. She forgets things, misplaces things so
easily these days. Soon she has forgotten all about her colleague, all about her grandson.

After a while she glances at her watch and realizes it is
considerably later than she had thought. The sun is high, and
it is hot and still, the house dead quiet. She runs up the stairs
and peeps into the bedrooms: Rose still sleeps, sprawled unti-
dily across the double bed in her pink pajamas amongst a pile
of Beanie Babies, but Mark's room is ominously quiet. She
runs down the stairs and out the front door. She looks across
the shadowy driveway, but can see no sign of him.

Her heart beating like a drum, her hands sweating with
panic, she climbs onto her bicycle and pedals recklessly down
the street, looking left and right. The hot sun pierces through
ragged cloud, the sun and shade fall on her face. Perspiration

pours down her forehead and her back. She rides to the beach where she abandoned the little boy, and strides wildly up and down, pushing her way through the people who are now arriving in large groups and stare at her with curiosity, as she makes her way rudely, stepping on people's towels, knocking over baskets, rushing down to the sea.

But there is no sign of him here. She thinks of her daughter's words: *He's totally unaware of danger*. She stands at the edge of the waves which seem to have gotten higher, the sea much rougher now. The waves pound the sand with an angry crash. She puts her hand to her forehead, scrutinizing the water, the sun cutting a wide silver swathe on the slate-colored sea. She imagines Mark's little body tossed onto the beach before her. Her mouth is dry with fear. Could he have gone swimming, after all? Could he have gone into this rough sea in a rage, and drowned? But surely the lifeguards would have seen him? She glances up at the bronzed lifeguards who now sit aloft in their chairs like young gods, unconcerned, flirting with pretty, bikini-clad girls, who have climbed up there. She stalks back and forth along the beach and again through the crowd, not sure what to do.

He is not on the beach, nor is he anywhere on the road. She remembers suddenly the man with the tattoo. Where has he gone? What might he have done to her darling boy? How could she have left her grandson alone with a stranger on the beach?

She sees a couple with a small child sitting near the spot where she left Mark whom she gathers, from the state of the sand castle the father is building, have been there for a while. She approaches and asks the woman if, by any chance, she has seen a small blond boy, a nine-year-old, in blue sweatpants? She has lost him, she says, he's been gone several hours, and as she says the words her throat constricts, and she feels tears come to her eyes. The woman, who is holding her own little boy safely on her lap, looks up at her with sympathy. "How terrifying!" she says, rising to her feet and shading her eyes to peer along the beach. She asks her husband if he has noticed a little boy on his own.

Stella adds now, her own terror increasing with the sharing of it, as though the whole thing has not been quite real until she speaks of it, "He might have been with a man, a man with a foreign accent and a tattoo of a snake on his arm." Her voice trembles.

The father says, "I think I did see a man here with a tattoo on his arm—yes, I'm sure of it, a snake, I noticed that, and he may have spoken with a foreign accent. I think he was with a little boy. It seems to me the child was crying. Didn't you see them?" he asks his wife, who now nods her head and says, "Yes, I think I did. Could this man have taken your boy, do you think? Do you think you should go to the police?"

"I don't know what to do!" she exclaims in despair. Panicking now, she runs back up the beach trying to find her bicycle which she had flung down on the road. Eventually she finds it, climbs back on, and races toward the house, saying a prayer. *Please, God, let him be safe. Please, God! Please!*

Now, in her confusion, she makes a rapid, reckless turn into her driveway and miscalculates the angle. She falls from her bicycle, sprawling across the stones, scraping her leg and hands. She lies for a moment winded, brushing off stones embedded in her palms. She rises with difficulty, blood trickling down her throbbing shin, the pain returning so piercingly in her hip she can hardly walk.

She abandons the bicycle in the driveway and hobbles into the back garden and stands at the edge of the pool, where she sees the little boy calmly swimming laps. In the seclusion of the back garden he is swimming naked, his body strong and smooth, unharmed.

"Why didn't you tell me you were home? I was so worried!" she screams at him in a rage.

The boy turns his head and smiles back at her with some satisfaction, she thinks.

She says, almost in tears, beating her fists against her thighs, "But I have been looking for you everywhere, and I couldn't find you! I was afraid something awful had happened. And now I've fallen off my bicycle and scraped my leg!"

He swims to the side of the pool and draws himself up on his arms to look, his blue eyes shining with sympathy. "Oooh! Poor Grandma! It looks awful! Maybe you need stitches? You better wash it and put on a Band-Aid, at least."

She glances down at him and thinks he resembles his Irish father as he was when she met him for the first time. He had come toward her, not a tall man but blond and blue-eyed. He clasped her hand in his and stared at her with admiration, exclaiming, "But you are much more beautiful than your daughter told me you were!" Looking at this fine, lively boy, she can't help feeling warmly toward her ex-son-in-law, despite everything. Perhaps she has judged him too harshly.

She feels the sharp pain down her leg and puts her hand to her side and sighs, "And my hip hurts horribly. I can hardly walk."

Mark cocks his head and grins at her. "I thought you said we weren't supposed to complain, Grandma."

She gives him a dark look but can't help laughing. "Well, you are certainly no fool, I'll say that for you."

He shrugs and laughs. "Come swimming with me, Grandma. Maybe it will be good for your leg." He turns on his back and looks up at the cloudless sky and bobs in the water. She sees his little penis bobbing about hopefully.

"I'm going to make us some eggs and bacon and heaps of toast," she says, suddenly starving, but when she breaks the egg a few minutes later, she drops it onto the floor.

That evening, after she has put away the Monopoly board and told the children to go to bed, the telephone rings. At first she almost hangs up on the caller, a man whose voice she doesn't recognize who asks for her. Something in the cultivated and stricken tone of the voice makes her hesitate.

"This is she," Stella says, and then, the pain in her leg piercing again, she thinks of her daughter, her darling girl, her pet, of the flight from Texas, which is to bring her back to them the next day. She remembers Emma standing on the stairs in her blue jeans and faded shirt, waving to her mother through the window. What if something has happened to her, the love of Stella's life?

But the caller, who then identifies himself, is the head of the history department at the university where she teaches. "I'm afraid we have just heard some very bad news," he says.

"What has happened?" she asks. As she sits down on the chair in the kitchen, her knees giving way beneath her, he tells her that her colleague, Eleni, has committed suicide this morning. While Stella was running up and down the beach frantically looking for her grandson, Eleni was cutting her wrists, after those of her little boy. There were signs of a struggle in the room, chairs overturned, he tells her. She sees the scene vividly, the little boy she held on her lap running from his mother in terror, knocking over chairs, struggling in her arms to avoid the knife. He must have fought for his life, but in the end he and his mother died together. They were found lying side by side in a pool of blood on the bed, while Stella and her grandson were eating their eggs and bacon by the pool.

After they are gone, unexpectedly, she misses the children. She runs alone up and down the beach in the early mornings in the mist and almost bumps into the man with the tattoo who, this time, is followed by a woman and a little boy who must be his own.

She wanders through all the empty rooms of the big house to see if the children have forgotten anything. With a little pang of remorse, she finds Rose's Beanie Babies, the stuffed animals she had thrown on top of the canopy bed in some childish game and forgotten, a little elephant, a rhinoceros, and a yellow bear.

She looks into Mark's room, which he has left neat and orderly. She goes downstairs into her big bedroom and tries to work, but in her mind she sees her grandson with his hair carefully slicked back with water, walking into her room in the morning, and she hears Rose clomping down the stairs at midday in her high heels. She sees the girl in all her hopeful finery, her hair swept up onto the top of her head, the dark makeup around the green eyes, the spangles shining on the innocent breasts.

But mostly she remembers Eleni, as she walked under the trees across the beautiful campus, where Stella will teach again in the fall. She sees her walking ahead of her in her bright orange skirt, carrying her dark, glossy head high, her slim hips swaying with dignity and life.

CONTENTS OF HOUSE

BY JANE CIABATTARI

Sag Harbor

I f you're watching this, I'm dead. But don't stop. Watch all the way through, and I suspect you'll know who did it. This is my confession, and his . . .

The most hostile thing Casey did after the breakup was sell off the contents of our house on the beach, the place we bought and furnished our first summer together in Sag Harbor. I chose each chair and lamp, each dish and towel, anticipating life together.

I left him on the first day of April. April Fool.

He retaliated by putting an ad in the *Star* for the Saturday after Memorial Day: *Contents of house. Eleven a.m. to five p.m. No early birds please.*

My best friend Sally had the nerve to go.

"By nine-thirty there were a hundred people lined up outside the front door," she reported as we ate dinner the following Friday night at the crowded sushi place in Sag Harbor. "By eleven a.m. the house was empty." Poof.

This was all clearly against the separation agreement, but Casey believed rules were for idiots. *Id-juts*, was the way he pronounced it.

"He was virtually giving it away," Sally said. She had taken notes. "He got ninety dollars for the brown leather couch."

"He could have gotten more," I said. "I bought that on sale at Ikea for five hundred, marked down from a thousand.

How about the four Italian stacking chairs?" I'd found them on the Design Within Reach website for eight hundred.

"Ten dollars each. He sold all the crystal wineglasses for two bucks each."

"Just like Casey to sell my stuff cheap."

"He had bins of stuff in the backyard, he told them everything there was free." She paused.

"And what was it?" I prodded.

"Well, I saw leather thong panties, a couple of whips, a Polaroid camera."

"Oh."

The bastard. He'd put it all out there for everyone to see. The zippered leathers, the leopard-print miniskirts and stiletto heels, the homemade videos, all pawed over and carried off by neighbors and assorted strangers.

"I didn't know if I should tell you this part," Sally said, "but I figured you should know."

She looked away. She was shocked. Sally was loyal, and she kept her mouth shut, which was more than I could say for my other friends during the divorce. But she was a bit of a prude. How could I explain what went on between us?

"We were just being . . . theatrical."

"Whatever," Sally said.

One humid morning a few days after the yard sale, drinking coffee at the Candy Kitchen after getting a haircut, I spotted my former sister-in-law Patty, the monster gossip, talking to a skinny blonde with a tight face. She was describing the costumes and videos Casey had given away. Looking out for her big brother. God knows what Casey did to her when they were kids. I stared straight ahead at the sign over the croissants: *PLEASE DO NOT TOUCH THE BREAD.*

"Nothing is ever what it seems," the blonde said.

"You never anticipate this stuff," Patty continued. "She seemed so good-natured, volunteering at the LVIS on Saturday mornings. More like she was twisted, if you ask me."

Did Patty really think it was my idea? Casey was thirty years older than I. I was still in college when we met. I was tentative, malleable. From the time I was small, I'd been trained to "behave." My dad was a contractor, brawny and tanned year-round from being on construction sites, prone to drink too much beer on winter weekends when work was slow. My mother used him as her enforcer. She liked to joke that all he had to do was look at me sideways and I'd stop doing whatever it was she didn't want me to do. The habit of obedience served me well through the Sag Harbor school system and into college, where I studied computer science and web design. It didn't prepare me for Casey.

When we met, I was a college senior, a tall, long-legged runner with curly strawberry-blond hair pulled back from my face. I was given to wearing jogging shoes, tank tops, and shorts, adding a sweatshirt when the weather was cool.

Casey was nearing fifty, tall and lean, with a firm jaw and silvery hair. He painted massive canvases of large-breasted women dressed in suburban drag.

"What do you think?" he said when he approached me at the drinks table at his show in a gallery near campus. I was flattered. I had seen the sharply positive reviews of his work in the *New York Times*. From his bio on the gallery wall I knew he had paintings hanging in museums all over the world. He took me out for lobster after the opening. He laughed a lot, a low chuckle. He reached out a couple of times and flipped my hair off my face, but otherwise he didn't touch me. He drove me back to the gallery to get my car, and asked me out to dinner again.

I was used to guys my own age. He talked more than they did. I listened. Every time he sold a painting at his gallery in the city, he boasted, the dealer sent him a check for $150,000. That was minus the commission. "Someone out there likes my work," he said. He was getting another $60,000 a year as a consultant to a museum in Amsterdam. He didn't say what he did for them.

The first time he took me sailing, I nearly got knocked out of the boat several times, blindsided by the boom or whatever it was called. He laughed a lot at that. He had grown up on sailboats. I had seen them from the beach, and from the Sag Harbor Long Wharf, where I took ice cream breaks from my summer job waitressing at a fish restaurant. But I'd never been aboard.

I wore a relatively modest black-and-white-striped bikini and sandals. He wore a white jersey and khaki shorts, boat shoes, no socks. He sailed to an inlet he knew, served grilled tuna, orzo salad, and sauvignon blanc. He asked if I wanted to sunbathe topless. "No one around but us," he said.

"No," I replied. He chuckled and called me *old-fashioned*. He reached over and dabbed zinc oxide on my nose.

Casey waited until I was wearing his engagement ring before he brought me by his older sister Patty's house in Bridgehampton.

He made a point of mentioning that I'd grown up in Sag Harbor. And he told her my age.

"Ah, twenty," Patty said. "Where were we when you were twenty, Casey? Italy? Yes, that was the summer we all had such a ball in Cortina. I was dating that awful Englishman." She turned to me. "He used to drink two bottles of red wine at lunch and simply pass out." Back to Casey. "And you were with, which one was it? Glenda the good witch. Came from the Midwest, looked like Grace Kelly, had promised her parents she would stay a virgin until the wedding deed was done."

Patty was tall and lean like Casey, with the same startling blue eyes. Casey had let his hair go gray. Patty colored hers a shade of beige I assumed was expensive.

"What color was Casey's hair when he was my age?" I asked.

"Strawberry-blond like yours," he said.

"Dishwater, ashy, not really blond, not really red," Patty said.

By the end of the afternoon Casey had convinced Patty to handle the wedding. "Rhonda's parents are of modest means," he said teasingly. "Let's make it easy for her."

We were married on a warm September day on the beach behind Patty's house. As we stood in the receiving line afterward, I couldn't keep my eyes off the surfers riding the incoming waves.

"Think of this room as a place in which you can do anything you want, anything you can imagine," Casey said on our wedding night. He had ushered me into his master bedroom a few hours after all the guests had driven back to the city and Patty had sent us off on our "honeymoon" at Casey's house in Southampton.

That night he began taking the Polaroids. He'd put together costumes for me to wear, isolating one or another erotic part of my body. "Just for us, later," he explained.

He talked constantly in bed. If he brought up something he wanted to do and I resisted, he called me *neurotic*. He began to use that word a lot. He also used the word *lick* and the word *crave* and the word *orifice* a lot. I assumed that was what happened when you got married. You adapted to each other's tastes. Just as later we chose the beach house together.

In the new place, he brought home tropical-tasting lubricants, moved on to "first-time" appliances with several speeds and pop-it beads he'd originally tried in Tijuana before I was born. Over time I realized that the quality of agreeableness that had served me well with everyone else in my life to date might, with him, become a liability. As he pushed me past each threshold, I began to say no. He cajoled and pressured. Over time, that became his favorite part of the game. He needed the accoutrements, the sense of sport.

One night I watched him watching me and watching himself in the mirror over our bed with a cold gaze. No doubt he was calculating curves he could use in his next painting. There was a growing resemblance between his new paintings and my body. My body was selling well.

Finally I pushed him away. I told him I wanted what *I* wanted.

I used the word *hate*. And *despise*. Feathers appealed to me more than spikes and leather and cameras and videos, I told him. I imagined birds, floating and perching here and there like carnival creatures. Leda and the swan.

He produced a whip.

I refused.

He insisted.

I said I didn't want to hurt him.

He said I wouldn't be hurting him.

He pushed the handle of the whip into my hands.

I refused to grip.

"Damn it," he said. He slapped me.

I shoved him away and ran downstairs. I threw on a shift and thongs I kept in the mudroom for after the beach, grabbed my shoulder bag, and left.

"The bastard," Sally said. "And that sister of his."

She and I were sharing avocado-shiitake sushi and vegetarian miso that Friday night. The restaurant was across the street from the tiny apartment I'd rented over a bookshop on Main Street. After I left Casey, I got a job right off the bat managing the college website. It was demanding work, coping with viruses and updates and system maintenance and trying to keep the design clean and easy to use. Not as creative as I might have wanted, but it paid well, and I had to cut back on expenses, living on my salary alone.

The minute I was single again, Sally had suggested we meet for dinner at a different restaurant each Friday night. Sally knew the ropes. She was almost thirty, single a long time, picky. She only went out with men she met through someone she trusted, and only on Saturday nights. The rest of the time she filled with dinners with girlfriends, Italian classes, hikes, bike rides, kayaking. Sally was barely five feet tall. She kept herself trim, wore her dark hair short and her skirts just above the knee. Standing next to her, at five-eight, I felt monstrous. And I felt worst about myself on Friday nights. During the week work kept me busy.

"When did that stuff start?" Sally asked while picking at her sushi with chopsticks. I was eating mine by hand.

"You mean the costumes?"

"Well, whatever it was."

"I'm not sure you want to know . . . or I want to say."

"Did you know when you got married?"

"Beforehand, he was, *Whatever you want*, as if I were calling the shots. Hah."

"Do you think you ought to see someone?"

"See, like date?"

"I mean a shrink. Maybe there's some sort of emotional damage?"

"Nothing that wouldn't disappear if I could think of some way of getting back at him."

I didn't feel hurt anymore. I didn't feel shame. When Sally

asked, it took me awhile to define what I felt. I was furious. *How dare he.*

"Think about it," Sally said. "If you decide you want to talk to someone, I can suggest a friend. And you should know that Patty is spreading the worst rumors."

"I know. She's busy pumping up Casey's profile. There was a photo of him in the local paper, honored for donating a painting to be sold at auction with the proceeds going to a re-treat for abused women. Meanwhile, I'm getting these heavy-breather phone calls at all hours. I think it's him."

"You know how to stop that, don't you?" Sally explained how she could punch a few keys on the telephone pad and give the caller a shrill whistle. "A cop friend told me about it. As for Patty, I suspect she's helping set you up for a bad settle-ment in the divorce."

"It's hard enough living on my income out here."

We split the check and I headed back to my apartment. I missed the sound of the ocean at night. I missed my things.

A few months after the split, some stock I had inherited from my mother's father suddenly went up from $25,000 to $200,000. I had money to play around with. When Sally came by for coffee early one Sunday morning, I got an idea for the game I wanted to play.

"Guess who just rented a house in Sagaponack?" Sally asked.

"Someone I know?"

"Exactly. Your ex. Six bedrooms. A sauna. Walking dis-tance to the beach. Did you see the *Science Times* this week?"

"I didn't have time."

"I saved it for you. Take a look at the piece on revenge. It's so you. Listen to this: *Acts of personal vengeance reflect a* biologically rooted sense of justice that functions in the brain something like appetite."

I nodded.

"And here's the kicker: *The urge for revenge is even stronger than lust.*"

Casey's new house was a nondescript McMansion across from potato fields. I drove by several times a day to get a sense of his routine. He was still living the artist's life, with irregular hours. But every morning he spent a few hours at the gym.

Breaking-and-entering was new to me. Luckily, the lock on the back door was flimsy. I slid in with my backpack of equipment.

The wireless video camera was tiny, impossible to detect. It fit neatly into the smoke detector in the ceiling of his new bedroom. The hookup took awhile. He had a new duvet cover in a faux-leopard print. He had his pants press set up in one corner. I slid open the closet door. A neat row of dark shirts and pants. He was addicted to Armani. The floor was littered with his shoes. I opened the drawer of the bedside table. Condoms, half a dozen sticky bottles of lubricant.

The bedside clock told me I had been there more than an hour. Time to go. And I was eager to see if the setup worked.

Back in my office, I logged in the coordinates of the site. With a click of the mouse I could see the empty room, ready to fill with images.

I wanted to give him a name that fit his persona. *Kinky* was the first word that came to mind. I Googled *kinky*. There were millions of sites. Under Casey's first name I discovered an Antarctic webcam: *Casey Station. Nineteen degrees below zero Celsius.* Frozen tundra was too good for my darling.

I tried *kinky sex.* There were about three times as many

sites as *kinky*, ranging from the direct—*kinky sex, strap-on dildo sex, kinky girls*—to the educational:

> *Restraint, role-playing, domination, erotic punishment, and discipline are all parts of the BDSM scene. The term "fetish" is used loosely to describe any general turn-on that might not fall into mainstream sexuality, such as leather or vinyl clothing, food-play, or certain parts of the body not normally associated with sexuality . . . Find other like-minded people in your area or around the world!*

I didn't want Casey to be watched by others like him. I wanted him to attract a broader audience. People who would be shocked. I decided on *kinkycasey.com*.

I inserted Casey's new webcam data into the *virtual voyeur's hub of choice* to kick up the traffic. With a few clicks of the mouse, the camera was broadcasting live over the Internet from his bedroom. Anyone could watch whatever he was doing. It was all there. I had access to that, and whatever kinky sex sites linked to him in return. I would archive it all. And someday, when the time was right, I would send him the link and wait for the fireworks.

It wasn't long before the traffic numbers began to spike. Three months in, Casey was becoming notorious among the "peeping toms" on the web. I waited until he was at his bedroom computer alone one night before I shot him the link. I watched on the webcam as he scrolled for a few minutes, then stood up, hefted his laptop, and threw it against the wall. Aha.

On the off chance I push him over the edge, I am making this podcast and uploading it to a spot on the web where only you, Sally, have the password. I know I can trust you to leave it alone unless something happens to me . . .

PART IV

AMERICAN DREAMERS

SEMICONSCIOUS

by Steven Wishnia

Lake Ronkonkoma

Jefferson stirred to semiconsciousness. Dim and distorted, like his brain was a dark dungeon of bruised meat. Terrible *dolor* in his head. Tongue groping around in his mouth. Something was very wrong here. It tasted dry and foul and metallic, scabby and membrane-oozy textures, only empty spots where several teeth used to be.

In a grove of thin trees. Next to a pile of beer cans and 40s. Budweiser. Pabst Blue Ribbon. Coors Silver Bullet. Olde English 800. Steel Reserve.

Must be behind the strip of shops.

Fuck, my head hurts.

Ribs in agony. Worse than the head. *Ay Dios*, and I thought that was the mother of all hangovers. Memory cracked open in the rain of pain. Fucking *cabrones* kicked the shit out of me, an evil centipede of Nikes booting my chest like a whole fucking team taking penalty kicks.

He tried to lift himself up. One elbow. Failed. Fell. Never mind the knees, they're collapsed like a cane-stalk house in an earthquake.

The bloody crust on his lips tasted faintly of tomatoes. He made it up onto his left elbow and puked. A pink-brown-red sunset of stale beer and bloodclots. He passed out again.

That's where they found him two hours later. Strapped him onto a stretcher, head belted and braced to avoid any further damage, rolled him up and clipped him into the ambulance. Outside and above red and yellow and blue strobe lights and sirens cleared the way, assaulting his wounded brain.

Danny Seltzer said goodbye to his aging parents in Delray Beach, in one of the waveform high-rises that walled the coast of South Florida. He drove down I-95, dropped off the rental car, and got on line. He removed his sneakers and watch, emptied his pockets, and placed the lot in the gray plastic bin—the national-security jailhouse rigmarole of flying, empty your pockets, take off your shoes and belt, get patted down. To complete the metaphor, foreigners coming into the country had to get fingerprinted and mug-shot.

The bottom of the bin had an ad for Zappos, a shoe-selling website. What would history have been like if other cultures had the same mania for advertising and sponsorship? Paris 1793: a billboard on the guillotine proclaiming, *Bic: The National Razor!* Valencia, Spain, 1491: an *auto-da-fé* framed by pillars depicting the tonsured head of Torquemada, his outstretched arm wielding a small torch, touting, *Fuego de Dios: The Official Matches of the Holy Inquisition.*

His cell phone rang the minute the plane taxied toward the gate at LaGuardia. Lisa Vitaliano, his editor at the *Paumanok Weekly*. She'd already left two voicemails and three texts. There'd been an assault in Lake Ronkonkoma, possibly fatal. It might be racial.

༄

Bloodofpatriots says:
The Federal Octopus is pursuing me. Osorio is an illegal alien. He's from Mexico.

RealAmerican says:
He's from Puerto Rico. He's an anchor baby.

Mike from Smithtown says:
His real name is Castro. He's covering it up to hide that he's a Communist. He's Fidel's son.

LiptonLady55 says:
That's his mother's name. He's a bastard. She was a prostitute in the South Bronx.

A cybermassive grapevine proliferated with accusations that the new U.S. president, Juan Ernesto Osorio, was not born in the United States, but in Mexico. Or Cuba. Or one of those bean-queen places.

His birth certificate said he was born in the Bronx, on July 16, 1965, at Morrisania Hospital, the son of Juan Wilmer Osorio, a solo-practice lawyer with a small office on Courtlandt Street off 149th, and the former Aracely Castro, who would take a leave of absence from her job as a sixth-grade teacher. Both were born in Puerto Rico, Juan in San Juan, Aracely in Carolina, where her older brother Papo played shortstop on a team whose right fielder was a rifle-armed kid named Roberto.

On April 24, 1966, the *Daily News* printed little Juan's picture on its "Bronx Cuties" page, along with Maureen Gallagher, Teresa Ippolito, Elijah James, Jacqueline Barretto, Ramona Puente, Yvonne Bronson, Joseph Anthony Genzale, Gerald Nolan, Deona and Matthew DiMucci, Michelle Romero, Shelley Renee Koslowitz, Glenroy Neville, and James Slattery. A busload of big-eyed babies immortalized on newsprint in ashy gray ink.

From www.letfreedomring.com:

Yes, my fellow American patriots, they say the facts are obvious, they say the documentation is there, they say we are deluded fools for caring that our great nation is led by a dangerous alien. They say they have evidence, that it is not so.

Their so-called birth certificates and newspaper announcements are forgeries. And remember that there are powers greater than those of man, powers that we must call on God's help to resist and constantly defend our homeland's security against.

There is only one entity in the universe that has the power to perform such a forgery. There is only one entity in the universe that has the power to plant such an evil seed and care for it until it bears its poisonous fruit: The Evil One. 666. The Number of the Beast.

We have the number of this beast. Osorio is the Antichrist. It is our sacred duty as God-fearing, freedom-loving Americans to stop him in every way we can.

Thank you for reading, and Let Freedom Ring!

C.T. says:

We oughta deport all of them, send them back to whatever pisshole they came from. They're like cockroaches, millions of them hiding in the dark and when you turn the lights on they run for cover. How do they get in the country? They just come here and nobody stops them, like they're real Americans or something.

LiptonLady55 says:

They won't let the Border Patrol do their jobs. They're

bringing them over to work cheap and take American jobs.

RealAmerican says:
First we got Obama, now we got this f*ckin' beaner. What's the country coming to?

Skeptic says:
You have got to be kidding. Puerto Rico's part of the U.S. They're American citizens. And he was born in the Bronx. They got his birth certificate, his baby picture in the paper.

Avenger says:
STFU, moonbat!

WhiteMale14 says:
[comment removed for violating guidelines]

C.T. says:
Puerto Rico's a foreign country, duh! They don't speak English there.

∾

Danny drove south on the Nicolls Road Highway and got off at Portion Road. It was a clear, beautiful, blue-green day. Coffee buzz of radios and gas pumps and America-runs-on-Dunkin'-Donuts. Eighty-seven degrees and sunny on this Sunday afternoon, traffic headed to the beach, construction and delivery, a white van with *We Buy Junk Cars* in red.

He pondered the story.

One victim.

Many vague threats.

No specific suspects.

Grass growing in the sidewalk cracks. Leaves undulating in the light breeze, middle-aged maples and scrubby pines. A strip mall off Portion Road west of Nicolls, one of the scores filling in the sides of this once-country road. A brown-brick slab topped by a shingled façade, housing a pizzeria, deli, Chinese takeout, paint store, RE/MAX real-estate office, a vacant Pilates gym, and the Dos Grandes Varones bar, where the night before an amiably rowdy crowd had watched Cruz Azul tie Club America 1-1, followed by the Yankees at Oakland.

This was the scene of the crime. Jefferson had stepped out for a slice of pizza after the soccer match. The slice had been slammed into his face.

The patch of woods behind the stores was taped off. A woman from the cops' Public Information Office patrolled outside, keeping the media, the forest of working legs and camera tripods, from getting too close. The victim was believed to be an immigrant from Ecuador, based on an ID card found in his wallet. Identification was being withheld pending notification of relatives. He was in critical condition at University Hospital in Stony Brook.

Any suspects? Motive?

"The matter is under investigation and we can't comment any further."

Nothing more here. Danny took a walk. To feel out the atmosphere. The bar wasn't open yet, but Portia's Pizzeria was. *The Quality of Our Pizza Is Not Strained*, the sign boasted. He ordered a slice, sat down, and flipped through his notes.

A familiar face came out of the bathroom. Detective Peter Restino.

"Hey, Pete, how ya doin'?"

"Hanging in there. You writing about this mess?"

"Yeah, you know anything?"

"Yeah." He dropped his voice low, leaned over the table. "You didn't get this from me, but we're looking at a pattern of assaults in the area. Victims a couple Hispanic males, one black male, one homeless male. The actors probably a group."

"Thanks."

"Don't mention it. If you do, I'll feed your balls to my dog."

Monday morning Danny parked his car by the *Weekly's* eastern Suffolk bureau, upstairs in back of a row of storefronts by the railroad tracks in Port Jefferson Station. He knocked once on the open door of Lisa's office and walked in. She looked up from her computer.

"Lisa, what's your take on this?"

"You talk to the cops?"

"Officially, they said it was under investigation and they couldn't comment. Privately, it might be a gang assault, might be racial. We can't use that, though."

"Not surprising. I don't think Calero wants this to blow up. But I bet he puts his foot in it sooner or later."

Suffolk County Executive Paul Calero was a former county police commissioner, brought in from Philly in the '90s with promises of an easier life and a bigger paycheck. In turn, he'd promised to bring urban tough-guy policing to the white-flight suburbs to make sure they didn't fall like the inner cities had. In his first campaign, he'd been racially conciliatory, dropping hints in Brentwood and Central Islip that his name might be Spanish, but when he'd won reelection a year and a half ago, he'd switched to swearing to crack down on the hordes of drug dealers, rapists, and drunk drivers allegedly inundating the county from points south of Key West and the Rio Grande.

That year, Brentwood high school boys had altered his name, chanting "*cul-ero, cul-ero*," Mexican soccer fans' version of the Yankee bleacher creatures' "ass-hole, ass-hole" singsong. The paper translated it as "an anatomical insult."

"You should talk to Jason," Lisa told him. "There's all kinds of stuff on the web about this. Some people are celebrating it." Her phone beeped. "Lisa Vitaliano," she answered, then raised her forefinger, signifying it was a call she had to take.

Jason Settles turned down the music, old-school Strong Island hip-hop, when Danny walked in, fading the segue from De La Soul's "Plug Tunin'" into EPMD's "Strictly Business." He was the *Weekly*'s resident computer geek. He resembled a nerdy Gil Scott-Heron, a retro Afro and big black glasses over a long-sleeved black jersey advertising some ultra high-end technobeast gaming machine. But he was a digital wizard, at least to this observer's untrained eyes. A computer-science major at Suffolk Community and then Stony Brook, he'd been one of the few black guys in the Silicon Valley of the '90s, when everything was going up-up-up, the money doubling every eighteen months like it was ordained by Moore's Law. After the dot-com bust, he'd come back East. He'd lived with his parents in Gordon Heights for a year, then lined up a job setting up and running the paper's fledgling website.

Jason called up a screen, drilled down through a succession of URLs and pages, and hit paydirt. "Yo, Danny, check this out."

ChristianSoldier says:
Osorio can't be the Antichrist if he's Mexican. The Antichrist is from Rumania.

WhiteMale14 says:
I don't give a f*ck where he's from. I'm ready to defend myself. Remember—if it can't break a sternum, it ain't worth sh*t!

RealAmerican says:
Like that illegal alien in Ronkonkoma last night. That's how to deal with them. A few more like that, and they'll think twice about crossing the border.

WhiteMale14 says:
F*ck yeah!

LiptonLady55 says:
He was a crackhead. He tried to rob somebody to get drug money, and he got what he deserved.

ItalianStallion says:
Build a fence on the border. An electrified fence. And leave the bodies there so the snakes and rats and vultures can eat them. Show them what happens when you try to sneak into the USA illegally!

C.T. says:
If the vultures don't die from eating human garbage! :)

Skeptic says:
Hey, ItalianStallion, where did your people come from?

ItalianStallion says:
What part of ILLEGAL don't you understand? My fam-

ily came here legally and worked. These people broke the
law coming here. They're breaking the law by being here.
They're criminals.

"Jason, you got any idea who's putting this shit up?" Danny
asked.

"You want to find out? You'll have to put yourself in touch
with the higher spirits. You have to smoke hemp."

"Okay, Maharishi Triangle Offense. Get serious."

"Okay, I'll be serious. You are undertaking a journey into the
netherworld of the political realm." Atop the twin computer tow-
ers, a raging green Incredible Hulk stared at an implacable black
Darth Vader. "This site is LongIslandforAmericans.com. It's a
far-right one, like LetFreedomRing or FreeRepublic. Then
these people also post comments on sites like ours, and they
troll on liberal ones."

"So can you tell who they are?"

"It depends. Most media sites now require registration, so
they can track identities and IP addresses and keep spam off. We
do. People can get around that pretty easily if they know anything about computers. Nobody knows if their name is real and
they can have ten different e-mail addresses, but it's your first line
of defense. It's like locking your car and not leaving the keys in
the ignition. If they don't want anybody to know their IP address,
that's a little more work. These are the trolls you eighty-six from
the site because they just come around to flame-war. You can
block their IP address, but they can use a public computer or
get privacy software for their own. And some sites don't track
IP addresses, 'cause they say anonymity protects people's privacy and freedom of speech. If they're paranoid and digitally
savvy, they'll hide. But if they're not hip to privacy, or they're
just too raging to care, it's not that hard to find them."

"Thanks. You know, they said the Internet was the most revolutionary invention since the printing press, but sometimes it's more like the world's biggest toilet wall."

"Word."

Danny spent the next couple of hours going through old local weeklies and the *Newsday* police blotter. March 31, Federico Ibanez of Farmingville reported being punched in the face by a group of young men on Horseblock Road. No arrests. May 15, Tommy O'Halloran, 58, no known address, reported being beaten up while collecting empty cans in Holbrook. June 21, two Mexican day laborers reported being attacked by a gang of whites in a wooded area off Nicolls Road. They said they had been taken there from the Kohl's parking lot on Ronkonkoma Avenue by two young men who'd offered them $100 a day for construction work. They'd fled and didn't get a good look.

Restino was right. There definitely was a pattern, and it fit geographically. And there were probably a lot more unreported. If the victims were illegal, they'd be too scared to call the cops.

Afternoon oozed along quietly, interrupted by occasional cars, in the Morningwood Estates development in Farmingville, a former potato field a mile and a half northwest of Exit 63 on the Long Island Expressway. Blocky beige and yellowish two-story clapboard houses with peaked roofs and diminutive windows, built in the last burst of the great postwar urban sprawl. The American Dream and white people's escape from the city had taken a big hit from leaping gas prices, and the satellites orbiting the city could only go so far out without losing heat and light.

It looked nicer now. The pitiful saplings staked into the

lawns had grown into curbside shade trees. Houses that had sold for $39,990 new in 1974 went for $339,000 even after the bubble popped.

Five youths in baggy shorts shot hoops aimlessly in a keyhole-shaped driveway.

"Hey, Tyler. You hear about the guy we fucked up? He wasn't Mexican, he was from Ecuador."

"Where the fuck is Ecuador?"

"It's on the equator, stupid."

"Am I supposed to know that? Was I the teacher's butt-boy?"

"Who cares? He was a fuckin' beaner, right?"

Danny headed down Nesconset Highway to Hauppauge. Calero was having a press conference at five. Police had identified the victim as Jefferson Nuñez, twenty-four, an Ecuadorian immigrant from Lake Ronkonkoma.

"We are doing and will do whatever it takes to apprehend the perpetrator or perpetrators of this crime," Calero said.

"Mr. Calero, do you think this attack might reflect on some of the language you have used in addressing the immigration issue?"

"We enforce the laws equally. That is the job of our law-enforcement personnel, and they do it very competently and with a great deal of dedication. The perpetrators of this reprehensible crime will be brought to justice, but we cannot and will not ignore our nation's immigration laws."

Danny pushed forward, got his question in: "There have been several assaults on immigrants in the area. Is there a connection?"

"We have no evidence at this point that this was racially motivated. Next question." Calero delivered his denial in a curt, clipped tone, like you were somewhere between a retarded tinfoil hat and an undersized cockroach for asking. When he was less tense he was more genial.

Danny called Nydia Perez for a response. The "outspoken county legislator" said the county exec was denying reality.

"We know of about ten attacks in that area in the past six months, by a gang of young men, usually calling racial names," she told him. "It's hard to get people to tell their stories. Obviously, the undocumented are scared to talk to the police. But you know, Danny, sometimes people who have their papers have fear too."

"How do you know this was another one?"

"We don't know who the attackers were yet, but it fits the pattern. And when some elected officials have built their political agenda on innuendoes about our community, it does not inspire confidence in their commitment to protect us."

"Are you referring to Calero?"

"I'll leave that to your readers to decide."

Evening. Danny sat in his ground-floor garden apartment off Nesconset Highway, his aging car in the parking lot, the neighbors' TV infiltrating the walls, a kid blasting hip-hop somewhere outside.

He filed a four-graph quickie for the website and pecked his notes into his laptop. He felt impotent and frustrated. Desire stunted by hopelessness. Cut off, isolated. You couldn't walk anywhere here. You had to drive even to get a quart of milk or a can of coffee.

He'd been cast out east by successive waves of layoffs and two divorces. Like human flotsam or jetsam, whatever the difference was. It was one of those job-application test questions they used to give back when they cared that people knew the language and had some command of nuances. Like *Distinguish between parole and probation*. Not anymore.

He'd been at the *Eye*, an alternative weekly in the city, until it got bought out and the new owners dejobitated him and three-fourths of the staff. A short stint at *Newsday* followed, until the former General Mills CEO they called the Cereal Killer had swept in and scythed through the newsroom. Lisa had been his editor there, and she'd swooped him up when she landed at the *Weekly*.

He took a sip of beer. Nice apricot-tinged hippie craft brew. Only one. Only one.

We're fucked. We need a miracle. Concrete behemoths roam the land crushing everything in their path, barreling around on tracks greased with corruption. I'm banging my head on the wall trying to tell these stories. Maybe five people care. They tell me, they praise me, it's gratifying, but the rest of the world doesn't give a shit. They're obsessed with celebrities.

The bosses want crap like that. They hire clueless twits who call some multimillionaire health-insurance exec or real-estate speculator a "populist outsider" because he bashes "Washington insiders" in his campaign ads. They want superficiality and snark from career-blinded yuppies whose knowledge of history doesn't go past Monica Lewinsky.

9

LiptonLady55 says:
Illegal aliens are two-thirds of the drunk drivers who kill people.

C.T. says:
Their poisoning the country. They come out of the jungle eating monkey meat and fried bananas. Their never gonna be sivilized human beings.

LiptonLady55 says:
We're sick and tired of these politically correct eletists ramming them down our throats.

❧

Tuesday morning a spokesperson for University Hospital issued a statement. Jefferson Nuñez remained in critical condition with a fractured skull and other injuries. He had strong vital signs, but the main danger was cerebral edema. Doctors were working to reduce it.

❧

LiptonLady55 says:
He came here to be on Medicaid and suck off of our tax dollars. All of them do.

C.T. says:
Why should we pay his bills? Let him go back to El Bananastan and have THEIR taxes pay for a witch doctor.

WhiteMale14 says:
Kick him in the head a little harder next time and save the taxpayers some money!

❧

The night before, the phone had rung at Nuñez's house, on a side street between Portion Road and the Expressway. Nine people shared the four-bedroom dwelling, three pairs of men, including Jefferson and his cousin Juan Carlos, in the smaller bedrooms, and a family, Santiago and Carolina and their baby girl, Xochi, in the big one.

Carolina answered. "*¿Hola?*"

"Good evening, this is Michelle from Atlas Health Insurance. Can we speak to Jefferson Nuñez?"

"*Mi ingles* is no good. *Momentito.*"

She went to look for Gabriel, one of the two Salvadorans, who spoke the best English of anyone in the house.

Jefferson Nuñez had insurance with Atlas, thanks to the regular job he'd scored in March with Ozzy's Demolitions in Holtsville. The side of the company van declared, *EVIL MINDS WHO PLOT DESTRUCTION.* Ramon, the long-haired Mexican *rockero* whose *tatuajes* covered his arms like sleeves, had to explain the joke.

Gabriel got on the phone. The woman repeated her inquiry.

"He's in the hospital. Can I take a message?"

"We're just reaching out to you to make arrangements for payment."

"I don't understand. He's in the hospital."

"Sir, we have to make arrangements for payment for medical services. His claim has been denied. There was alcohol in his blood."

"Say what?"

"He is ineligible for reimbursement. His policy does not cover alcohol-related injuries, so it is his responsibility to make payment in full. He is legally obligated to do so."

"*¡Puta!*" Gabriel cursed, slamming down the phone.

* * *

Jason called Danny and Lisa into his office. "I think I got something," he said. "The IP address for both ItalianStallion and WhiteMale14 is the same as the one for the website of the Farmingville Civic Protection Association."

"That doesn't prove anything, but it makes sense," Lisa observed. "Those were the people trying to get a town ordinance prohibiting landlords from renting to illegal immigrants last year. Tom Montanelli was the head of it. I remember him saying, *If we don't stand up now, we're gonna be overrun.*"

"Yeah, they're scary," Danny reflected. "When Jay Knight had a congressional town hall meeting there, he got booed off the stage. There were all these people screaming at him, *Keep the government out of our Medicare!* And others chanting, *No amnesty! Build the fence!* The cops had to escort him to his car."

"Yes, but why two names?" Lisa asked.

Jason Googled Montanelli. "He's got a teenage son, Michael," he explained. "Goes to Sachem East High."

"Fourteen is a white-supremacist code," said Danny. "It stands for the *fourteen words*, one of their slogans."

"A lot of them use it in their online handles," Jason added. "That and 88."

"Fourteen could be his age when he started posting," injected Lisa. "Or the year."

"There hasn't been a lot of organized white-supremacist activity on Long Island," mused Danny, "but they've been trying to make inroads into the anti-immigrant movement. That stuff really doesn't play very well here. People moved out of the city to get away from the blacks and the Puerto Ricans, but they'll insist they're not prejudiced. They want to keep their towns white, but they'll say it's about schools and crime.

They lower their voices when they talk about race."

"Yeah, but the kid could be a wannabe," Jason put in. "You know teenage boys, they always want to be the most bad-ass. The closest they've ever been to South Central is watching the Lakers on TV, but put on a red bandanna and presto change-o, they're a Blood, you know what I'm saying? And if you read what WhiteMale14 is posting, it sounds like he's bragging about it."

Lisa had the last word. "That makes sense, but it's all speculation. We're not cable TV. It still doesn't give us anything we can use. Let's get back to work. Production's tomorrow night."

St. Matthew's Church in Central Islip, a few miles away, was abuzz with grief and outrage. People from middle Suffolk's Latino communities agglomerated, commiserating and pondering what to do. In the basement, nine people met around a long fold-up table, draining a metal urn of coffee. There was no formal leader, but they deferred to Nydia Perez and the priest, Father Miguel Martin Reyes.

Father Reyes had just celebrated his sixty-first birthday. He'd been at St. Matthew's since 1990. A year in El Salvador had marinated him in liberation theology. These children, these thin, young boys in cheap sandals kicking a ragged soccer ball in the dirt street between their houses of cinder blocks and cane stalks, these children and toddlers skittering about like a litter of kittens, they are the future of our world. And without justice, what will happen to their lives? What will happen to their souls? Their parents slaving away, their teenage brothers and sisters succumbing to the temptations of drugs and gangs, trading the flower of their youth for a few gaudy trinkets and a poisonous solidarity.

The hierarchy hadn't liked him preaching those lines in Brooklyn and the South Bronx. The last straw was when he'd led a sit-in protesting the closing of a firehouse in Bushwick, the city neighborhood scorched almost to the ground by looters in the '77 blackout and by landlord-hired arsonists in the decade surrounding it. They'd bounced him out to a suburban parish where he occasionally heard dark mutterings. *We moved out of the city to get away from THEM. Now they give us one as a priest?*

Demography played a trick on them. The parish now gave more Masses in Spanish than in English.

Still, the gringos here had tested his faith. Ignorance you could cure, but theirs was different. It was a willful, belligerent ignorance that insisted it was right and didn't want to know anything else. You couldn't tell them nothing.

He remembered the young woman teacher who, almost in tears, spoke about the parents at her school telling her, "Why does my son have to learn Spanish? This is America, we speak English!"

You needed to have faith. Without faith there was no hope. Without hope you were in the abyss, like the glue-sniffing kids in San Salvador, the boys in Brooklyn, barely teenagers, who if you asked where they were going to be in ten years, they'd tell you "dead" or "in jail." If they were optimistic, you'd get some variant on "big-time drug dealer."

Bolivar and Susana, Jefferson's older brother and sister, arrived at the ICU around noon after taking a red-eye from Guayaquil. His pulse was strong but jittery, the oxygen mix okay yet his breathing irregular, the EEG slowly fading to a flat green line. He was brain-dead. Father Reyes gave him Last Rites.

At 4:07 p.m. on Tuesday, Jefferson Tomás Nuñez Yagual

left this world for whatever lies beyond it, *paz en el cielo* or eternal nothingness.

The funeral was at 9:30 Wednesday morning in Central Islip. Danny headed west on 347 and then south on Nicolls Road toward the LIE, steering with his left hand, his right alternating between delivering bites of buttered bagel and sips of deli coffee. The Expressway jammed up just after he got on. Stop-and-go, inching forward, then jumping up a few yards when the car in front moved. Shit, I'm gonna be late. No time to find a good position, unobtrusive but close to the action.

Traffic opened up just before Exit 60, then slowed again when he passed the ramp. The car barely moved when he stepped on the gas. White smoke spewed from the engine. He pulled over. It smelled like burnt rubber. He opened the hood. The radiator was jetting out smoke and steam. There was a big crack in the top.

He called Lisa. "Don't worry about it," she told him. "Deal with the car and come back to the office. I'll reimburse you." He called a tow truck and took a cab from the garage.

Top-of-the-hour news bleeps teletyped out of the radio.

Five Farmingville youths have been arrested in connection with the fatal beating of a South American immigrant in Lake Ronkonkoma last weekend. Suffolk County police said they made the arrests after one of the suspects posted pictures of the assault on Facebook. The victim, twenty-four-year-old Jefferson Nuñez, died yesterday afternoon.

Danny desperately checked his phone for messages. It was hopeless to try to get online in the cab. His phone beeped with a text from Jason. *Michael M. 1 of 5 charged. Other names TK.*

The story's blowing up and I'm out of the action. He furiously recalculated. It's a backstory/reaction piece now. The dailies and TV will be all over the arrests, we've gotta go for depth, and I have twelve hours to do it. I should've been at the funeral.

He got another message a couple of blocks from the office. Jason had grabbed some screenshots off Facebook. The photos were dim and impossibly blurry, but the comments were readable. *Another spic smackdown! M&M do it again! Mark, u should of kicked that hard when we played Newfield :)*

They really were that fuckin' stupid, he mused. Or narcissistic.

In Lisa's office was an executive-looking woman he couldn't recognize, but she seemed familiar. Like bad news. And Lisa looked like she'd just run over a cat and was trying to figure out how to tell its owner. Oh yeah, she's from Human Resources at VNT Media, the parent company, the one you'd see once or twice a year at staff meetings where she explained our benefits or how they were being "adjusted." The knowledge hit him before its full import could flower.

"We're sorry, this has nothing to do with the quality of your work, but your position is being eliminated."

Father Reyes delivered the funeral oration.

"His name was Jefferson. His family, thousands of miles away in a different land, gave him the name of an American hero. They named their youngest son after the man who wrote the Declaration of Independence. The man who wrote that *all men are created equal.* And we believe that Jefferson Nuñez was brutally beaten, cruelly murdered, by a gang of young men—still boys, really—who thought that he was not American enough to have the right to life.

"He was one of the legions of immigrants who have come here, seeking a better life for themselves and their families. Who fled the green fields of Ireland when a deadly plague turned the potatoes black. Who fled the grinding poverty in the mountains of Sicily and the marshlands of Poland so their children would not be trapped in the same fate.

"Who taught his killers to hate people like him—and us? Was it the descendants of those who came before?

"*Dios conoce el camino de los justos.* God knows the way of the just. Let us make that road, and let His love and wisdom guide us as we build it."

BLOOD DRIVE

BY KENNETH WISHNIA

Port Jefferson Station

The envelope was addressed to Mr. *James F. Keenan III*, a name he never used.

Jimmy tore the envelope open the minute it arrived, barely flinching as the chaotic results of his frenzy sent a wayward piece of glue-stiffened flap slicing into his little finger.

His meaty hands had no trouble grappling with an I-beam swinging on a cable ten stories up, but now they tingled as if they belonged to someone else as he unfolded the letter, leaving a thin smear of blood on the plain white paper.

His long-overdue severance pay.

He stared at the numbers on the check and recoiled as if he'd been whacked in the head with a cue ball.

Something was wrong. Dead wrong. There were only three numerals, and two of them were zeros that meant less than nothing. There was an awful lot of emptiness on the page, where there definitely should have been something. Something *more*.

"Seven dollars?" His temples pulsed, and the room flattened out behind the sheet of onionskin bearing the name *Brady Construction*, the walls and furniture turning paper thin. "Seven fucking dollars?"

He'd been waiting all week for this lifeline, or at least for a sign that he had a *chance* of being pulled from the rising tide of debt before his strength failed and he went down the drain completely.

The envelope fell to the floor.

Even the white noise of daytime TV couldn't drown out the giant sucking sound in his ears.

You work for a company twelve years . . .

Time enough for the navy-blue anchor on his wrist to go fuzzy around the edges and fade to match the dull grayish blue of dead people in movies.

His muscles were still hard, and he could hump a ton of rebar up a ladder as fast as any kid half his age. But the company could get away with paying the kid a whole lot less.

He crumpled the check and threw it at the TV screen. It fell three feet short of the target.

"Honey, what's wrong?" Rusti called from the kitchen, her voice cutting through the whirlwind like a chain-smoking Siren of the seas.

He saw himself in the supermarket aisles, the prices jumping out at him: $4.99 for a gallon of milk. $3.99 for a half-gallon of juice. $12.99 for a twelve-pack of Bud Lite. Thirty to forty bucks a week for pads and lotions and all the other female stuff. Even hunting for the three-for-a-dollar bargains on canned peas and carrots, the total quickly shot past $100 to $150, then easily cleared the bar at more than $175 for a week's worth of groceries and other needs. And how the heck were they supposed to get through five months of winter with the price of heating oil rising faster than a Wall Street guy can drop a thousand bucks on drinks at a high-class titty bar?

"I'm going out," he said, pulling his faded denim jacket off the hook. "You need anything?"

"Sure. Coffee, sugar, paper towels—"

"Better make a list." He really didn't want to carry all that crap around, but he'd already offered.

"You need a list to remember three things?"

"All right, never mind." He yanked the door open while stuffing his arms into the sleeves.

"I'll write it down for you."

"I said never mind." He pushed the screen door so hard it bounced back and nearly smacked him in the face. "Damn it!" He kicked the bottom panel, leaving a dent in the aluminum, and marched out. But the door swung back like it always did and the latch-hook caught the sleeve of his jacket and tore it.

"F-*aargh!*"

He had to let fly at something, so he punched the wall and his fist went right through the sheetrock, which swallowed his arm up to the elbow.

"Jesus . . ." He pulled his arm out, astonished by the size of the hole he'd left, and brushed the white dust off his sleeve. The last time he'd lashed out like this, in the brick house on Ocean Avenue, he just hurt his hand on the old-school plaster and lath. But these cheap tract houses were made of toothpicks and cardboard.

And now he needed to go to the hardware store to buy a sheet of wallboard, a roll of paper tape, and some spackle.

A swirl of pale green caught his eye. Rusti was on her knees in front of the TV in her faded bathrobe, flattening out the check on the coffee table, a cigarette dangling from her fingers. Her stringy red hair hung loose, covering her eyes, but the smoke curling upward darkened the freckles on her chest, and all he wanted to do right then was find a dark hole he could crawl into and hide out for a while.

He scrambled out the door, but not fast enough. He still heard her sigh, heard the disappointment in her voice when she called after him: "You can forget about the sugar, okay? We can do without."

The new Spanish supermarket had just opened up on the other side of Route 112, so at least they'd save some money on gas, instead of having to drive to the Pathmark on Nesconset Highway. But he wasn't ready to face the narrow aisles just yet, or contend with whiny toddlers spilling out of shopping carts, so he kept walking north past the strip mall and the funeral home.

Traffic was heavy on 112, as always, and he had to deal with the crush of cars, battered pickups, and SUVs idling at the light, leaning on their horns and spewing carbon monoxide into the air.

The 104 Bar was closed, and foreclosure signs were sprouting like jagged milestones around the bare trees along the road. And the Claddagh Inn, in a fruitless effort to bring a few tourists up the hill from the port, had switched over to live music, which should have meant Clancy Brothers look-alikes in thick wool sweaters playing Fuck-Them-English-Bastards reels and jigs, but usually meant way-too-loud tribute bands playing lame-ass covers of Van Halen and Led Zeppelin hits from another era.

He desperately needed to walk off the frustration, but the sidewalks were cracked in so many places he had to watch his step, so he couldn't find a rhythm that would allow him to burn off some of his blinding rage. The wind whipped at the power lines, and dead leaves swirled around his feet. He passed Dano's Auto Clinic, his eye lingering on the poster-sized graduation photo of Dano Jr. in the window, a seventeen-year-old kid who was shot dead in a booze-and-testosterone-fueled confrontation on a black guy's lawn.

As if there weren't enough problems in the world.

He crossed the LIRR tracks and felt like he was crossing the border into enemy territory, into alien turf.

Except for the Army-Navy store, which had owned a piece of Main Street for decades, half the storefronts were empty, and the rest had been taken over by *bodegas* and phone-card stores catering to the latest wave of suckers who actually thought they had a shot at the American Dream. Even the pool hall announced itself in bilingual red-and-yellow neon, and salsa blared from every other doorway.

"Should have brought my passport with me," he grumbled, as three dark-skinned guys hanging in front of the Spanish deli narrowed their eyes at him.

He started down the hill past the biker bar with the misspelled sign, *Harley's and Honey's* (didn't anyone know where to put apostrophes these days?). There was already a row of gleaming Harleys lined up along the curb outside the bar, and God help you if you rode anything less than a Harley. How could these geezers afford them, anyway? And doesn't it matter that Harley-Davidson just royally screwed its workers?

He glared at the aging bikers, almost daring them to start something. But they picked up on the intensity of his anger, and refused to meet his gaze.

Harley-Davidson, he thought. Proudly made in the U.S.A. Except that the bubble had burst and his brother steelworkers in Milwaukee had just caved, approving a seven-year wage freeze and a two-tiered pay scale that screwed the new hires and paid the temp workers even less, *even when demand for the cycles went up*, which sure wasn't how they taught the laws of supply and demand at the local community college.

He paused at the corner when the lights changed. On a clear day you could see all the way to Connecticut from where he stood. But the power plant's red-and-white-striped smoke-stacks were belching twin plumes of thick gray smoke that blended seamlessly with the clouds and obscured the horizon like a moldy blanket.

A flier for the annual Dickens Festival was flapping in the breeze, half-glued to the lamppost across the street. Every year, on a Saturday in mid-December, the well-to-do Port Jeff villagers dressed up in Victorian costumes and strolled around the center of town reenacting their favorite bits from *A Christmas Carol*. Maybe they should have gone with *A Tale of Two Cities* instead, since they elected to split the town in half to keep their tax revenues from going up the hill to the bums in Port Jeff Station and to keep the riffraff out of their school district.

Port Jefferson Village was once a sleepy town with little more than a post office, a diner, and a used bookstore where you could get fifty-cent paperbacks (and macramé supplies, back in the day). Then somebody got the bright idea of building a couple of fishermen-themed restaurants, including one in the shape of a ship's hull, and things started to take off.

And now the windows were going dark up on the hill.

Jimmy let the dead weight of his mood pull him further down the hill. But even with a black hole where his heart should have been, he managed to formulate a plan of sorts to head to the docks and watch the waves come in and maybe let the cold November wind chase the dark clouds from his thoughts.

There were fewer foreclosure signs on this side of the tracks, and the houses got bigger and nicer and further back from the street. Suddenly a Spanish chick with dynamite tits and a clipboard in the crook of her arm stepped in front of him.

"We're having a blood drive today," she said. The entranceway to Infant Jesus R.C. Church arched up behind her, framing her face like a monk's hood, which made for some strange associations with the dynamite tits.

But the pleasure was short-lived. He was about to say, *Screw you, I need every drop,* and step around her, when she added, "In memory of Jefferson Nuñez."

Jimmy knew the name. It had been in the papers for weeks. Nuñez was a hard-working guy, an Ecuadorian immigrant who never made trouble for anybody, until one night a bunch of teenagers hopped into a late-model SUV and went looking for a "Mexican" to jump. They spotted Nuñez outside a bar in Ronkonkoma and "beaner-hopped" him, kicking the crap out of him, then a kid with an Irish name delivered the final blow and left him lying in a pool of blood like a piece of roadkill, not a guy who had as much right to breathe as any of these punks from Sachem East High School.

"We're also raising money for a scholarship in his name," she said.

Jimmy recognized some of the day workers from the Home Depot parking lot lining up outside the parish house. Then a teenage girl with short black hair stepped out to talk with them, snippets of Spanish floating down to him in the street. A tiny red spot bled through the gauze bandage on her arm, and one of those bright red *I Gave Blood* stickers adorned her chest like a badge of honor.

And Jimmy found himself saying, "Yeah, sure. Why not?"

The woman smiled, handed him a sheet of instructions, and directed him up the steps to the parish house.

The plastic ID holder pinned to her scrubs said her name was *Gabriela.* She had dark wavy hair, full lips, and an oval face with a few lines around the edges.

"We just need to get a sample to test for anemia," she said, pricking his finger and pressing a thin clear tube to the wound to draw out a drop of his blood. "Just routine, 'cause you don't look very anemic to me," she said with a slight accent, her eyes running up and down his body.

She took his blood pressure, and after confirming for the fourth time that he hadn't had sex with a fag, a whore, or a junkie in the past three years, she made him lean back and roll up his sleeve.

She pulled the elastic band tight and tapped her gloved fingers on the pale skin of his forearm, feeling for a vein. Her other hand gripped his upper arm. An impish grin stole across his face and he flexed his bicep for her, but when he looked into her face, she was frowning.

"Is it that bad?" he asked, his smile fading.

"Sometimes it can be hard to find the vein. But on you, it's easy."

She stuck him with the needle, and his ass clenched reflexively. She held the needle in place with her finger, secured it with a piece of surgical tape, then slid the tube into position and twisted it tight.

"That's not what I meant."

"I know what you meant," she said flatly. She must have heard every dumb pick-up line that guys use on nurses a million times.

She eased the valve open with her thumb, and dark red blood invaded the clear plastic tube, flowing so fast it felt like she was sucking the life out of him through a silly straw. She adjusted the tiny plastic wheel and got it under control so his blood was dripping slowly into the pint-sized bag.

"Don't know why I'm giving it away," he said. "I should be selling this stuff."

"Then why don't you?"

"Got nothing else to offer, I guess."

She reached across his chest and took his other hand, felt its weight, ran a finger over the scratches and calluses, eyed the wedding ring on his fourth finger.

"Oh, a man like you has plenty to offer," she said, a bit of boob peeking out of her V-neck. Had a few miles on them, but they were still nice to look at. "There's something special about you."

"What's so special about me?"

"Look around," she said, her eyes flitting from side to side like a scam artist checking the street for cops before offering a hot tip on the fifth race at Belmont. She brushed a few wayward strands of hair out of her eyes with a gloved finger. "We don't get many Anglos in here."

"Just caught me at the right time, I guess."

"Maybe. Timing is everything. I bet you could get good work as a—what do you call it? Un abogado."

"A what?"

"Sort of like a lawyer—"

"You kidding me?" A jolt went through him, causing a gurgle in the plastic tube.

"I'm sorry. Is that the wrong word?"

"Right word, wrong guy. Me and lawyers don't always see eye to eye, know what I mean?"

Gabriela straightened up and massaged her neck, and the bag swelled with his blood as she flitted over to the supply table and spoke in low tones with another volunteer.

She came back and looked right at him with those big, dark eyes. "Okay, my friend Marissa says that abogado usually means lawyer, but in this situation it's closer to advocate."

"What's the difference?"

"An advocate is someone who offers what you might call extra-legal assistance."

"And what does a pretty lady like you need an advocate for?"

Her face hardened at the compliment. "Because we have laws that are not just, so we must have justice that is not lawful. That's why we need an advocate."

There was a fire in her eyes that wasn't there before.

He understood why. At least he thought he did. And if she was serious, then money was involved. "I'm listening."

She leaned in close and whispered things in his ear, nasty things about her job at the hospital and what the nurses' aides had to endure to keep their jobs—the demeaning comments, the unwelcome contact, the . . . well, if it wasn't truly consensual then it was rape, wasn't it? According to the laws of New York State, it was, although they could never prove anything. Nothing could be done because he was an administrator and most of the staff were of questionable legal status and were too afraid to speak up.

And she had the scars to back it up.

"You ever think of calling the cops?"

She nailed him with a look. "Maybe you're not the right man for the job, after all." The blood bag was full. She closed the valve and detached it, sealed and labeled it.

"Okay, now hold it, hold it. If you got a job for me, I said I'm listening."

She yanked off the surgical tape, pressed a cotton ball over the spot where she had punctured his skin, and pulled out the needle. "Hold that for me."

He held the cotton ball in place while she tore off another strip of tape, and explained that the girls had agreed to pool their resources in order to send the boss a clear message that it was time to start rethinking his priorities.

"And what do you want me to do?"

"We want you to deliver the message in the only language this man understands. You can roll down your sleeve now."

He obeyed. He was feeling a bit lightheaded from the loss of blood, so she helped him over to one of the cots, where the volunteer handed him a cookie and a plastic cup of cranberry juice and Gabriela gave him some kind of pill to bring up his blood pressure and told him to lie still for at least twenty minutes.

"Well? Will you do it?" Gabriela asked, peering down at him through the haze.

"Listen, sweetie, a job like that has got to cost at least—" What did it cost? What should it cost? He'd never put in a bid for a job like this. "Three hundred bucks," he said, pulling a figure out of the air.

She spun on her heel and walked away, disappearing behind the screen, and he figured that was the end of it. Maybe he should have said two hundred. *Ah, screw it.* Why should he run the risk of felony assault charges for a lousy couple hundred bucks? If anything, he should have asked for more.

He lay back, chewing on the crumbling cookie, and stared at the TV on the wall. It all felt a bit unreal to him. He was still kind of dizzy, and it was hard to concentrate on the image of a newly elected congressman with a bright red tie who was proposing to reduce the federal deficit by cutting Social Security and raising the retirement age to seventy-two. The words and numbers swirled around in Jimmy's head, but they weren't adding up to anything until the truth crept up and bit him in the cerebral cortex. *What a bunch of crap.* Retiring at seventy-two might be fine for corporate-funded assholes like the guy on TV, but not regular working people like him. *What a fucked-up country we turned out to be.* What happened to paying people a decent wage and taxing the rich for all the high-end crap they're always showing off? Cars, clothes, jewelry. We could turn this whole shitty situation around in a minute if we just got back to basics.

So his mind wasn't really on the deal he'd made when Gabriela stepped out from behind the privacy curtain and stuffed a wad of grimy, mismatched bills in his fist.

Good thing it's getting dark early because there are cameras everywhere that would burn him in a second. Shadows are blending into the night and a stiff breeze off the Sound is blowing through the hospital parking lot and there's nowhere to huddle to get warm, so he just has to wait it out on the lee side of a dark green minivan like a burl of briarwood clinging to the side of a cliff. The SOB's shift ends at four-thirty, she said, but it's way past that now and he hasn't called home yet to tell Rusti that he'll be back for dinner, he just has a job to do first.

The glass doors keep sliding open and shut, open and shut, and people who don't match the description she gave keep coming and going, and the nasal echo of the public address system keeps releasing snippets of doctors' names into the night: *Paging Dr. Andresen, Dr. Andresen? Paging Dr. Contreras, Dr. Husseini? Paging Dr. Andresen? Dr. Andresen?*

Yeah, where the hell is Dr. Andresen? Not the guy he's waiting for, but still . . .

Then a young nurse with the soft, clear voice of a water nymph cuts through the clutter: "Goodnight, Dr. Clinton."

That's him.

"Goodnight, Becky."

Footsteps scrape the pavement, loose gravel rolling under his shoes as this Clinton guy gets louder and closer until his shadow pierces the space just beyond the edge of the van, and Jimmy looks around for the hundredth time and lunges and suddenly it's all knuckle and bone and teeth and pain and pleading and a knee to the groin and another look around and ducking the weak swing and kicking out sideways and driving the kneecaps in a direction they were never meant to go till the SOB finally goes down and kicking him in the ribs over and over till the guy's arms fall flapping to the ground, and then stomping again and again until he hears the satisfying crack of boot on bone. Boot on skull, it turns out, but he can't skip out yet, not before he delivers the message: "Lay off the girls."

Red bubbles dribble down the guy's cheeks as he struggles to draw breath. Then he says, "Which ones, asshole?"

Which calls for one more kick in the jaw.

By the time his pulse returns to normal, he's wiped most of the blood off his hands, but there are bruises on his fists and places where the skin is broken and the flesh beneath glistens like raw meat. Must have happened when he knocked out some of the guy's teeth. Those teeth sure hurt like hell. But he thinks of his old boss, Mr. Brady, and wonders how many guys would chip in to pay five hundred bucks a pop for every tooth he knocked out of *that* guy's mouth, and a slow mean grin blossoms across his face.

And he thinks of all the other assholes who need a beating that nobody else is willing to give them, like the abusive jerks who smack their girlfriends around for smiling at some guy on the supermarket checkout line, and the pimply faced punks who call their own mamas bitches when they get caught stealing from their purses, and all the deadbeat dads who always seem to have money for beer but never seem to have money for child support, and all the false profiteers who get rich preaching about how making piles of money is God's way of rewarding the faithful, and *definitely* all the bosses who push their workers harder and harder, demanding concessions or else the jobs will go to China, so the workers make the concessions but the jobs *still* end up going to China, and hell, maybe even a newly elected state senator or a congressman who sails into office on a sea of fat-cat money and the first thing he does is make plans to slit the throats of the people he's supposed to help. I mean, they don't get serious Secret Service protection or anything like that, do they?

He sees himself printing up business cards saying *Jimmy Keenan, Advocate*, but can't figure out what else to say or how to say it, and decides that word-of-mouth will have to do for now.

His knuckles bitch and moan as he ignores the approaching sirens and feeds a couple of battered old quarters into the pay phone and dials the number, a warm feeling spreading in his chest as he tells his wife the good news.

"No worries, honey. Looks like I got steady work for the next six months, at least."

JABO'S

BY **AMANI SCIPIO**

Bridgehampton

Though we lived a little over a mile from the famous ocean shoreline in the small but quaint town of Bridgehampton, the ocean was a place we hardly knew. The glitz and glamour of the Hamptons were far beyond our reach; we lived tucked away on Sag Harbor Turnpike, an area made up of generations of migrant workers, many of who had come up from the South as early as the 1800s. My mother and father migrated north from Georgia in 1958, to get away from poverty and racial injustice.

The season for watermelons was winding down when May and Shangy decided to catch a ride on the back of a watermelon truck passing through Lyons, Georgia. They had heard stories of how black people had good lives up in New York. Shangy had been released from the army and was seeking a better life and May, she was a young teenager fascinated by the tall caramel-colored man. Shangy's family warned my mother that he was no good and that she shouldn't leave Georgia with him, but at eighteen years old May felt she had the right to do what she wanted, even if it meant dropping out of school.

Shangy was known for his gambling, drinking, and womanizing, why would she think he would change when he arrived up north? May was a quiet girl who had lost her mother as an infant and was raised by her grandmother. All May knew about her own mother was that she was a very good painter and was only nineteen years old when she died giving birth to her. My mother's world was so small and limited she actually wrote down her life plans—to have three children and be on welfare, just like the many generations of women in her family before her.

With their worldly possessions stuffed into pillowcases and small suitcases, the eager group of migrant workers jumped on the back of the old GMC truck that had a wooden dump bucket. The truck provided very little protection from the cold and rainy days and nights heading north, but the workers didn't mind because they were all thinking about a better life than the one they'd lived in Georgia. The trip was long and hard. The group spent time working on farms in South Carolina and Virginia, until finally settling at Rosco's Camp, a potato farm in Bridgehampton.

May and Shangy had made it to Long Island, to Sag Harbor Turnpike, a part of the Hamptons few really knew or talked about. The work camp was sometimes overcrowded, forcing some of the workers to sleep outside in makeshift tents. They would gather around fire-filled steel drums for warmth, drinking moonshine. My mother tried not to be scared, because her grandmother had told her that there was good in everybody, you just had to find it. Times were particularly hard for Shangy; he could not find enough work. He spent his time gambling and drinking, and to make matters worse, my mother was now pregnant.

Word had gotten around about the living conditions in the migrant camps, so social workers were often dispatched to see if they could be of help. One such social worker saw my mother, almost eight months pregnant, kneeling down by a stream with no shoes on in the cold, trying to catch fish. The campers were tested for TB and sent to treatment centers, and my mother's test came back negative. The social worker, still overwhelmed with concern, had my mother admitted to a nearby hospital so she would at least have food to eat. When she was released after giving birth to my brother and me, the social worker found her a place to stay.

My mother became good friends with Mrs. Cora Lee, who ran the small nursing home where she was sent. That was the first time she was separated from Shangy, but May would not return to the camp. Mrs. Cora Lee allowed my mother to stay until she got back on her feet. Here May met Mr. Roosevelt Lee, and got pregnant with my brother Mark. But they didn't stay together. By the age of twenty-one May was alone and had three kids. She eventually found a small four-room place of her own on Sag Harbor Turnpike.

Like many of the other women who lived on Sag Harbor Turnpike, my mother scratched out a living doing house cleaning for the rich white folks on the other side of town. House cleaning was backbreaking work and it didn't pay much for a single woman trying to raise three kids, so our mother would clean two houses a day, leaving very little time for us, which meant my brothers and I were left alone most of the day, when school was out.

Behind the scenes of the famous and super-rich people who lived and vacationed in the Hamptons were parts of Sag Harbor Turnpike that were full of pain and suffering. Some people had and some didn't, and the ones who did have were often cruel and heartless. There was a place called Jabo's, a two-story house on the Turnpike that was run by a husband and wife, but because the husband was sickly, his wife Mrs. Ella was in charge. She was a mean-spirited woman who thought of no one but herself.

Everyone who lived on the Turnpike knew about Mrs.

Ella's place. Jabo's was considered the local hangout for loose women and alcoholics. Mrs. Ella and her husband Jabo sold everything out of their house—fried chicken dinners, cigarettes, alcohol, and soft drinks—which was convenient for those who didn't have a car to get around.

The place also catered to those poor souls who had returned from the army with no family, or came up on the season and had nowhere else to go. Some had simply lost their way, fallen on hard times and found themselves trapped by alcohol, living each day for their next drink. Mrs. Ella would accept their Social Security benefit checks in exchange for booze and a cot in the basement of her house. I never understood why those men couldn't do better for themselves, or why Mrs. Ella herself wouldn't help them. Jabo's was a sore covered up by the neighborhood that grew along Sag Harbor Turnpike. Though Jabo's was not a labor camp it encouraged camp-style living for the numerous men who lived there in the basement. Everyone knew what went on at Jabo's but everyone acted as though nothing was wrong. Children were not allowed to go down to Jabo's. Friday and Saturday were the busiest and most dangerous nights because that's when people had money.

My parents hadn't been living together for several years. One night, Shangy was drinking and gambling at Jabo's when another player accused him of cheating. A fight broke out. By the time it was over my father lay on the floor with a knife broken off in his head. Everyone thought for sure he would die, but he didn't.

After surgery removed the broken knife, my mother stayed by his side, and when Shangy was released from the hospital she brought him home. Shangy had to learn all over again how to talk and walk. Soon he was almost good as new, except now he was prone to seizures. The man in the wheelchair was kind and slow to anger and once let us eat a whole five-pound bag of sugar.

When Shangy could take care of himself, once he was on his feet again, he moved out and took a cot in Mrs. Ella's basement down the street, so that he could be close to my brothers and me. After that we only saw him on Sundays, a day he reserved just for us.

One Sunday I wore a red-and-navy-striped baby-doll dress with a navy bow pressed between a wide white collar with white ankle socks and black patent-leather Mary Janes made by Buster Brown, waiting for Daddy to take me for our Sunday walk. Though it had been said that my daddy was as mean as cat shit, when I was with him I felt special and like I really belonged. But this Sunday, for some reason my mother refused to let Shangy take us, and I stood behind the broken screen door begging May to let us go, and she said no. I watched my father walk angrily down the dirt path back to Mrs. Ella's. Later that day the news came that Shangy was dead. He had suffered a seizure and fallen down the stairs leading to the basement. He died instantly. I was only five but I can still smell the overwhelming scent of spring flowers and I can see his casket and the military officer removing and folding up the flag and his frozen face as he gave it to my mother. Shangy was only thirty-two years old.

When I was nine, we still lived in that same small four-room shack on the Turnpike. One evening May's new boyfriend, who had been drinking, decided to fix the stove in the kitchen. In a matter of minutes the place we called home went up in flames. None of us was hurt but all we had left was on our backs. Thanks to the local kindergarten teacher, Mrs. Thomason, who put together a collection of clothes and even toys, my family began to heal. The woman infused us with a little hope.

After a few months of living in a neighbor's basement, we moved into a two-bedroom house that had a beauty parlor in the front. The beauty parlor had gone out of business so Mrs. Ella, the owner, rented the back portion out to my mother, and that's how we ended up living next door to Jabo's, where my father had died.

Anyone living outside of Sag Harbor Turnpike did not know what was truly happening at Jabo's, the gambling and the drinking and the poor souls who were held hostage in the basement because of their inability to do better for themselves, or were just down on their luck like my daddy. What bothered me the most was that Mrs. Ella would take their welfare checks in exchange for boarding and alcohol. Those men were always going to be stuck living each day drinking away their future.

Often I would climb on top of my brother's bunk bed, crouch on my knees, and softly sing "Summertime," a song I occasionally heard my mother singing as she washed the morning dishes. The window looked right out on Jabo's basement next door.

"Little May, is that you, is that you singing?" a raspy voice would call from outside. The voice came from Red, one of the local vagrants who lived in Mrs. Ella's basement. He was a tall, light-skinned man with black curly hair who called me Little May because I looked so much like my mother.

I would pretend that I could not hear Red calling. Though he seemed nice enough I was afraid of him and the other men who lived in Mrs. Ella's basement. There was CJ, a skinny, wiry, dark-skinned man with thick matted hair that never looked like he combed it. I can't ever remember seeing CJ sober. Earnie, on the other hand, was neat and clean; the difference between Earnie and the other men was that he had family who looked after him even though he had lost his way. I didn't like Earnie because whenever no one was looking he would expose himself. One day May's boyfriend caught Earnie exposing himself to me in our living room. My mother's boyfriend slapped Earnie, cursed him out, and told him if he ever saw him around me again he would kill him.

Then there was Red, who got his name because of his complexion. In those days, light-skinned blacks were called *red-bone*. Red stood about 6'4", and always wore jean overalls and dirty work boots. His caramel skin was oily and prone to acne. Red only drank when he wasn't working.

At nightfall the loud music and cussing would start over at Jabo's. The women would all be wearing pencil dresses that looked so tight I wondered how they could breathe. They smelled of loud perfume and had painted-up faces, ready to enjoy the night. The music would be blaring but not loud enough to drown out the loud cackles spewing from the mouths of the women who'd had too much to drink. Once the serious drinking started, the cursing and arguments escalated, almost always turning into a fight. Then someone—usually Red—would pull out a knife and May would call us back into the house, but we would sneak out again and watch. CJ was the first person I ever saw get cut. I smelled blood for the first time, and sweat mixed with moonshine, in the heat of the night, and it made me sick inside. Most of the time these outbursts would end with Mrs. Ella sending somebody down to the basement to sleep it off.

We got to know Red best because he was the only one our

mother trusted to stay with us when she went to have a drink next door. He would talk about his childhood in South Carolina, and how scared he was of the Ku Klux Klan.

Later that year CJ had the DT's so bad he lost touch with reality and one morning Red found him under his favorite tree; he had died there in the dead of winter. What a lonely and fruitless life Red and CJ led and how cheated God must have felt.

The summer I was twelve, I learned how to do my own hair and I learned how to sew. Even though we only saw our mother late in the afternoon, we didn't miss her, because her being there was like she wasn't there at all. She came home from work, poured a vodka and orange juice, and sat at the kitchen table, smoking until she got tired, and then she would sleep on the couch, and by the time she woke up we would be in bed. My brothers and I knew how hard our mother's life was because she would never let us forget.

I spent a lot of time in my usual place, on the top bunk in my brothers' room, looking out at Jabo's basement, rocking back and forth, and singing "Summertime."

"Little May, is that you, is that you singing?" I pretended not to hear Red's raspy voice. I didn't want anyone to know I sang. I knew after a while he would stagger away. I hated my life, and I hated myself; the only comfort I had now was that school was out for the summer, and I wouldn't have the daily stress of the other kids picking on me.

May worked so much, she wasn't aware of what it was like for a girl child among all these men. I felt bad so I closed my eyes and remembered sitting on the beach with Daddy, smiling as the runoff from the crashing waves pulled the sand from beneath my feet.

* * *

When you hear of eastern Long Island or the Hamptons you are reminded of the super rich, the famous, the fine homes, beautiful beaches, but poverty stared us straight in the face. We had Mrs. Hattie's shack across the street, shadowed by a huge honeysuckle bush. Mrs. Hattie still used oil lamps for light and a wood-burning stove for heat and cooking. Though by community standards we were all poor, we always had food, clothes, and a roof over our heads, and at the time that had to be enough.

Most of the people living down on Sag Harbor Turnpike, including our mother, brought along with them from the South the heavy baggage of their self-hatred and bitterness. If my brothers and I did something wrong, like playing around in the house or our grades were bad, we got beat severely, especially my younger brother Mark.

Sometimes she would be at the table helping him learn to read, and every time he missed a word she would hit him. The doctor told her to stop beating him but it was already too late. I would occasionally catch Mark looking at our mother with undisguised hatred. My younger brother was full of rage, and I was scared of him. My twin brother Eugene was the oldest but he seemed to suffer even deeper than Mark and me. Eugene was small in body and always teased about being weak, especially by Mark, who was eight inches taller and a hundred pounds heavier.

Eugene had to prove that he could protect anyone, even if he could not protect himself. Mark and I got the worst of it because unlike Eugene, we wore our anger and frustration like dirty clothes, and because we stopped caring, we did not fear as much. The harder May would hit Mark, the less he would cry, until he did not cry at all anymore. Because Eugene was so frail, he could not allow himself to be in a position where he would get beat, so he worked on being more agreeable to our mother, until she thought he could do no wrong. Eugene did everything he could to make her happy. We always ended up forgiving May for the things she did because she never had a mother herself, making it very hard for her to know how to be a mom. She would tell us stories of how she was beaten as a child, just as her grandmother told her about her own brutal childhood. All this seemed perfectly normal because that's how it was.

But my brothers and I found ourselves alone and on our own most of the time. We all shared the same desire to stay away from our mother, so we would make up adventures that would lead us into the forest for hours, and in our minds we returned victorious and strong. Nothing could hurt or break us, not even our mother. We were a team; we were our own family.

One day that summer we were playing when Eugene punched me in the back and I started to howl. Mom ran down the hall with the electric cord. We were all about to be beat. Something inside of me broke. I knew that I couldn't take another beating so in one instant I decided to run away. I ran out the front door and down the street. My mother went next door and told Mrs. Ella that I had run away and could she help bring me back. I did not get far; just as I was about to cross the railroad tracks near Narrow Lane, Mrs. Ella's long, black Cadillac pulled up behind me. My mother hurried out of the car, grabbed me by the arm, and shoved me into the backseat. They brought me back.

My mother made me go into my brothers' room and get undressed. She tied my hands and feet to the top of the bed and gagged my mouth. Each strike with the electric cord felt like a hot knife cutting into my back and legs. The gag came off my mouth and I screamed and begged her to stop, but she just hit harder. For the first time I thought she was going to kill me. I probably would have died if Red hadn't run in from next door and made her stop.

When I got dressed and returned to the room where my brothers were sitting, the expressions in their eyes made me feel that hope was gone. Eugene looked like he would be scared for the rest of his life, and Mark would just continue to hate from the inside out. The cocoa butter took away the physical scars, but Mark grew up so filled with rage that he always drinks and thinks about suicide to contain it.

Our parents came up to Bridgehampton on a watermelon truck seeking a better life, but because of their many overwhelming personal struggles, life was not what they had hoped for on Sag Harbor Turnpike.

SNOW JOB

BY TIM TOMLINSON

Wading River

Bob Foote backed his 1982 Monte Carlo into a space near Macy's at the Smith Haven Mall. He was nibbling chocolates from a Whitman Sampler someone had left at the house on Christmas Eve—a regift: two of the chocolates were missing. From the backseat, his two little dogs, a poodle and a schnauzer, observed his motions, anticipating the opportunity to lick his sticky fingers. He nudged the bumper of the car behind him, pulled a few inches forward, and cut the engine. The dogs sat up, excited. "Not yet," he told them. He split another chocolate in two and tossed a piece to each. He licked his own fingers this time, and got out of the car.

His desert boots sank into snow four inches deep. It was coming down over an inch an hour. The roads were hazardous, yet that hadn't stopped the shoppers—the day after Christmas was the biggest sale day of the year. But Bob Foote hadn't gone out in a blizzard for bargains. He went out to watch people be people—that is, phonies, hypocrites, con men, and petty thieves. They never let him down.

He popped the trunk and removed a box the size of a large suitcase, wrapped with festive holiday paper depicting ice skaters and snowmen alongside green trees covered with brightly colored ornaments. The paper fit on the box like paint, the ends taped down tight as hospital corners without a wrinkle on the entire surface. Bright red ribbon circled the box diagonally at either end, coming to a bow near the top, a silky red dahlia—practically a work of art. He closed the trunk. The dogs peered through the back window, but neither could see him. The poodle was near blind, and the window had fogged over. Both dogs began to whine.

"Yeah, yeah," Bob Foote said, trying to convince himself that the dogs' cries didn't pierce his heart. The dogs *owned* him—he let them do just about whatever they wanted, and he couldn't bear to deny them anything. Since his retirement six months earlier, his greatest joy was to put on a stack of Jerry Vale records, lie down on the living room floor, and have each dog fall asleep on his chest.

With the gift-wrapped box under his arm, he walked toward the Macy's entrance, carefully placing his shoes into the steps others had left in the snow. Scores of shoppers bent into the snow and rushed past him as if they were in a race, as if a hundred people had arrived for a smorgasbord set for ninety-nine, and they were going to make good and sure Bob Foote was the loser. Wait till they find out, he thought, smiling. Wait till one of them claims the booby prize in this box.

A *Leave It to Beaver*–type family approached, Mister and Missus, Junior, and Sis, their arms filled with bags and boxes.

"Merry Christmas," Mister said to Bob Foote.

Junior corrected him. "Christmas is over, Dad."

"So it is," Mister agreed, winking at Bob Foote.

Sis said, "Happy New Year."

"Yeah," Bob Foote muttered. "Sure."

Other shoppers passed—mothers shouting at kids, fathers shouting at mothers, kids shouting at nothing. The kids slid, packed snow in their hands, and threw it at parked cars and each other; they fell into the snow and made what might have been snow angels if anyone could see through the snowfall. Bob Foote was glad to be beyond it all—the kids, the gifts, Christmas. He hated all the holidays, but Christmas was the worst. The most phony, the most costly, the most disappointing. In his whole life, he couldn't remember receiving a single gift he truly valued—even from his wife and his sons.

On the sidewalk outside Chess King, a group of teenagers loitered. They were all underdressed—unzipped denim vests, studded leather jackets, sneakers, and no gloves. They smoked cigarettes and shivered, pimples underneath their soft whiskers. Their hair looked like it had been hacked with hedge clippers, then slept on. Why, Bob Foote wondered, would anyone want to raise children today? At least when he'd had his kids, he had no idea that they'd turn into punks. They could, of course, and they did, but that hadn't seemed a sure thing. Today, you were either a Kennedy, in which case your kids would wind up news anchors or congressmen or the leader of some charity in Africa, or you were a nobody, your kids, punks. These kids weren't Kennedys.

The unmistakable smell of marijuana drifted his way. Bob Foote recalled a day fifteen, sixteen years earlier. He'd parked his car at Port Jefferson Harbor for a nap when he saw his fourteen-year-old son Cliff sucking a joint in the midst of a crowd like this. From his earlobe a shiny ring hung. Bob Foote shuddered—the kid had become the embodiment of a nightmare. He had slid down behind the steering wheel and driven slowly away. Maybe he shouldn't have, maybe he could have helped . . . but it was painful just to look at Cliff's dopey stoned puss.

The kid with the joint exhaled. "What are you looking at, fat fuck?" he said.

Bob Foote recoiled—he hadn't realized he was staring. "Sorry, sonny," he answered, shaking his head. "Merry Christmas."

"Hey," the kid said, cupping his crotch, "sonny this."

The other teenagers laughed. "Sorry, sonny!" they shouted. "Merry Christmas, sonny."

Bob Foote moved on. To himself, he counted *one, two,* and a snowball caught him square between the shoulders. Another two flew past.

Punks, he thought. Complete punks.

At the mall's entrance, he stomped the snow off his shoes. Then, as if he'd forgotten something, he tapped his trousers and dug his hands into his coat pockets. Shaking his head as if he couldn't believe what a putz he was, he started back in the direction of his car, taking care to avoid another embarrassing exchange with the teenagers. The well-wrapped box in his arms reminded him, he had his own prank to pull.

He squeezed between a pair of cars and turned back into his own lane, cursing the snow edging over the tops of his desert boots and into his socks. Opposite the Monte Carlo was a large Buick and a small Toyota, each covered with snow, parked front end first. He set the gaily-wrapped box down in the snow and leaned it against the Buick's rear bumper. Undetected, he crossed the lane and returned to his Monte Carlo, where the dogs waited behind fogged windows.

Back in the car, he tapped the front seat for the dogs, and started the car. He set the heat on high, blasted defrost, turned the windshield wipers on low. He pulled the desert boots from his feet and set them under the floor heat vents, then draped his socks over a vent on the passenger-side dash. The poodle got on the floor between his feet and licked his toes.

"Atta girl," he said, laughing against the tickling sensation. "Atta girl."

The schnauzer settled into his lap. And Bob Foote settled back for the show.

When he retired, six months earlier, he'd canceled garbage collection and began dumping the trash himself. He gathered it into large lawn-leaf bags and flung it into dumpsters behind strip malls or 7-Elevens or at the ends of the drives of local schools. He did a rotation, making sure not to visit the same place twice in a month. He found the routine relaxing and refreshing. New places, new views, fresh issues to ponder, such as the relative merits of plastic dumpsters on wheels, as opposed to the heavy metal dumpsters plonked directly onto pavement.

But before long, it started to seem like a pain-in-the-ass obligation, and he hit on a new idea: regifting the trash. Instead of bundling it up into one big bag, he created small parcels, little boxes, neat grocery bags. He made some trash look like postal packages, with tight string securing the flaps. He made other trash look like recent purchases in shopping bags with the tops folded down evenly. He took these creations to shopping areas and left them in conspicuous places—in carts, on top of car trunks, or against the walls near pay phones. And then, from the front seat of his Monte Carlo, one dog licking his feet, the other curled up on his lap, he watched the parade of phonies, thieves, con men and women, make their discoveries and hatch plans for sneaking his trash into their cars and, eventually, home. He loved watching the shenanigans—the abrupt halt, the slow circling, the pacing back and forth looking for outraged observers. Then the pounce, the tension between the casual departure and the racing heart. The careless deposit into trunks, or onto back-seats. The slow exits from the parking lots into the safety of traffic. Sometimes he followed them. They drove around the corner, parked in front of a house, or up the road to another strip mall, a gas station. They couldn't wait to see what they'd scored. The anxious unwrapping, the tearing away of paper or tape, the sawing at string with the edges of keys. And then, revelation—the looks on their faces! The frantic looking around. Who did this? Or worse, who's observing this? Who's seeing them for what they really are: moral amoebas without a scintilla of virtue. God, did Bob Foote love those moments! The best were the ones he tailed all the way home, the ones who slid into their houses with packages under their arms, the lights flashing on and the furious unwrapping, followed by the exclamations and the expletives. Sometimes he covered his schnauzer's ears.

And the range of them—the doctors and lawyers didn't surprise him, but twice he'd seen close friends of his wife, and once a pair of nuns. He had to rub his eyes and make sure he wasn't the one getting duped.

Today's package was the *crème de la crème*, if he could get French about it. This one packaged all the wrappers, all the bows, the cards (with the names crossed out), and all the tinsel from the meaningless gifts that had been exchanged over the previous two days—excluding the Whitman Sampler, whose chocolates remained good, if compromised. There were the gifts from his two sons. From Cliff, the younger punk, a book about nautical semaphores. Always something about the sea from Cliff, as if someday they might ship out together. On the back it said, *Used*. From Wally, the older punk, a subscription to a golfing magazine he didn't read—he didn't golf. By chance, Wally did. He'd pissed on them both, wiped the dogs' asses with the pages, tossed them into the box. The gifts from his wife—a card without his name or hers, and a book about famous battles of the U.S. Navy (The fucking Navy! He'd been a Marine) . . . he used the card to scoop up a few frozen turds from the backyard, bing bang boom, into the box. The box had come with the gift his sons had given their mother, Samsonite luggage that must have fallen off a truck and had about as much utility for his wife as tits on a nun. To that mess, he added the past several days' debris: chicken bones, the heels and waxes from cheese, cracker boxes, broken ornaments, tissues, napkins, plate scrapings, turkey bones, chicken gizzards, stale bread, burnt lasagna, half-chewed meatballs, pie tins, cupcake wrappers, soup cans, empty milk cartons, half-a-week's kitty litter. For good measure he threw in the watch he'd received for thirty years retirement, a gold-tone Jules Jurgensen with a twist-o-flex band, water resistant to ten meters, that fogged up and stopped the first time he wore it in the shower—a piece of crap. Like his job, his sons, his life. And that's what he felt about Christmas, a piece of crap—a holiday when garbage got wrapped up and recycled and presented as gifts to hapless suckers who oohed and ahhed at it, then returned it or gave it away to some other loser.

He'd wrapped the box carefully in the garage, his sons and his wife shaking their heads. And now he was sitting back, waiting to enjoy the fruits of his labor.

Two women spotted the box at the same time. One came from the shops, her arms full. The other came from her car, she was just heading in; she had two boys who ran in the snow in front of her. Bob Foote saw the boys first, or rather his schnauzer did, and started barking. Bob Foote shushed her, and she curled back down on the seat beside him, her throat grumbling until his fingers tickled her calm.

Then the women converged. Bob Foote couldn't hear what they said, but he could imagine. "That's my box." "You're full of shit." "Well, it's not your box." "It is now." "No, it's not." "Yes, it is." "No, it's not." Each with a hand on the ribbon, pulling this way, pulling that.

Someone, Bob Foote thought, is going to get hurt if this keeps up much longer.

So he honked the horn. Both women jumped, startled. The woman with the bags lost her grip, and her feet seemed to shoot straight out from below her hips. She fell straight back, flat as a plank. Then the soft dull thunk of her skull hitting the Buick's bumper. The other woman covered her mouth with her hand. She screamed for her boys to come back. She turned and ran. She didn't forget to take the box.

Bob Foote jumped out of the car and rushed toward the fallen woman. His bare feet in the snow sent his mind hurtling back to Korea. So did the blood, the helmet-like puddle seeping into the snow around the woman's head. He slid his fingers under her scarf and felt for a pulse—he pressed on one side, the other, nothing. A pair of headlights glowed blurrily at the end of the lane, coming his way. He straightened up, hopped back to the Monte Carlo. The oncoming car slowed, and Bob Foote slid below the wheel.

Lonnie Lonigan sat in a booth of the Good Steer Inn on Jericho Turnpike. A True Blue curled smoke from his lip. He hated True Blue—the smoke was so thin he barely squinted. But his Lucky Strikes made him hack like he had a pint of pus in each lung.

On the wall at his elbow was a personal jukebox. He flipped through the offerings looking for the Italian love songs that gave Bob Foote such a kick. They'd both married Italian girls from Bushwick. Lonigan got stuck with a mutt. Janet Scaturo—one pregnancy and she pooched out. Two, she pigged. By the time she divorced him, she was pulling a caboose wider than a Volkswagen bus. Bob Foote got Jackie Capello, pick of the Bushwick litter. A pain in the ass, worse than a Jewish princess, but two kids hadn't blown her figure, and she held on to her looks, more or less. Even back then, eighteen, nineteen years old, she knew how to lick an Italian ice. It should have been the two of them, Lonnie always thought, but Korea, all the rest, shit got mixed up. Now all he cared about was the dirty movies. Was there a greaseball song about that? He punched in "Amore Scusami," "Mala Femmena," and "Addio, Mi' Amore." These days, three was all you got for fifty cents. There's your morning in America.

With his sleeve he wiped off a clear spot in the window. Thick fat snowflakes fell. Headlights glowed on traffic slowed to a crawl. Bob Foote was ten minutes late, but that was okay. No rush. The plan was a lunch, a few beers, and Bob Foote would go home to the wife he couldn't stand, Lonnie would pick up a six-pack and head to the dirty movies—the second best thing about being divorced. For the holidays the Rocky Point Adult Cinema featured all the skins nominated for the Adult Video Awards. And every day they drew stubs for a free first-class flight out to Vegas for a stage-side table at the ceremony. Ginger Lynn, Nikki Charm, Christy Canyon—the winner got to sit with them all, three nights, in the flesh. And since seeing this year's *New Wave Hookers*, Lonnie had become obsessed. Every time he closed his eyes he saw Traci Lords doing very interesting things. It was going to take more than a blizzard to keep Lonnie Lonigan away from a crack at that freebie. And he had to win—Janet had cleaned him out.

He'd thought of asking Bob Foote for a loan—he knew his friend could spot him. But there was a funny thing about Bob Foote: he didn't approve of the skins. Even in Korea, when they were twenty, twenty-one years old. He wouldn't go along to the brothels. He wouldn't look at the magazines. The guys both hated him and respected him for it. And Lonigan learned it was best just to avoid the topic.

Outside, a Suffolk County Police patrol car crept by, blue light flashing, the siren muffled in the snow. Then another cop car. And another. An ambulance followed. Lonigan shook his head—he'd driven a jeep at the Frozen Choisin, snow up to his kneecaps, and the only accident he had was pissing his pants when a bomb blew his vehicle into the drifts. This snow—he could drive it blindfolded, he could drive it drunk, and would.

Bob Foote couldn't. Lonigan saw him pull into the diner's lot, watched him slide and fishtail, then try to wedge into the space close to the entrance.

"Slow, you dumb bastard," Lonigan muttered.

Bob Foote spun his wheels again and again, and gave up. He motored over to a wide open area in the lot's far corner, then lingered outside the car, saying goodbye to that blind goddamn poodle. The guy was becoming a crackpot. When he came through the door near the register, his hair and beard glistened with snow.

"Bob, you fat bastard," Lonnie said, "I thought I was going to have to come out and park for you."

Bob Foote fell into the booth. He tried to speak, and choked back a sob.

Lonnie jumped up and waved off the waitress. He threw his arm around his friend and said, "Okay, Bobby, okay. Whatever it is, you hear me? Okay."

Lonigan knew all about his tricks with the garbage. Sometimes they went together, drank quarts of Schaefer and watched the show. But from what Bob Foote was blubbering, this one went haywire. His friend had crossed a line. He'd made himself vulnerable. Shit could happen.

When he finished, Lonigan returned to his side of the booth. "Look," he said, "it's two ways. Either she's dead and you did the right thing, 'cause no use getting fucked for something not your fault. Or she's not dead, which case someone finds her, they call the cops, she's all right. You keep your name out of it." He sat back and put a match to a True. "I'd rather get the cancer than smoke these goddamn things. I gotta suck twice to get half a puff."

"Can we keep the focus here?"

"I'm saying, Bob, you got nothing to worry about."

"She had no pulse, Lonnie, did you hear me?"

"Yeah, I heard you."

"The woman died."

"That we don't know."

"What do you mean, *we don't know?*" Bob Foote said. "Were you there? Did you feel her?"

"Let me ask you something: are you a doctor?"

"She had no pulse."

"Oh, so you are a doctor. Maybe you could have a look at these hemorrhoids?"

"She didn't have a pulse, Lonnie."

"You didn't *feel* a pulse. You, a retired schmuck used to climb poles for the lighting company. You don't know a pulse from a putz, my friend."

Bob Foote smiled weakly. "I know a putz," he said.

"I'm a putz, I know. But seriously, Bob—nothing. All right?"

"How do you figure?"

"Nothing legal, I'm saying. Spiritual, that's between you and *Il Papa.*"

"It's not the Pope I'm worried about."

"Look, legal—they got dick. Two women fighting over a box not even theirs. Freaking blizzard, no one sees past their nose. One falls, cracks her skull."

"And they call that manslaughter, Lonnie."

"No fucking way."

Lonnie Lonigan signaled for the waitress. She brought two schooners of Pabst.

"Remember," Lonigan said, "my brother-in-law's on the Suffolk County force. I'll give him a call, see what they have, careful like . . ."

"You talking about Jimmy?"

"So?"

"The one you broke his nose?"

"That's a long time ago."

"The one I held his arms for you."

"Hey," Lonnie said, sitting forward, "the son of a bitch deserved it, number one."

"Number two, he hates my guts. You don't tell him shit about what happened."

"I didn't say *tell*, I said find out, all right?"

"What are you gonna tell?"

"Hey, Bob, let me handle this, all right? You do the garbage and the dog walking, yeah? And let me handle the cops and the skins, *capiche*?"

"The guy's an asshole," Bob Foote said.

"So he's an asshole. Who isn't? Now come on, finish your beer. Then we get a pint and a six-pack and go to the dirty movie festival."

Bob Foote shot him a look.

"These broads today, Bob," Lonnie said. "You heard of Nikki Charm?"

"What is she?" Bob Foote said. "Eleven?"

"They're all legal, Bob. Strictly professional."

"That's part of the problem."

"Yeah, well, spare me the sermon."

Bob Foote said, "Spare this."

Lonnie sat back. He looked at the storm. They hadn't called it this big, this intense. All this snow, blankets of it, coming down thick and sticking. Plows banging down the Turnpike, sanders scattering sand like fertilizer on a lawn. If he left for the theater now, he'd miss only the first nut, maybe a facial, depending on how well the plows were working out east. Looking at his watch, he said, "We better roll."

"*Adios*," Bob Foote said, standing.

"But Bob, we okay here?"

"Sure."

"I talk to Jimmy, give you a shout at home, yeah?"

Bob Foote said, "After the dirty movie?"

Lonigan shrugged. "A man's gotta do what a man's gotta do."

"Don't make a mess."

Lonigan got the tab, and they walked out together.

"How's Jackie?" Lonnie asked.

Bob Foote said, "How's Jackie? Her bedroom is pink and she scrapes the cheese off pizza, that's *how's Jackie*."

Lonnie shook his head. "How'd two guys like us marry two broads like them, you ever wonder that?"

Bob Foote took his friend's hand. "Not too much anymore."

Lonnie said, "I hear you." He watched his friend scrape an inch of snow from his windshield. He watched the Monte Carlo recede into the slow traffic on Jericho, then he went back inside to the phone by the men's room. He was feeling a little guilty, but he was starting to get the beginnings of something that felt like an idea.

"Yeah, meet me at the mall," he said into the receiver.

"The mall?" his brother-in-law replied.

"The mall," Lonnie said. "The fucking mall, over by Macy's. Half an hour."

He hated talking to his brother-in-law like that, but what could he do? Bob Foote was right: the guy was an asshole. An asshole who hated Bob Foote.

In the men's room he took a leak, one palm flat on the wall. You shake it more than three times, you're jerking off. He heard that when he was, what, twelve? Thirteen? Right around the time he met his wife. And Jackie Capello. He shook it more than three times. "I'll show him a putz," he muttered.

The ride home, Bob Foote kept the wipers and defrost on high, and still the windshield looked like it had been smeared with unguentine. He felt as blind as his poodle. Plows and sanders—modified garbage trucks—pounding all over the place. Snow covered the sand a minute after it spread. Every ten yards an accident. Even four-wheel-drive pickups abandoned. Some of them already snowed under. He wondered if the woman's body was snowed under as well. He wondered if he should have waited with her, should have called the cops . . . But this was manslaughter, plain and simple, no matter how you looked at it. He hadn't intended to kill her, but he had intended to deceive, to expose, to embarrass, and the chain of events his garbage instigated led directly to the woman's body splayed out in the snow. He wondered if anyone had found her. Someone would have to have found her. But what if they didn't? What if she got plowed? Bob Foote shuddered. He almost wanted to puke.

The radio was no help—just news about the storm and a lot of the bullshit songs that were hits after Sinatra and before the Beatles. The only songs for him were Jerry Vale—there was a singer. The rest of these clowns . . .

Clowns made him think about Lonigan, wasting his retirement in the dirty movies, not that Bob Foote had the answer. He slept past noon, walked dogs, and gift-wrapped garbage. Not exactly a retirement lifestyle breakthrough. But at least it was something, a worldview. Lonigan, day after day, with his beer or his whiskey and his dumb Danish broads with the New Jersey accents. Once, he passed out in his seat. The manager threatened to call an EMS.

Still, Lonigan wasn't always a clown. He was crazy brave, and crazy strong. They almost had to issue him a new chest for all his medals in Korea. He was loyal, and he was a goer. He'd fly at a man twice his size, Bob Foote had seen him do it. And it didn't take much to make him fly. One cross look, one dumb remark. He'd been in four fights just since retirement, and he lost only one, to his ex-wife. He'd missed a support payment, and she found him at the dirty movies. She hit him with her wedding ring right in the orbital bone. Hairline fracture blackened his eye damn near two weeks. Looked like he was wearing a hockey puck for a monocle. He had to squint to see the skins.

Jackie Foote sat in the kitchen reading editorials in *Suffolk Life*.

"You got a call from someone," she said. She slid a note on the table his way.

"Who?"

"Your friend from the mall, he said."

"My friend from the mall?"

"That's what he said."

"I don't have any friend from the mall," Bob Foote said. "What mall?"

He punched in the number he didn't recognize.

"Hello, asshole," a man's voice said.

"Who's this?"

"No," the voice said. "Who are you?"

Bob Foote pulled the phone from his ear. He looked at the receiver. Something about the voice was . . . peculiar. "If this is a joke," he said, "I'm not laughing."

"No one's laughing on this end either, motherfucker."

"Hey, there's a woman in this room, you son of a bitch. If I knew who you were I'd smack you in your goddamn mouth."

"You want to know who this is?" the voice said. "This is the guy whose wife picked up what you dropped at the mall."

"The mall?"

"Ah, we're gonna play games now, asshole? The mall, where the blood is still wet in the snow."

"You must have—"

"Okay, so we play games," the voice said, and the line went dead.

Slowly, Bob Foote set the phone back in the cradle. He stared at the side of the refrigerator with the calendar. For months every day was blank. The kitchen was yellow. The refrigerator was yellow. You open the fridge, the Saran wrap is yellow. He fought for his country so his wife could match the Saran wrap to the wallpaper. So his kids could become punks.

"Who was that?" his wife asked, not looking up from her paper.

Bob Foote said, "Wrong number."

"Wrong number?"

He grabbed the leashes hanging off the front door knob and his dogs jumped up.

Every car that passed him on his walk to the Wading River Beach scared him shitless. With the snow, it was like they were driving on cotton—he couldn't hear them until they were right at his back. And how could they see him? He could hardly see the dogs at the end of the leash. Any one of the cars, he thought, could be the caller. And any one could strike him, run his fat ass over, and who could ever accuse the driver of negligence?

It made perfect sense, when he thought about it. He always expected a bum deal. In this life, you don't get even laughs free. And if you live honestly—a simple life full of sacrifice, climbing poles all winter with your fingers numb so your wife can drive a Volvo and your sons can study poetry in college—you deserve what you get. He had nothing but disgust for his life, and resigned dread for his future. He was almost better off back at work. At least there he had guys he could talk to about how there was nothing to talk about.

At the beach, he unleashed the dogs and they charged down to the shoreline. How did they even know the way? He started walking blind, and every now and then one of them raced by, the wind lifting the dog's fur. He should have helped the hurt woman. Lonnie was right—what was he afraid of? But it was the whole horror of it—the utter nonsense of the fight over a booby prize, and then the sound, the dull thunk of her skull catching the Buick's rear bumper, like a softball pinging off a backstop pole. How in the hell, he kept wondering, did someone know it was him? Was it the woman in the car? Did she make his plates? If she made his plates, how did she track them?

When he'd had enough of the cold and the wind and the paranoia, he turned back toward the parking lot. His eyes were half frozen. He whistled for the dogs. Only the schnauzer appeared. He called and whistled after the other. But she'd done this before. She was getting old, she was less enthused about challenging walks in the weather. More than once she'd turned around, slipped past him, found her way back home alone.

His wife's car was gone, the garage empty. He thought, I don't even get dinner in a snowstorm.

He went out back and called for the poodle. Nothing. A hedgerow of hemlocks trimmed the backyard. He slipped through a pair that had been chewed away by the red spider, and kicked several yards into the woods. He called for her again, but the heavy snowfall threw a blanket over his voice.

Inside on the stove, a can of Campbell's Chunky—beef and country vegetables—sat inside a small pot with dark burn marks across its bottom. On the top of the can was a Post-it. *Don't forget to add water. The boys are out with friends. Your friend called again.*

He threw the note, the can, and the pot in the garbage. He crumpled two slices of Kraft's individually wrapped American cheese together in each fist and dropped them in the dogs' bowls.

"Don't eat your sister's," he told the schnauzer.

The schnauzer ignored him. She went straight to the poodle's bowl and cleaned it out, then she cleaned out her own.

Bob Foote slid out the side door.

At Bernie's on Sound Avenue, a pair of young couples hugged each end of the shuffleboard table. The guys and the gals wore flannel shirts and jeans. Bob Foote was glad he wasn't a young man now. The way they dressed, how did they know who was who, which was which? And when they figured it out, what would it matter.

He ordered a boilermaker, threw back the whiskey and sipped the beer. Then he ordered another. *The boys are out with friends*, she wrote. So what? What did he care? What did they care? It was another phony Christmas, just like all the other ones. Once, they gave him a bathrobe—it had the hotel's name on the pocket. A pair of punks. Did they think he was that stupid?

The news was on. During his second beer, the incident at the mall appeared—a woman in the parking lot, found dead from injuries sustained from a fall. Anyone with information could call this number. Bob Foote took change from the bar and entered the phone booth.

He dialed Lonigan while watching one of the flannel-shirted gals lean over the shuffleboard, her ass like twin halfs of a large cantaloupe. Maybe it wasn't such a bad time to be a young man after all.

Lonigan picked up on the second ring. "You watching the news?"

"I thought you was at the dirty movie," Bob Foote said.

"I went to the mall. See what I could see. A buddy of mine's in trouble."

Bob Foote said, "Semper fi."

Lonigan said, "You got that right."

"So what did you see?"

"Cops eating donuts behind yellow tape."

"You know 'em?"

"I know all the cops."

"And?"

"And nothing. They think the broad slipped by accident. The bumper she hit was her own. They scraped some hair and skin and blood off it, but no one suspects shit."

Bob Foote said, "Not no one." He told Lonigan about the call his wife took, about the conversation he'd had with the caller, about the new note.

Lonigan went bat shit. The kind of this-is-what-we-fought-for obscenity-laced rant he threw when things got grim. In the background, he could hear Lonigan throwing things, breaking things, stomping on their broken pieces.

"For Christ's sake, Lonnie, stop. You wreck anybody's house, make it the caller's."

"You know what you do?" Lonigan said when he'd calmed. "You set up a meet."

"A meet?"

"Call his ass back, ask what he wants, and where."

"And then what?"

"Then I show up and break his goddamn nose."

"What if—" Bob Foote said, but his friend was already off the line.

He bought a round for the girl with the cantaloupe ass and her friends and took his change. The back roads hadn't been plowed for hours. He crawled the five miles home to Wading River in second gear.

His low beams swept along the front yard. Scattered across the snow were the contents of the package he'd left at the mall. He idled the Monte Carlo and kept the headlights on the mess. Sinking to his knees in the snow, he grabbed at the debris. There it all was again, the paper and wrappers and pie tins. He carried it with both arms to the garage where he dumped it into a large refuse bag.

That's when he saw the poodle, on its back, four paws in the air, rigid. Its head had been twisted completely around. The schnauzer crept over to Bob Foote's boots and nuzzled. He picked her up and lightly scratched her belly while staring at his dead dog.

Somehow it all made sense, he always knew he'd get a bum deal.

He stuffed the dead dog into a grocery bag and hid her body behind a row of hemlocks in the backyard. He'd bury her when the ground thawed. Then he called his friend from the mall.

"Hey, we missed you, big guy."

"You won't miss me again," Bob Foote said.

"Ooo," the man said. "That's the way, uh-huh, uh-huh, I like it, uh-huh, uh-huh."

"What do you need me to bring, asshole?"

"Uh-huh, uh-huh," the man sang again.

The morning was cold and quiet. Nothing in the harbor stirred. Way off at the breakwater, the fresh white snout of the Port Jefferson-Bridgeport ferry pushed into the calm harbor, its horn a flat *wonk, wonk, wonk*. The docks and the boats in their moorings were heavy with snow. Everything seemed dulled, arrested, killing time. Pylons looked like they were wearing chef's hats.

From a second-story deck of Danford's Hotel, Lonnie Lonigan swept the marina parking area with a cheap pair of field glasses, the kind that pop out of a wallet-sized packet.

"I can't see a fucking thing with these," he said. "This is what they give you on the force?"

His brother-in-law Jimmy, the cop, said, "Fix the focus. You gotta fix the focus."

"I did fix the focus."

"You can't see the ferry?"

"Of course I can see the ferry," Lonnie said. "Of course I can see the ferry. The ferry's big. We're not looking for big things, are we?"

"I'm just saying," Jimmy said. "Let me see."

He took the glasses from his brother-in-law. Lonnie was more like his older brother—fourteen years separated Lonnie from his sister, Jimmy's wife. Sometimes he acted like Jimmy's father. Lonnie had walked his sister down the aisle, and the one time Jimmy got caught cheating on her, Lonnie broke his nose. Bob Foote held his arms, and Lonnie broke his nose. "Not for cheating," Lonnie had told him, "for getting caught." Jimmy never forgot it.

Jimmy peered into the parking lot with little satisfaction. "They worked okay in Vegas."

"You brought these to Vegas?"

"Fucking A, I brought 'em. I wanted to see everything up close."

"How much closer can you get to a hand of cards?" Lonnie said.

"Not for the tables—the shows, the shows."

"You saw shows?"

"Sure I saw shows. They got shows everywhere."

"What kind of shows?"

"Everything, Lonnie, I told you."

"Tell me again."

Jimmy's shoulders slumped. "Is this some kind of test?"

"I'm interested," Lonnie said. "I'm just asking."

"You're never just asking."

"Come on, Jimmy, tell me. I can't stay at the skins show the whole time."

"You will."

"But if I don't—what else they got?"

Jimmy shook his head. "I told you. They got tigers, white tigers . . . everything."

"You're a goddamn idiot." Lonnie grabbed the glasses.

"You know—" Jimmy stopped himself.

Lonnie asked him what.

"Nothing."

"No," Lonnie said, "what? I want to hear this—are you fronting off?"

"I'm a goddamn cop, Lonnie, you know that? You could show a little respect."

"Or what?"

Jimmy pointed to the parking area's entrance. "There he is."

"There's who?"

"Your friend."

"I don't see shit," Lonnie said.

Jimmy pulled the field glasses from his eyes. There, in the distance, was Bob Foote's Monte Carlo, smoke puffing from its exhaust.

Lonnie said, "Right on time."

"You sure he don't know who's calling?"

"Bob? He don't know shit."

"He's smarter than he looks," Jimmy said.

"You're smarter than you look. What's that tell you?"

Bob Foote rolled to a stop at the pair of orange traffic cones that reserved a parking space. The car next to the reserved space, a Plymouth Gran Fury, was just like the voice had described it: a cream-colored, four-door sedan with cardboard folded over the license plates. He put the Monte Carlo in park, got out and moved the cones, got back into the driver's seat, and pulled alongside the Fury and cut the engine.

Bob Foote got out of his car. He went to the passenger side, opened its door wide, and stepped aside. He counted to ten, then he pulled the seat forward and stepped aside again. This, he assumed, was in order to indicate to whoever was watching that no one was in the car with him. He counted to ten again. Then he opened the trunk, stepped aside, counted. He got back inside his car, his heart pounding.

On the seat alongside him was a shoebox, wrapped in Christmas paper, a big red bow in the middle. He'd followed the instructions exactly, exactly how his "friend from the mall" told him. He'd gone to the bank, he'd withdrawn $5,000—almost every nickel in his account—and he'd stacked it in the box, using newspaper to fill up the open space. Now he waited, his eyes fixed straight ahead at the ferry. It seemed almost still in the water, but a few more loud blats on the horn and into the dockside it bumped. Moments later, its wide mouth opened slowly, slowly, slowly, down toward the algae-green and brown concrete ramp.

Three sharp taps on the Monte Carlo's trunk startled him. A hooded man walked briskly past. When the man had reached the docks, Bob Foote got out of his car, the box in his hands. He didn't look anywhere but at the ground. He approached the hood of the parked Fury, placed the shoebox just behind the ornament, and returned to his car. He started up, backed out, and gave three toots on the horn.

Lonnie watched the Monte Carlo roll the length of the parking area. It followed in line behind the half-dozen cars that had disembarked the ferry, and turned right onto Main Street heading up the hill toward Setauket.

"Good boy," Lonnie said. "And my apologies to the Missus."

He was about to pocket the field glasses when he noticed the punk—a greasy kid with hacked-up hair, jeans painted-on tight, and an earring reflecting sunlight off his lobe.

"What the . . ." Lonnie muttered.

The punk lingered at the Plymouth's hood, looking this way and that. Then he went for the box.

Lonnie burst out onto the Danford's deck.

"Hey!" he shouted.

The punk tucked the package under his arm and ran.

He ran like a gazelle.

Lonnie ran too. He ran like a hippo. Three car lengths, he was sucking air so hard it burned. Four, he doubled over, clutching at his left arm, coughing from his throat into his colon. He tried to call out to Jimmy, but he couldn't get enough air to squawk. The kid hit the docks, his feet flying, before Lonnie hit the pavement facedown.

The moment he heard Bob Foote honk, Jimmy started back toward the Fury from the docks. He walked slowly, the hood pulled tight around his face. He wanted this to work perfect, he wanted to pay Bob Foote back, even if it wouldn't get him a nickel. He wasn't sure how, but he was certain Lonnie would scam him on his cut. By the time he saw the punk with the package, the guy's Converse sneakers were slapping the dock and coming straight for him.

"Hey!" he shouted. "Police!"

The punk threw a shoulder into Jimmy's rib cage and sent him flying onto the deck of a moored cruiser. The snow broke Jimmy's fall, but the thud took the wind out of his lungs. The kid swung onto the ferry, and took a staircase up to the passenger deck.

* * *

That's when Bob Foote returned in the Monte Carlo. He took the same spot alongside the Fury and leashed up his schnauzer. He walked her over to the fallen man, Lonnie Lonigan, facedown in the snow. Several people had gathered around.

"Shouldn't he be faceup?" Bob Foote asked.

One of the onlookers said he didn't have a pulse.

"Oh," Bob Foote said. "You're a doctor?"

He continued to the dock, where he advised the dockmaster to call an EMS.

Jimmy pushed himself up from the deck. He brushed snow from the rungs that led back to the dock, and carefully pulled himself up one slow, slippery step at a time. Something had gone out in his back; it hurt him to reach, it hurt him to step, it hurt him to breathe. Probably a busted rib at least, he thought, maybe two. When he reached the top rung, his face even with the dock, he looked straight into the tips of a pair of desert boots.

"Oh, hello, officer," Bob Foote said. "Do you need a hand?"

He snapped the right boot square into Jimmy's teeth. The cop flew back flat on the deck. The schnauzer peered over the edge and barked at Jimmy's prostrate form.

"You have a happy holiday," Bob Foote said, "you hear me?"

He turned and boarded the ferry. It felt colder than he'd expected. With the successful outcome of their little prank, the idea of taking a ride on the water seemed a bit unnecessary, if not absurd. But it's what his son had insisted—his price for helping out—and he climbed the steps to the passenger deck to find him. That might not be as easy as it seemed. Cliff wouldn't be the only greasy little punk with hacked-up hair and the jeans painted-on tight. But he would be the only one who'd ever given him a Christmas gift worth a shit.

ABOUT THE CONTRIBUTORS

QANTA AHMED, MD is an associate professor of medicine at Stony Brook University. Her first book, *In the Land of Invisible Women*, was a memoir of life as a doctor in Saudi Arabia. She contributes regularly to the Huffington Post, and her articles and essays have appeared in the *Jerusalem Post*, the *Christian Science Monitor*, the *Guardian*, and the *Wall Street Journal*. She is the first physician and Muslim woman to be selected as a Templeton-Cambridge Fellow at the University of Cambridge, England.

JANE CIABATTARI is the author of the collection *Stealing the Fire* and has had stories published in the *Literarian, KGB Bar Lit, Chautauqua, Literary Mama, VerbSap, Ms.*, the *North American Review, Denver Quarterly*, and *Hampton Shorts*, among others. She has received three Pushcart Prize special mentions and fiction fellowships from the New York Foundation for the Arts, the MacDowell Colony, and the Virginia Center for the Creative Arts.

REED FARREL COLEMAN, author of thirteen novels, has been called the "noir poet laureate" in the Huffington Post and a "hard-boiled poet" by NPR. He has won the Shamus Award for Best Novel three times and has been twice nominated for an Edgar Award. Coleman has also won the Macavity, Barry, and Anthony awards. He is an adjunct professor of English at Hofstra University and lives with his family in Suffolk County on Long Island.

JULES FEIFFER is a cartoonist, playwright, screenwriter, and children's book author and illustrator. He won a Pulitzer Prize and a George Polk Award for his cartoons; two Obies for his plays; an Academy Award for the animation of his cartoon satire *Munro*; and lifetime achievement awards from the Writers Guild of America and the National Cartoonist Society. Feiffer lives in Southampton and is a visiting professor at Stony Brook Southampton.

JZ HOLDEN has settled in East Hampton after living in Israel, Switzerland, England, and New York City. She lives part-time with the love of her life and their two cats, a Maine Coon called Maximillian and his regal sister Sophia. Holden was a journalist for twelve years prior to devoting her heart, creativity, and passion to fiction. She holds an MFA degree in creative writing and literature from Stony Brook University and a BFA from Pratt Institute.

William Prystauk

KAYLIE JONES moved to Sagaponack in 1975, where her family continued to live for more than thirty years. She is the author of five novels, including *A Soldier's Daughter Never Cries*, and the memoir *Lies My Mother Never Told Me*. She teaches in the MFA program at Stony Brook Southampton, and in the Wilkes University low-residency MFA program in professional writing.

Marion Ettlinger

SHEILA KOHLER is the author of eight novels, including *Becoming Jane Eyre* and *Love Child*, and three collections of short stories. She has won the PEN/O.Henry Prize twice, the Open Voice, the Smart Family Foundation, the Willa Cather, and the *Antioch Review* awards. She was a fellow at the Cullman Center and teaches at Bennington and Princeton. *Cracks*, a film directed by Jordan and Ridley Scott and based on Kohler's work, was released in spring 2011.

NICK MAMATAS was born on Long Island, in Port Jefferson, and attended college at Stony Brook University. His books include the Lovecraftian Beat road novel *Move Under Ground*, and the satire *Sensation*. He has published sixty short stories in *Asimov's Science Fiction*, *Mississippi Review*'s "postmodern pulp" issue, *Supernatural Noir*, and many other venues. Mamatas's work has been nominated for the Bram Stoker Award four times, and the International Horror Guild Award

Joanne McGevna

MATTHEW MCGEVNA received his MFA in creative writing from Southampton College in 2002. His fiction has appeared in *Ozone Park Journal*, *Karamu*, *Confrontation Magazine*, and *Epiphany Magazine*. The story included in *Long Island Noir* is part of a collection based on his experience growing up in Mastic Beach. He currently lives in Center Moriches, New York, with his wife Joanne and his son Jackson.

Renette Zimmerly

TIM MCLOUGHLIN is the editor of *Brooklyn Noir* and its companion volumes. His debut novel *Heart of the Old Country* is the basis for the motion picture *The Narrows*, starring Vincent D'Onofrio. His books have been published in seven languages, and his writing has appeared in *New York Quarterly*, the Huffington Post, and *Best American Mystery Stories*. He lives on the western tip of Long Island.

Denise Vazquez

RICHIE NARVAEZ received his BA and MA at Stony Brook University on "Lawn Guyland." His work has been featured in *Hit List: The Best of Latino Mystery, Indian Country Noir, Mississippi Review, Murdaland, Plots with Guns, Storyglossia, A Thousand Faces,* and *You Don't Have a Clue: Latino Mystery Stories for Teens.*

Dana Benningfield

CHARLES SALZBERG is the author of a number of nonfiction books, including *From Set Shot to Slam Dunk,* an oral history of the NBA. His novel *Swann's Last Song* was nominated for a Shamus Award for Best First P.I. Novel. The sequel, *Swann Dives In,* will be published in October 2012. He has been a visiting professor of magazine writing at the S.I. Newhouse School of Public Communications and he teaches writing at the New York Writers Workshop, where he is a founding member.

Kaylie Jones

AMANI SCIPIO, a native of Bridgehampton, Long Island, wrote her first short story, "The Cain Bridge House," for a high school competition; though the story did not win, she continued to write. Her work has appeared in numerous poetry anthologies, including *Painting Daisies Yellow* and *A Time to Be Free.*

Deedle Tomlinson

TIM TOMLINSON was born in Brooklyn and raised on Long Island. He's a cofounder of the New York Writers Workshop, and coauthor of its popular text, *The Portable MFA in Creative Writing.* He teaches in NYU's Global Liberal Studies Program. His stories and poems have appeared in print and online in many venues, including the *Missouri Review, North American Review, Pank,* and *Underground Voices,* among others. He lives with his wife in New York City.

Edward Champion

SARAH WEINMAN has written for the *Wall Street Journal,* the *Los Angeles Times,* the *Washington Post,* and many other print and online publications. Her fiction has appeared in *Ellery Queen's Mystery Magazine, Alfred Hitchcock Mystery Magazine,* and various anthologies, including *Baltimore Noir* and *Dublin Noir.* She lives in Brooklyn, just a mile away from the Atlantic Avenue LIRR hub.

Bob Hall

KENNETH WISHNIA'S novels include *23 Shades of Black*, an Edgar and Anthony award finalist; *Soft Money*, a *Library Journal* Best Mystery of the Year; *Red House*, a *Washington Post Book World* "Rave" Book of the Year; and *The Fifth Servant*, a finalist for the Premio Letterario ADEI-WIZO. He thanks Michael and Mary Mart and SCCC students Vinny Bivona, Aaron Bryant, Lauren Pelisson, and Brian Ratkus for their comments on an early draft of this story.

Karen Wishnia

STEVEN WISHNIA is the grandson of two illegal immigrants. He went to Ward Melville High School and Stony Brook University before escaping to New York and respected but marginally successful careers as a journalist and bass player. He is the author of *Exit 25 Utopia* and *The Cannabis Companion*. He recently completed a novel entitled *Very Bad When Drumming Stops*.